"DO YOU ENJOY YOURSELF, MISS LINDON?"

"That seems an unlikely question coming from a marquess and former ship's captain, my lord," Penelope said sharply.

Lucas smiled. "From a ship's captain, perhaps. The sea tamed the rogue but didn't drown him, and you haven't answered the question."

"The question's impertinent, my lord." She took several deep breaths and looked away from him, toward Lindon Hall.

Lucas ducked his head, but only for a moment. "Perhaps it is. But I owe you a debt, and providing you with some diversion seems to be the only gift I can give you. You have a merry wit, Miss Lindon, when you relax. Let me give you the chance to use it. As you said, the hunt will be upon us soon. I could have a house party and invite gentlemen and—"

Miss Lindon became whitely rigid. "No. I will not."

"Miss Lindon—"

Miss Lindon turned her back on him. "Thank you for your offer, my lord, but you must see that socializing with you like that would cause talk."

"What kind of talk are you particularly worried about, Miss Lindon?" he asked, his voice dangerously even. "Your being associated with a former rake or a potential murderer?"

BOOK YOUR PLACE ON OUR WEBSITE AND MAKE THE READING CONNECTION!

We've created a customized website just for our very special readers, where you can get the inside scoop on everything that's going on with Zebra, Pinnacle and Kensington books.

When you come online, you'll have the exciting opportunity to:

- View covers of upcoming books
- Read sample chapters
- Learn about our future publishing schedule (listed by publication month *and author*)
- Find out when your favorite authors will be visiting a city near you
- Search for and order backlist books from our online catalog
- Check out author bios and background information
- Send e-mail to your favorite authors
- Meet the Kensington staff online
- Join us in weekly chats with authors, readers and other guests
- Get writing guidelines
- AND MUCH MORE!

**Visit our website at
http://www.kensingtonbooks.com**

A SLIGHT CHANGE OF PLANS

Glenda Garland

ZEBRA BOOKS

Kensington Publishing Corp.

http://www.kensingtonbooks.com

To Scott:
For pacing

Chapter 1

Spring, 1815

Lips upcurved, Penelope Lindon quickly sketched Lord Worthington's large recumbent backside. Judging by the open picnic basket, the two glasses, one tipped over to leave a red gashing stain on a fine white blanket, and the bottle of wine glistening in the dappled sun, Penelope surmised Lord Worthington had indulged himself to the hilt.

But in such a strange place, Penelope thought, sketching the lace-edged handkerchief he held in one plump, outstretched hand. Lord Worthington's dislike of the outdoors, which he ascribed to constitutional delicacy, was well known. Even on a beautiful spring day, the townsfolk would have expected him to chase his skirts within the controlled confines of Wildoaks, his magnificent Elizabethan manor house, not here by the swollen, rushing river, its untamed banks a maze of budding shrubbery and scattered apple blossoms.

There, a couple strokes to show how Lord Worthington curled up like a baby when asleep. Penelope looked forward to telling her younger brother about her happening upon Lord Worthington's nap by the river. How Chad would hoot with laughter when he saw the sketch. Penelope would have to get his promise not to spread the story about. Lord Worthington's position might be very beneath his dignity, but it would not do for them, a viscount's son and daughter, to spread vulgar gossip, especially since the son was soon to go to Oxford and the daughter was in caps.

A shot rang out in the distance. Penelope jumped. Never say, she thought with exasperation, that her father had a shooting party out in May. She backed up quickly, sketchbook under one arm, toward a large tree.

Or maybe there was a poacher in the woods. It would be amazing cheek for someone to poach in broad daylight, yet Penelope knew many of Lord Worthington's tenants were unhappy.

Safe by the tree, her back pressed against its rough bark, her heart pounding, Penelope tossed off her irritation. She was having an unexpected adventure, and it felt marvelous after the boredom of the past month. The twins had both had spring colds, one after the other, and complained as vigorously as cranky and uncomfortable five-year-olds can.

Penelope glanced around the tree. Lord Worthington would be annoyed if he woke and thought Penelope was spying on him. The shot had not roused him. Could she creep away?

Then she realized the only sounds came from the birds and the river. At the very least, she expected Lord Worthington to be one of those unfortunate people who snore. Was he ill?

Tucking her sketchbook into the leather pouch she carried over her shoulder, Penelope took a deep breath. "Lord Worthington? Pardon me, my lord?"

No response. Another single shot rang out, then another. It was a shooting party, then, not a poacher, and it was drawing nearer. Still Lord Worthington did not move.

Penelope's heart began to pound anew. She raised her

voice. "Lord Worthington, there is a shooting party coming this way."

Nothing. She touched his shoulder with shaky fingers, then shook him. Lord Worthington rolled abruptly onto his back. Sightless eyes stared at her from a blue, contorted face. Penelope pressed her knuckles against her mouth. She heard a whimpering noise from her own throat. She pulled up her skirts and ran, lungs burning, leather bag bouncing against her back.

Lindon Hall's red brick wings and gleaming blond stonework rising above the hills and trees seemed like a beacon of safety and security to Penelope. As she ran up the Hall's wide pebbled drive, she saw her eighteen-year-old brother, Chad, stretch his arms above his head and take long, relaxed steps down the broad stone stairs.

"Chad!" Penelope threw her arms about him, panting.

"I say, Pen," he said, teasingly, "what's the rumpus?"

Penelope tried to get her breath. "Lord Worthington, I was sketching him. By the river. I think . . . I think he's dead."

"Show me," her brother said, all trace of playfulness gone.

"Have Masters send for Doctor Anderson," said Penelope, gasping. "Meet us at Sycamore Bend. Might be alive. Couldn't tell. Hunting party. Out."

Chad snapped his fingers at a groom who had stopped in the drive, round-eyed, when Penelope had run up. "You heard Miss Lindon. Be quick, man." Chad took her hand. "Show me."

They walked briskly through the fields and copses to the river. They heard the hunting party move off west.

Lord Worthington lay undisturbed. His blue, sightless face stared at the bower of branches above him. Penelope stopped about ten yards away and shuddered.

Chad's hand tensed in hers. "Stay here. I'll take a look."

"Be careful."

He shot her an irritated look and knelt next to Lord
Worthington. From his waistcoat pocket, Chad with-
drew his new watch and pressed its shiny back under
Lord Worthington's nose. Chad shook his head. "He
looks deuced strange."

"How do you know?" snapped Penelope. "Have you
ever seen a corpse before?" Then she shook her head.
"I'm sorry, Chad."

"Apology accepted," he said stiffly. Then his blue eyes
sparkled. "He does look gruesome, the old libertine.
Don't poker up, Penny. I'll not speak ill of the dead in
anyone's company but yours." He stood up. "We must
inform Sir William."

"Yes," said Penelope. "He'll arrange for an inquest. It
will all be quite horrible."

Chad put an arm about Penelope's shoulders and nodded. "We're in for a delicate time if the jury comes back
with death by misadventure, for no tenant farmer with
a daughter will weep into his ale over this day. In fact, I
suspect more than a few people will be ecstatic."

Late Summer, 1815

Captain Lucas Pargetter, newly the sixth Marquess of
Worthington, walked about Wildoaks marveling at the
poor taste with which it had come to be decorated. Too
many colors and patterns fought for attention in every
room except the study. Although no particular statuette
or wall hanging or sofa appeared cheap, somehow their
combination did. It was like a pirate's den, Lucas
thought. The image of pudgy, languid Edmund as a pirate, however, made him choke back laughter.

Lucas supposed he should show more respect for the
dead, but Eddy's dying on him, worse, getting himself
murdered, had to be the lowest joke Eddy had played on

him. Nor could it be said that Edmund was unacquainted with playing jokes on Lucas.

Edmund had doubtless looked upon sending him into the navy as one such. Mercifully for Lucas, the joke had saved his sanity and his self-respect.

Thank God for his steward Jarvis, Lucas thought, who had taught him so much of the sea and agreed to accompany Lucas into his forced retirement from being captain of the *Atlantia.* What would Lucas do with himself, landlocked in Derbyshire? How would it feel not to have a ship under his feet?

And, most important, would people ever look at him as the man he was now? Only three months ago, when he had been home briefly, he had stopped at the local pub, The Green Duck. The hatchet-faced proprietress had told him the whereabouts of every woman he had ever flirted with. The list had been lengthy, but she had talked fast, as though wanting to dispose of a loathsome task. Then she had told him Mary Smith no longer plied her trade there, thank you very much.

Mortified, Lucas had dropped a coin on the table and left before he lost either his temper or his dignity.

What would he do now? His naval "exile" had come to an end, but an end forced not only on himself, but on those around him. Would the Four Corners, as the neighborhood was known, miraculously forget his past indiscretions in the blinding light of the Worthington title?

Maybe. Unlikely. Downright long odds.

It should not matter to him. He knew he had changed.

A large, garish Chinese vase in the entrance hall made Lucas wince. He wished that Jarvis had been able to clear the bedroom Lucas had appropriated so he might have someplace private to brood. The very size of the house seemed confining.

He would walk the land that was now his and, he told himself with a determined nod, he would remind himself that he need not stop at a quarterdeck railing. There must be some advantage to being back on land.

"Tina, Timothy, wait for me," Penelope called.

Tina turned her head and smiled, her five-year-old face cherubic. Then she blithely followed her twin brother into the forest. Exasperated, Penelope quickened her pace. She blinked as she passed from bright sunlight into the dim pine canopy. Then she spotted their blond heads bobbing toward a clearing.

When Timothy saw she was gaining on them, he grabbed Tina's hand and pulled her forward. Tina giggled. Within a moment, they were out of sight. Lifting her skirts slightly, Penelope broke into a slow run.

It was times like these that made Penelope feel in complete charity with any mother who wondered why she had had offspring. But Penelope never wondered for long. Her sister's children were the center of her life, the best part. She had taken them in after Helen had died in childbirth, and their father, Lord Eversleigh, could not look upon them for his grief and guilt.

So at nineteen years of age, Penelope had cared for the twins, found them a wet nurse, overseen their budding education, their play, held their screaming bodies close when they were sick. Her mother was little help; she made vague references to the necessity of avoiding childhood ailments, then returned her attention to whatever novel she was reading. Her father hunted, usually someplace other than Lindon Hall. Chad had been too young.

They were good children, her twins. If they had a flaw, it was the way they let their infernal curiosity inspire them to disobey her. They were always bounding off to investigate some small sound Timothy heard in the bushes, or something Tina saw high in a tree. Soon the governess she had hired would harness some of that energy into useful learning, but since Lord Worthington's murder, Penelope did not trust she would find only pleasant things in the woods.

Hiring the governess had marked a change in their lives, and made Penelope wonder again when or if Eversleigh would take interest in them. For their sakes she hoped he would. For her sake, she hoped he stayed away for the next fifteen years.

"Hell's bells," a male voice bellowed.

Tina screeched. Penelope ran. As she crested the hill leading to the clearing, she tripped and, fighting for balance, careened down the hill into the quick arms of a tall stranger.

"Is there no order in the country?" the stranger inquired, lifting one brow.

Penelope blushed and tried to push out of his strong embrace. He kept a hand to her arm. "Steady, miss."

Now Penelope recognized him. Lucas Pargetter, the rake who behaved himself only when surrounded by hundreds of miles of ocean. The sea had filled him out into a powerful figure, that power emphasized by his casual breeches and ruffled shirt. He wore no coat. The sun had kissed his light hair in white streaks and turned his face a golden brown. Looking at him made her heart race in a way that had nothing to do with running. Although, she thought, she should be running away, twins in hand.

"Auntie Penny, Auntie Penny!" The twins ran to her and hugged her legs, almost knocking her down and pushing her from the reach of his strong hand.

He raised his brows. "You should keep better control of your charges, miss. They nigh pretended I was a pin in a game of skittles. Who is your employer?"

"Tina and Timothy are my niece and nephew, my lord. I have no employer." She was strangely breathless by the time she finished uttering the words.

"You know who I am?"

"Certainly. Although you are returned more quickly than we had anticipated."

"Who had anticipated me?" he asked, frowning.

"Who is he, Aunt Penny?" Timothy asked, round-eyed.

"The new marquess," replied Penelope, in her excitement substituting what he was for who he was. "I mean—"

"We had a marquess here," said Tina. "But you do not look like him."

" 'Course not, stupid," her twin said. "He's dead. He was murdered."

Tina clutched Penelope's leg more tightly and whimpered.

"Enough, Timothy. And your sister is not stupid." Penelope blushed again as Lord Worthington regarded her quizzically.

"Well, now that we have established that I am a marquess, but not dead, perhaps we should back up. Would you be so kind as to tell me who you are, ma'am?"

"That's Aunt Penny," declared Timothy, pointing.

"So I gathered," Lord Worthington said.

"Do not point, Timothy. It is not polite."

"Sorry, ma'am," replied Timothy and chewed his lower lip.

Lord Worthington's lips twitched.

Penelope straightened her shoulders. "I am Miss Lindon, my lord, daughter of Viscount Lindon of Lindon Hall, and the children are the Honorable Mr. Timothy Eversleigh and Lady Christina Eversleigh."

"Very pleased to meet you," he said with a bow. "Please pardon me, Miss Lindon, for mistaking a walking dress in half-mourning for a governess' garb. And please forgive my language. I am unaccustomed to being on the watch for children under full sail, particularly on Wildoaks property."

Stung by the implied rebuke, however lightly delivered, Penelope retorted, "Lord Worthington—your late cousin, that is, my lord—granted me free rein of his land. I often visited his tenants. Since I did not know you had returned, I could not ask your permission."

Lord Worthington held up both hands. "Pax, Miss Lindon. I have no desire to go against tradition. You and your twins may wander where you like."

"Thank you, my lord."

"What did you mean, sir, 'full sail'?" asked Timothy.

"Your pardon, Mr. Eversleigh," said Lord Worthington. "I have been at sea for a long time. I meant only to compliment you on how quickly you can run, as a ship with all sail set."

"Oh," Timothy said, eyes round.

"Have you ever seen such a sight?" Lord Worthington asked.

Timothy shook his head.

Penelope heard Lord Worthington mutter something like, "Landlocked," as he looked toward the distant hills.

"Come, children, let us leave Lord Worthington to his walk."

She had his whole attention again. He said with a smile, "You need not desert Wildoaks today on my account."

Penelope felt as though the sun had suddenly popped out from behind a cloud and blinded her. "You are kind, but—"

"Since we are neighbors, we will see more of each other. May we not start as I would have us go on, as friends?"

Penelope flushed from anger and embarrassment. Physically he had changed, but his light, almost caressing tone could not have. Indeed, that tone was certainly half the reason he had gotten himself banished to the sea. The last thing Penelope needed was someone with such a seductive voice and the reputation to match paying her attention.

"Thank you, my lord, but I think not." Penelope grasped each twin by the hand and marched them, protesting, back through the pine trees.

Lucas returned from his walk feeling cross and dispirited. His first meeting with one of his neighbors, indeed, a member of one of the Four Corners' estates, and it had not gone well.

Miss Lindon's rustling gray dress had betrayed her agitation. Yet she had stood, straight and true as a masthead, and more or less wished him to perdition. No bowed spirit there, Lucas thought, remembering the animation shining in her light blue eyes, made all the more striking by the deep black of the curls peeping out from her cap. Surely, he thought, she was too young to be in caps. And whom did she mourn?

He shook his head. Doubtless he should pursue the matter no further. Doubtless he should set his sights strictly on cleaning up affairs here and take himself off to London or some other far corner of the world where no one thought of him as Lucas the Lothario or some other dreadful sobriquet.

On that happy thought, Lucas went into the study and surprised his uncle Albert from a sound snooze in a wing chair. The old man came awake with a series of harrumphs and splutters.

"My apologies, sir. I did not see you."

"No reason you should, my boy. No reason you should. Dashed good to see you again. When did you arrive?"

"Shortly after noon, sir."

"Sorry I was not about to receive you. We thought you would come day after tomorrow."

"Think nothing of it." Lucas rang for refreshments.

" 'Tis a bad business, this," the old man said, waving his hand in the general direction of the beamed ceiling.

Lucas nodded. "The solicitor sent to fetch me said there was some question about how my cousin died."

"Bet he almost sicked up trying to get it out. The solicitor, I mean. Marston the Younger. Nervous sort of chap."

Lucas silently agreed with his uncle's assessment of the nervous solicitor. "Was it poison, Uncle?"

"The physician said so, but I cannot remember what kind. Edmund's face looked like purple rice pudding when they carried him in. Put me off my feed that night, I can tell you."

Lucas would have smiled at the homely simile except for the image it conjured. "I am sure." A thought struck him. "Must have been awful for the person who found him."

"Didn't hear of any hysterics, but then Penelope Lindon is a mighty steady woman."

"Miss Lindon found the body?" asked Lucas, astonished.

The study door opened wide and a pretty young woman dressed in black flounced in. She wrapped white arms round Lucas's neck, kissed his cheek, and cried, "Lucas! You do remember me, I hope? I'm Cecily. When did you arrive? Silly man, you must tell us next time you come home so we can be ready for you. I heard you have been stomping through the woods for hours. What a perfectly dreadful thing!"

Lucas disengaged himself, correctly recognizing this beautiful creature as Edmund's widow from their first and only meeting in London when he had been made post-captain two years ago. "Your servant, Lady Worthington. I didn't know I would be returning myself. I had thought to see something of England before I came up."

Lady Worthington—Cecily, indeed!—blinked. Doubtless, Lucas thought, she did no looking at countryside. The countryside was supposed to look at her.

"I was just telling Worthington here about Miss Lindon," said Uncle Albert.

Cecily made a *moue*. "Old Faithful? Why ever would you want to talk about her?"

"She discovered Edmund's body. Why do you call her 'Old Faithful'?"

A second lady joined them, also wearing deep mourning. "Cousin, welcome back to Wildoaks." Lady Honoria Pargetter, Edmund's older sister, passed into the light from the large stained-glass window, and seated herself in an upright chair, her spine a foot from its back.

"Thank you, Cousin," Lucas said with a bow as correct as she. "I trust I find you well?"

"Well enough under the circumstances, thank you." Although Honoria still carried herself with the arrogance of a flagship, she had aged since he had last seen her ten years ago. Why, Lucas thought suddenly, she must be all of thirty-seven.

Honoria had seemed so young when her mother and Edmund had gathered the whole family in the drawing room across the hall and told him he would be sent to sea for his indiscretions. They had clustered together around two couches, some standing, as if for a family portrait. Or a jury pronouncing sentence.

"You were telling me about Miss Lindon," said Lucas to Cecily. "Why do you call her 'Old Faithful'?"

"That silly mourning she wears," said Cecily, absently picking up bric-a-brac from the desk.

Lucas debated asking for whom Miss Lindon mourned, for fear of showing too much interest. Fortunately Honoria filled in the blanks for him.

"Her fiancé was killed at Salamanca. Five years ago."

Five years, Lucas thought, astonished. What paragon merited five years of mourning?

"It is embarrassing to his parents," Cecily added, "as you may easily believe. She betrays a shocking amount of sensibility." Cecily put down a bronze bookend with a thump, dismissing the subject of Miss Lindon. "Now you are home, Lucas, we must make plans. I have hopes of your reputation being true, so you can lift this house's spirits. It has been deadly dull."

Honoria raised her brows. Uncle Albert snorted.

Edmund had certainly married his match for shallowness. "I am not the same person who left this house eleven years ago. Even if I were, I believe we owe Cousin Edmund, your *late* husband, madam, some respect. Whatever your opinion of Miss Lindon's mourning, you will continue yours. I will also don blacks for a month, though it is not required."

"You show excessive civility, Cousin," Cecily purred. She slid a delicate hand onto his bare wrist. "Is there any way I can convince you to relax your standards?"

Lucas reflected that he had approached French men-o'-war and vicious privateers with more enthusiasm than his lady cousin now inspired. "You must remember, *Cousin,* that Edmund was murdered. To show anything but the most scrupulous respect could invite talk we none of us need."

"He is quite right, my dear," said Uncle Albert.

"Indeed," Honoria said in freezing accents.

Cecily paled. The three were silent while Masters the butler brought in tea. When Masters had left, Lucas decided to throw Cecily a bone.

"I don't think, however, that there would be anything amiss in our calling on our neighbors."

Honoria's head tipped up. "They should call on you first. That is your right as Worthington."

Lucas thought suddenly of the cool condemnation in a

pair of blue eyes. No, the Worthington title was certainly not blinding anyone. He said, "I do not wish to stand on ceremony."

Cecily brightened. "Tell Masters. His younger brother is butler to the Lindons, and they know everyone. Of course, Miss Lindon is like to plan some staid affair where we all sit around drinking tea and eating cake."

"Which is all we should be doing," Honoria said.

Lucas agreed. Cecily poured them tea. Lucas considered her bowed blond head thoughtfully. Cecily seemed eager to forget Edmund had been murdered. Did she think no suspicion would ever fall on her? Or, was she hiding something that could be revealed should the least bit of probing come her way?

Lucas glanced at Uncle Albert and Honoria. Both studied something across the room. Were they consciously trying to avoid his eye, Lucas wondered. Had they been sailors aboard his ship and acting thus, he would have suspected them of some mischief.

This homecoming was turning out to be more awkward than Lucas had anticipated. Who had killed Edmund, and why? And what, if anything, should Lucas do about it?

Indeed, what *could* he do about it?

Chapter 2

Chad swiped a macaroon from the silver tray set to one side of the airy maroon-and-cream drawing room.

Penelope slapped at his hands. "Those are for our guests. How do you hope of getting on at Oxford if you have no manners?"

Chad merely grinned and took a healthy bite. "You look nice today, Penny," he said, chewing. "'Tis a good thing lilac becomes you. Makes your eyes look violet. And not too many ruffles. You look better in dresses that have fewer ruffles."

"Thank you," said Penelope dryly. "But whether it becomes me or not is not the question." Still, she was pleased. It never hurt to look one's best, even if one had given oneself a hearty disgust by thinking frequently of a pair of flashing hazel eyes and strong arms. Had not Lady Drucilla told her the truth about Gerald? He had been charming, too.

But not quite so intriguing, one part of her whispered.

"The twins said you met our guest of honor a few days ago. You did not tell me. What is he like?"

Penelope turned away to inspect a flower arrangement by a tray of fine cookies. "Like a ship's captain, I expect. Tall, tanned by the sun. Really, there is not much to tell."

"Does he look anything like the, er, former Worthington?"

"Not a bit," she replied, and her unruly thoughts

contrasted the late Lord Worthington's pale, pudgy complexion to the present one's bronzed vitality.

Chad leaned against the back of a maroon divan and folded his arms. "You are remarkably closemouthed about our new marquess. Give over, Penny, do."

"I will thank you not to use cant. As for Lucas Pargetter, do not forget, the late Lord Worthington ordered him into the navy because the family was afraid of him disgracing them further. If I am 'closemouthed' about him, 'tis because I have no interest in him beyond his status as our guest."

"Further?"

Penelope frowned. "Further what?"

"You said 'disgrace them further.' What had he done?"

"He managed to take as mistresses, simultaneously, I must add, two ladies who categorically loathed each other."

"So?"

Penelope plucked at a yellow rose to make it even with some of the spring lilies. "One of them attacked the other in a jealous rage at a ball, screeching his name. Old Lady Worthington had an apoplexy when she heard the scandal. She sent him down to the country, that is, here."

Penelope remembered seeing young Lucas Pargetter once or twice that summer, at church. She had not been able to keep her mind on the service for watching him fidget and then smile at young ladies who caught his eye. He had remained her epitome of male perfection. She had even felt peculiarly disappointed when she had accepted Gerald's proposal.

Penelope said, flatly, to dispel the heady remembrance of his arms steadying her, "He soon embroiled himself in another scandal here. Then he went into the navy."

"What was the scandal here?"

"I have neither time nor inclination to talk about it."

Chad grinned. "And to think, Worthington was only twenty-two then. Just four years older than I am now."

"These are *not* character traits you want to emulate," said Penelope, struck anew by her brother's good looks. Leaning against the divan, Chad appeared the picture of good breeding and elegance. How many young women would fall to his spell?

"Oh, tosh, Penny, what did he do that was so bad? Sounds to me it was the women's faults. Who were they, by the way?"

"That is not important. Besides, his crime here could not be attributed to anyone's behavior other than his own. Lucas Pargetter was indiscreet, which is a serious character flaw."

"Come on, Penny, now you must tell me."

Penelope pursed her lips. "He was caught in The Green Duck's barn with a serving woman, Mary Smith, and from all reports, it was a nasty little scene."

"Nasty?" Chad asked. "He was not . . . I mean, 'twas not—"

"No. 'Twas nasty because she asked him for a position at Wildoaks and yelled quite obscenely when he refused, and because he had also been flirting with Miss Aylsbury."

"The former vicar's daughter?"

"Yes. She spent a week crying over the incident."

Chad whistled and waggled his brows. Then, after taking a nibble of his stolen macaroon, he frowned and said, "Then why do we have him as a guest in our father's house?"

"Whatever his past reputation, Wildoaks still marches along our father's estate. What would happen to our Four Corners if two quarters of it could not get on together politely?"

"You and your concern for the tenants, Penny. By the

time I take on Lindon Hall, I swear they'll be the fattest, most contented lot in all Derbyshire."

"I hope so," replied Penelope soberly, "for there have been rumors of riots brewing up north." Penelope pushed that ugly thought away. "And if we did not, Lady Howath would."

Chad grinned. "Never tell me you are competitive, Penny."

Penelope smiled. A bell rang, and she glanced at the clock.

"'Tis a quarter to four," Chad said. "Who could it be?"

Penelope grimaced. "Likely it is the Reverend and Mrs. Simons. They are always early."

"And she, poor thing, often looks like she needed another half hour with the crimping iron."

"Go find Mother, will you?"

Chad grumbled, but went to collect their mother.

Penelope smoothed her own hair under her cap, wondering how well Lord Worthington's charm would work when she met him in a crowd. Too well, most likely. Be careful, Penelope Lindon, she told herself. You have too much to lose.

Penelope smoothed a stray wisp of hair under her cap, just before Masters announced Reverend Simons and his wife. Against the backdrop of the Lindons' tastefully restrained drawing room, Mrs. Simons did look disheveled. Frowzy locks of hair escaped the large knot she wore at the back of her head, and a ribbon on her blue dress was hanging at an odd angle. Chad's assessment of Mrs. Simons had hit the mark.

Reverend Simons, however, appeared as well groomed as always, from his closely shaven, square jaw to his styled hair and brushed black cleric's coat. Penelope knew many young women came to church to gaze on their vicar.

The vicar bowed over her hand. "A pleasure, as always."

Lady Lindon wandered into the drawing room, a book under her arm as usual. Penelope counted to ten as her mother said, "Chad told me there were people downstairs? Oh, Reverend Simons, Mrs. Simons, how nice to see you." She turned to her daughter. "Penny, are we having a party?"

Mr. Simons smiled slightly.

Penelope continued counting to twenty so she could speak with poise. She knew she should have given up all hope that her mother would regard what happened in her own house as real as what happened between the covers of her novels. "Yes, Mother. A tea party."

"How lovely. Whom else have we invited?"

"The Crimpins, Sir William and Lady Howath, Lord Worthington, Lady Worthington, Lady Honoria Pargetter, and Lord Albert Pargetter."

"Will Miss Crimpin be coming?" Lady Lindon asked, glancing expressively at the two trays of baked goods on the sideboard.

"Yes, and there will be lemon cakes," added Penelope. Lucia Crimpin's appetite for sweets was well known.

"Good." Lady Lindon sighed with relief. "You will pour, my dear?" asked Lady Lindon.

Penelope nodded and seated herself on a purple floral-patterned sofa behind the gleaming silver tea service. She had anticipated that her mother would pass the task to her. As she handed a well-sugared cup to the vicar, Chad entered. He whispered, "No trace of Father. He must have gone to ground."

Penelope compressed her lips and nodded.

"How fares the vicarage, Mr. Simons?" Lady Lindon asked.

"The Worthington party is here, my lady," said Masters.

"Oh!" said Lady Lindon. "Show them in."

A rush of excitement tickled Penelope. She smoothed her skirts. Would he notice her? Talk to her? Penelope scolded herself for being such a ninny.

But Lord Worthington's eyes did catch hers immediately upon his entering the room. He smiled, causing little flutters to fly in the back of her throat.

Lady Lindon performed the introductions. Penelope shivered again as she heard his liquid voice say, "I am pleased to meet you." When he said, "Your servant," to her while bowing low over her hand, Penelope thanked him silently for not mentioning their previous meeting. Perhaps some of her thanks showed on her face because he winked slightly before moving on to greet the vicar and Mrs. Simons. The nerve of the man, Penelope thought.

"Vicar, pleased to meet you and your lovely bride."

"My lord," said Mrs. Simons with flushed cheeks. Not an unusual reaction for a woman to have when receiving a compliment from Lucas Pargetter, Penelope thought, and scolded herself for being petty.

"I am honored to meet you, my lord," the vicar said smoothly. "I must say, I approve of the respect you show."

Lord Worthington bowed. He wore a black coat and black trousers. Indeed, only a dark gray waistcoat, an impeccably tied white cravat, and his sun-streaked hair relieved his black. It was a striking effect.

"Worthington is full of plans," said Lady Worthington, touching his arm with a black-gloved hand so that it appeared as if they were one flesh. Lord Worthington stood impassively, although Lady Honoria frowned, and Lord Albert smirked. Did Lord Worthington encourage the new dowager to think she would again enjoy all the privileges of being mistress of Wildoaks?

An irrational jealousy surged through Penelope. The

vicar, too, had tightened his mouth. Any self-respecting man would, Penelope thought, when presented with such blatant lust. Chad, however, worked his lips to contain an unruly smile.

"You must sit down and tell us about your plans," Lady Lindon said, "or perhaps your life at sea. You have been away from home for some years."

"Eleven, my lady." Lord Worthington sat down on a delicate chair opposite Penelope. Chad sat down next to her, and she began handing him cups of tea for their guests.

"No milk or sugar, thank you, Miss Lindon," said Lord Worthington, smiling warmly. "I joined the navy as a midshipman, ma'am, a very green midshipman. We set sail immediately for Jamaica. I do not think I would have survived if it had not been for Jarvis, my steward, who was a foretopman at the time."

"Were you in battle right off, sir?" asked Chad.

"No, but have you ever tried to climb rigging when your ship bucks like a two-year-old colt?"

Chad shook his head.

"Jarvis taught me how to do that," said Lord Worthington, "and many other things."

"It all sounds quite thrilling, don't you think?" asked Lady Lindon. "Full of adventure and travel."

"There are some, my lady," the vicar said gently, "who find more mundane pursuits as interesting."

Lady Worthington lifted her pointed chin, her eyes flashing. "I'm sure there are. I, however, think Worthington's life to be one of the most interesting."

"It had its moments, *Cousin,* but there were also times when I wished my ship and crew at Jericho."

Penelope could not help the twitching of her lips this honest comment caused. Lord Worthington smiled at her, and Penelope studied the cream Aubusson carpet to hide her embarrassment and pleasure.

Masters appeared. "Sir William and Lady Howath, Mrs. Crimpin, Miss Crimpin."

From the hallway, Miss Lucia Crimpin's voice sailed into the drawing room. "Stop poking at me, Mother, do. All my flounces are lined up, and we're late as 'tis."

Chad covered his mouth with his hand. To be sisterly, Penelope thumped him on the back. Lord Worthington smiled, a pure smile without artifice. Penelope gazed at him. How, she wondered, could a simple smile so change a person's face?

Startled by her impression, Penelope dropped her gaze again, this time to the embossed silver tea tray before her.

The newcomers exchanged greetings. With so many people in the room, one conversation gave way to many. Penelope remained by the tea tray, but the guests milled about, chatting and helping themselves to cakes.

Lady Howath soon ensconced herself in a curving Queen Anne chair across the room. When Lady Lindon passed by, Lady Howath hailed her hostess, forcing her to stop and converse. As if she were queen, Penelope thought. Lady Howath had the least right to play queen in this neighborhood. Her house, Swanning, might be one of the Four Corners, but it did not match the resources of Lindon Hall, nor it Wildoaks.

Perhaps that was why Lady Howath always looked as if she had just tasted unsugared lemonade and why she desired to know everything about everybody in the Four Corners. Penelope judged that Lady Howath was getting no information from Lady Lindon, for she was fanning herself vigorously.

Penelope hoped that when she reached her later thirties she would have other pursuits than gossip. But what else would she have? a little voice inside her whispered. The twins would be almost grown, Timothy to university, Tina to London for her Comeout. What would be left for her?

Penelope set her lemon cake down on the low table, suddenly discovering she no longer wanted it, and saw Miss Crimpin throwing herself at Lord Worthington. Penelope watched with distaste as Miss Crimpin demonstrated her allure with every flutter of eyelash, every blond curl, every perfectly aligned pink flounce. Lord Worthington participated in Miss Crimpin's antics with the greatest civility and good nature. Then as Miss Crimpin paused for breath, Lord Worthington turned his head and smiled directly at Penelope as though sharing a joke.

Penelope stifled a gasp. Lord Worthington extricated himself with one smooth remark and joined Penelope on the sofa.

"More tea, my lord?" She could not decide whether she should be angry at how quickly he had put aside Miss Crimpin or gratified that he had left Miss Crimpin to seek out her company.

"No, thank you," he said, leaning back and crossing his booted ankles. "I have not spoken to you yet. Do you care to indulge me?"

"In conversation? Yes, of course."

Lord Worthington laughed, causing several curled and beribboned heads to swivel their way. Lemon cake in hand, Miss Crimpin frowned. Lady Worthington pursed her lips, considering. Lady Howath, of course, noticed everything.

"I appreciate your caution, Miss Lindon," Lord Worthington said. "I suspect you know of my reputation, although you must have been quite young when I left Derbyshire."

"I was fourteen when you left, but my mother is of a romantic disposition. She spoke reverently—and often—of your story."

"Lady Lindon is most kind," said he, deadpan.

Penelope's lips twitched, but she agreed.

"Does it bother you to have a man with a reputation for being a rake in your drawing room?"

Although he smiled, Penelope thought he meant the question seriously. "I have seen many people change, too many to judge a person by his past before I know his present."

Her answer startled her. She had had the chance to put him at a proper distance and yet during their brief conversation she had discovered a well of sympathy for him. Was that how he had seduced so many women, by appealing to their sympathy? Or was Lord Worthington a shrewd judge of character and had discerned that Penelope could not be influenced by flattery like Lucia Crimpin? Penelope remembered her first meeting with him and tried to keep her caution.

"How are your two small sloops, Miss Lindon?"

Penelope realized he referred to the twins and was suprised he thought to ask after them. "I will endeavor to keep them under shorter sail. Is that the right term?"

Lord Worthington smiled. "Exactly right. But as I said, you needn't bother."

Chad strolled up, handed over his teacup for more, and sat down on Penelope's other side. As Penelope poured the tea, its warm pungent scent seemed to clear her rapidly clouding brain.

"Good to have you in the neighborhood, Worthington," Chad said, imitating their father's bluff manner.

"Thank you," replied Lord Worthington.

"Not that we are happy with the way you came to be here, if you take my meaning."

Penelope trod on her brother's foot. Chad blushed.

"Of course," said Lord Worthington " 'Twas a strange, nasty thing that happened to Edmund. And I understand, Miss Lindon, that you found his body. How distressing for you."

"At first," said Chad, enthusiasm for the subject

warming his voice, "She thought he was sleeping out there next to the river. 'Tis why she sketched him."

Lord Worthington leaned forward. "You sketched him? My dear Miss Lindon, that sketch could be a very important clue to finding out who committed this foul act."

"There was nothing there except picnic things." Penelope frowned. "At least, I do not think there was anything else. I showed it to Sir William, and I have not looked at the horrid thing since May twelfth. When it happened."

"May twelfth? Are you certain it was the twelfth and not the fourteenth?"

"Yes," said Sir William Howath, who had come up to them to have his cup refilled.

"Good God," Lord Worthington said. "I saw my cousin on May twelfth. The solicitor told me he died on the fourteenth. How could the man have made such a blunder?"

"You say you saw him that day? When was that?" asked Sir William, his round face intent.

Lord Worthington appeared surprised at the rapid questions, so Penelope said, "Sir William is the local magistrate."

One of Lord Worthington's brows rose as he glanced at Penelope then Sir William. "About noon."

"Where was this meeting?"

"At The Green Duck."

"What did you talk about?"

"Sir William," said Penelope, "perhaps this is not the best time. If you called on Lord Worthington tomorrow—"

Lord Worthington smiled at her, making her pulse race without warning. "I am quite comfortable answering Sir William's questions. I had written to my cousin requesting his assistance to buy a property in Virginia. Now that there is the peace, I find . . . I found myself often in the United States escorting merchanters. I had thought to invest. My ship, the *Atlantia,* had been held up in Dover during re-fitting, so I had the time to make the journey. My cousin denied my request for funds, and I rode back to Dover."

"What horse did you ride?"

"A bay gelding I hired."

"Ah," said Sir William, nodding. "That confirms what Will Trent said. He saw a man on a bay gelding riding away from the river. But The Green Duck is quite far from the river."

"I rode out to look at Wildoaks," Lord Worthington said. "I had not seen the place for several years."

"Why did you not meet Lord Worthington at Wildoaks?"

"It was a whim of his to meet me at The Green Duck, and I wasn't in a position to question Edmund's whims."

He spoke so precisely, with such a calm, cool air that for the first time, Penelope understood how he had commanded men. Doubtless he had also commanded their loyalty. She picked up her teacup, wondering where such errant thoughts originated.

"Quite so," Sir William said, but from his raised brows and the way he pulled at his lower lip, Penelope surmised that Lord Worthington's account had raised his curiosity.

"Sir William," Penelope said, "perhaps you might postpone any further questioning. This is a social occasion."

"You are correct, Miss Lindon. If I may call on you tomorrow, my lord?"

"Of course. I'll help in any way possible."

Sir William bowed and went to join his wife.

"I don't know how anyone could suspect you of being a poisoner," Chad said contemptuously. " 'Tis a coward's method."

Lord Worthington inclined his head. A sparkle danced in his eyes. "Thank you, Mr. Lindon. But you must know, I was sorely plagued by a pain in my right shoulder, which I had dislocated when my ship had a slight disagreement with another vessel."

Chad snorted. "You were still capable of shooting him, I daresay."

Lord Worthington raised his brows quizzically.

Chad blushed. "Were you so inclined, of course. Excuse me."

Penelope watched her brother pluck a cake from the sideboard and head across the room to do the pretty with Lady Honoria and Lord Albert. She was intensely conscious that Lord Worthington continued to sit near her. "Chad goes to Oxford soon. I'll miss him." Good Heavens, where had that come from?

He took her teacup and refilled it.

"My lord," Penelope protested.

Lord Worthington handed her the cup. "Sorry. I'm unused to such courtesies."

"This must be difficult for you. The change, I mean."

"Difficult," he said, looking grim, "and unwanted."

Miss Crimpin came up to them, sat down next to Lord Worthington, and handed her cup imperiously to Penelope. "La, my lord, I thought I would never shake Lady Howath."

Miss Crimpin flirted with Lord Worthington until the party broke up. Lord Worthington entered into her game with skill. Blush after blush he brought to Lucia Crimpin's famous cream complexion. Yet Penelope also observed him glancing several times at Sir William, who stood across the room talking to Lady Lindon and the Simonses.

How, Penelope wondered, did he manage to charm a lady and consider a problem at the same time? Did he merely charm without art, or did his long experience with the fair sex enable him to charm without thought?

Penelope found herself becoming increasingly annoyed

and angry to think about either alternative. She planned to favor him only with a cool smile when he left. Instead, to her horror, a tingle crept up her hand when Lord Worthington took it and bowed as he took his leave on Lindon Hall's front steps.

"Miss Lindon, today has been an enormous pleasure." He smiled, the smile without artifice, without extra charm, even.

Penelope found herself returning that smile. "Thank you, my lord, for coming."

Lord Worthington joined his family in their carriage. The coachman started the horses. The carriage sprang forward.

"Interesting fellow, Worthington," Chad said.

"And so dashing," sighed Lady Lindon. She turned inside.

Penelope watched the carriage retreat down the drive.

"What do you think of him now?" asked Chad, sidling closer to Penelope.

Penelope rested her hand above her heart, surprised to find it racing. "My opinion of Lord Worthington has not changed, but I fear I have underestimated the amount of interest he will generate in our little Four Corners."

Chad laughed, put an arm around Penelope's waist. "I believe Miss Crimpin became so distracted she left us some lemon cake. And I am still hungry."

Penelope allowed Chad to lead her inside, but not before she glanced over her shoulder to the drive. The carriage had disappeared.

Chapter 3

The bootmaker assured Penelope he would have
boots ready for the twins within three days and sent to
Lindon Hall. She tipped him handsomely and guided
the twins back to the road that led north out of town,
then branched west to Lindon Hall. The air warm but
soft on her face, Penelope listened with contentment to
the twins chatter about the pretty wildflowers and what
Cook had made them for tea the day before.

"Lookie, Tina, a patchy rabbit. Come on, let's follow
him."

"Not off the road, Tim."

The twins ran ahead. The rabbit must have understood Penelope's directions because it darted off the
road into the underbrush. A fine lizard caught their eyes
after that, however, and they proceeded down the road,
from curiosity to curiosity.

The sun was bright and had grown quite hot. The day
Lady Drucilla Pargetter had come to her and told her
about Lieutenant Gerald DeVine, Penelope's fiancé, had
also been hot. Remembering the sympathy she had felt
for Lord Worthington, Penelope welcomed that ugly
memory.

"Miss Lindon," Lady Drucilla had said, coming into the
sitting room and holding out her hands to Penelope, "I
came the moment I received your letter. How dreadful!"

"It is more of a shock right now," Penelope had said,

indicating they should sit away from the sunshine pouring through the windows. "I looked at the Lists every day, but I never dreamed to see him appear on them. A place called Salamanca. You are very kind to come."

"Stuff and nonsense! We have become friends this last year, have we not? Of course I would come."

They had become friends, although it was a constant source of mystification to Penelope why Lady Drucilla, who had known Penelope all her life, should decide to pick her up now. Many things had separated them. Lady Drucilla was two years older and much more beautiful, had already been to London for her Season, and, as sister to Lord Worthington, she enjoyed considerably more consequence. Most of the time she acted like it, too. But an uncertainty sometimes peeked out from her that made Penelope feel protective of her, for all her worldly manners.

Penelope had captured that uncertain expression in a drawing one afternoon. She thought it some of her better work, and without realizing it, transferred some of her affection for her work to Lady Drucilla.

"I thought you would need some consoling, and sure enough, I find you with dark circles under your eyes."

Penelope said, carefully, "I regret Lieutenant DeVine's death, but it has been six months since I have seen him. We had not known each other very well to begin with, either. My father arranged the match in a fit of fatherly feeling." And Penelope suspected he would be as annoyed as anything to learn that his fit had gone for naught and he would have to reapply himself.

"I think you are trying to shrug off my sympathy. The circles are there, you must admit that."

"They are from Timothy's teething. He cries far into the night, and will allow no one but I to give him any comfort."

How far into the night had she rocked his little five-month-old body? Had he quieted at two o'clock? Three?

"That does not surprise me, not in the least," Lady Drucilla said. "The connection I and everyone else see between you and your poor sister's children—why, I think it quite the most sensible thing Lord Eversleigh could do to leave the twins in your able care."

Penelope forced another smile. "Helen was my dearest friend, not just my sister. I could not abandon her children to nurses and nannies."

"I hear Lady Eversleigh approves of the arrangement," said Lady Drucilla, referring to the twins' grandmother.

"I think Lady Eversleigh would have been happy to have two infants disturbing her household were she not quite so frail."

"But she is, so it is an ideal arrangement."

Then, some impulse of bitterness, perhaps prompted by lack of sleep, provoked Penelope to say, "Lord Eversleigh has written a condolence letter to me that has little to do with condolence, and everything to do with his own ideal arrangement."

"Whatever do you mean?" asked Lady Drucilla.

Penelope regretted her outburst, but it was there, she did not want to be a tease, and she had no reason not to trust Lady Drucilla. "His letter says that while I remain unmarried, he will not object to my continuing in care of the twins."

"You are so lucky." Lady Drucilla turned her face, stood, and walked away a few steps.

Penelope watched in alarm and astonishment.

When Lady Drucilla turned back, her expression strained, she said, "I do not know if I should tell you this. I have kept silent because I thought you cared for Lieutenant DeVine."

Penelope stood and went to Lady Drucilla, who held

her hand over her mouth. "Kept silent about what, Lady Drucilla?"

Lady Drucilla gripped Penelope's arm. "Lieutenant DeVine was not worthy of you, Miss Lindon. He was not worthy at all."

"You must be very plain with me," Penelope said, trying to contain her alarm.

"Do you remember when the lieutenant escorted you to Wildoaks for Worthington's twenty-fifth birthday dinner? Do you remember the time after dinner, when my aunt asked me to see why Masters did not answer the bell in the withdrawing room?"

Penelope nodded. She well remembered how Lady Honoria's lips had thinned every time she had pulled the cord. And Lady Drucilla had not hidden her displeasure at being sent with the message like some common maid.

"In the hall, I met Lieutenant DeVine. He had excused himself from the port and cigars. He could not have known I would be there, but—"

"But what?" Penelope asked.

"He attempted to ravish me."

"My God," Penelope said. She remembered how agitated Lady Drucilla had been upon returning to the drawing room. She had said little and avoided Penelope's glance of commiseration.

"I would not have said anything if you had not told me your feelings for him. You do believe me, do you not?"

Penelope's heart went out to her friend. "Of course. How terrible for you. How did you get away from him?"

Lady Drucilla lifted her chin. "Worthington called for him. He cursed under his breath. I could smell the wine. Then he pushed me away. You do see now why I think you are lucky? It was filthy, having him touch me. And now Worthington wants to marry me off to one of his friends, Lord St. Alverrin. You, you have an excuse never to have to put yourself forward. You can pretend you will never get over Lieutenant DeVine and go on with your twins. You have your own family. Do whatever you must to keep them."

So they hatched the idea between them. Penelope kept on the blacks she had donned for her sister, for Gerald. She soon discovered her sad story was the romantic tale of the Four Corners, and her mourning of Gerald kept away other suitors.

Would such a ruse have worked for poor Lady Drucilla. After several agonized letters to Penelope about how horrid her marriage to St. Alverrin was, Lady Drucilla had died, ostensibly of some ailment. Penelope wondered with considerable pain, however, whether Lady Drucilla had taken her own life.

Penelope did not believe that all men were base, but it was disconcerting how normal Gerald had appeared. He had kissed her when he had asked for her hand. The sensation had been pleasant, although not the earth-shattering experience told in poems or her mother's novels. Could one ever glean clues to someone's inner self from his outward appearance and behavior?

Certainly she was no sterling example of one's outward appearance as indicative of one's inward self. At least, not until lately. Within one week of Lucas Pargetter's return to Derbyshire, she was dangerously close to putting the lie to the character she had constructed for herself.

"Auntie Penny, come quick!" called Tina from the top of the rise. Penelope hurried, seeing Timothy standing next to a tall, stocky man who held a red roan's front hoof.

"He's in trouble," Tina said, taking Penelope's hand.

The man straightened and doffed his cap. "Ma'am."

He was dressed as a well-placed servant, in a brown, plainly cut coat, and his craggy face was deeply tanned. Black brows drew a heavy line across his forehead.

"I am Miss Lindon. Do you require assistance?"

"Name's Jarvis, Miss. I work for Cap'n, that is, for Lord Worthington. Red here's come up lame."

"He has a boulder in his shoe," Timothy said happily.

"Did I not just see you in town?"

"That you did, Miss."

" 'Tis strange that your horse came up lame after so short a distance."

"Aye, Miss," said he slowly.

Penelope recalled Sir William questioning Lord Worthington and wondered whether Lady Howath had been working her mischief among the townsfolk. By and large they were fine people, but it had never been difficult to persuade them to mistrust someone.

"Perhaps you should bring your horse back to Lindon Hall. Our groom can remove the stone."

"Thankee, Miss."

"Can I ride him?" asked Timothy. "Can I?"

"No, dear. The horse is limping."

"Poor horsey," Tina said.

"Here," Jarvis said, pulling a small apple from his pocket. He waited for Penelope's nod before handing it to Timothy. "Palm flat, now, or he'll munch your digits."

Timothy fed Red the apple and giggled as the roan nuzzled his palm. "You can do it next time," he promised his sister.

The four started off, Jarvis leading Red, the twins skipping around the limping horse. Presently they tired of that, and ran ahead to investigate some wildflowers.

"You knew Lord Worthington when he was in the navy?"

"Aye, Miss."

"For how long?"

"Since when he was a midshipman."

Jarvis, Penelope surmised, was not in the habit of volunteering information. "He was good at it, I assume?"

"Miss?"

"Being a midshipman. Otherwise, I suspect he wouldn't have become a captain."

Did Jarvis's brown eyes betray a flicker of good humor? "At first he didn't know his tops'l from his t'gallant. Didn't know how to rig a line. Or even how to salute a superior officer."

Penelope smiled. She could well imagine Lucas Pargetter being unable to acknowledge anyone as a superior.

"He learned," Jarvis said. "I say he was one of the finest captains they've had in fifty years. Knew how to treat his men, could charm wind from Heaven, and took frigates, Miss, when he felt like it, even when he was lieutenant."

"That is unusual?"

"For most. For one not bred to it, aye, Miss."

Penelope asked a question without asking. "There are rumors in town about Lord Worthington."

Jarvis again turned his steady gaze on her. "Aye, Miss."

"And you are angry about them."

Jarvis pursed his lips. "Aye, Miss."

The twins sighted the gates to Lindon Hall's drive, and the four setters her father kept about the grounds galloped out to greet the twins. The twins threw their arms around the friendly dogs and giggled when the setters licked their faces. Jarvis's roan rolled his eyes at the dogs, but was too tired to prance and paw about.

"Timothy, Tina, take the setters up to the house."

The twins needed no further encouragement, but raced up the grassy hill to the house, the setters yipping at their heels.

"The stables are to the right," said Penelope. She and Jarvis took the path that wound round the Hall to the mews. Jarvis studied the manor and its grounds carefully.

Penelope suspected his approval would not be easily granted.

At the stables, a groom hurried up, wiping his hands on a towel he carried in his pocket.

"Higgins, see that this horse's shoe is looked to."

"Yes, ma'am." Higgins led the roan away, clucking at him cheerfully. The roan followed without hesitation.

"Would you like to wait in the kitchen? 'Tis on your left. I'll tell Cook to set aside something for you."

"Thankee, Miss."

"Good day to you." Penelope turned and walked up to the house, brows raised. She wanted to find Chad. This news would catch his interest, and maybe she could quench its newness before she had to face her neighbors.

Lucas tweaked the fold of his cravat into something a bit more appropriate to a lord than a sea captain. God, but he hated this dressing for dinner. He had begun to loathe all of country life, as a point of fact, except, perhaps, for the long rides and walks he took in the woods most afternoons. And then, there was a pair of honest blue eyes he would have sought out again if he could find some excuse that she would not see as an improper advance. There was something exhilarating about the way Miss Lindon forgot her implacability.

But first, Lucas thought, he must determine why Jarvis swayed in his dressing mirror as though performing some jig in half time. "You have something to say, Jarvis?"

"Aye, Cap'n. There're some ugly rumors about town."

"That I murdered Edmund, no doubt."

"That you're a filthy poisoner, beggin' your pardon, sir."

"I suspected as much. How did you hear about the rumors?"

"Stopped for a pint. When I left town, Red came up lame."

Lucas turned from the mirror to regard Jarvis. "Why didn't you tell me immediately? I'll not have you put in jeopardy."

" 'Twas just a bit of heckling, Cap'n." And Jarvis described what had happened.

"Miss Lindon, you say? Was she upset?"

"She'd figured out about the rumors, Cap'n, but seemed to take the notion quiet-like. No fits or faints."

That was high praise indeed from Jarvis, Lucas thought. He paced about, wondering if she had felt pain at the rumors, then cursed himself for assuming that she would care about someone she had met only twice. Then he cursed himself again for even wondering about it. He was growing back into his old habits of distraction if he could contemplate austere Miss Lindon so. And yet, he had seen fire in those blue eyes, too. Passion lay under the surface, and passion had forever intrigued him.

"Why did my cousin show such poor judgment as to be poisoned the one day I came into Derbyshire?"

"Sailors' luck."

"Thanks." Lucas took a few more trips about the room.

"Beggin' your pardon, Cap'n, but what do you intend to do about it?"

"The rumors, or my cousin's poor judgment?" Lucas smiled, but could not maintain it before Jarvis's affronted and disapproving expression. Lucas held up both hands. "Peace. Levity aside, they are one and the same question."

"Cap'n?"

"No one can prove that I murdered Edmund, but no

one other than Edmund or the bastard who murdered him can disprove it. From whom do I seek redress for the rumors? No one. The less I say about it, the better."

Jarvis shrugged, and warning bells sounded in Lucas's mind. "What have you left out?" he asked Jarvis. "Speak up, man. I asked you to come with me because I knew I would need someone who was not afraid to tell me the truth when I needed it."

Although his expression did not change, Jarvis appeared more uncomfortable. "'Tis only part of it, that you were seen riding away from here on that day, I mean."

"And the other part?" Lucas asked grimly.

"That you admitted to meeting Lady Worthington two years ago. The town folk are thinking that—"

"Given my reputation, I would naturally murder my cousin for a pretty woman and avenge myself for being buried alive at sea, away from all temptation. Of course, I see it all so clearly now. Damn and blast. I never thought my reputation would bite me in the face quite like this." A gong sounded from far off in the house. "Damn and blast. We'll pick this up later. At least now we know where the wind's coming from."

"Aye aye, Cap'n."

Lucas went downstairs in a devilish temper. He wished vehemently that he had never had the misfortune to step into The Green Duck that day eleven years ago and wink at Mary Smith. At the time, he had looked on her fresh cheeks and lush curves as his hope of salvation, for Mary Smith kept his mind from Miss Maria Aylsbury. Lucas had known he could not pursue gently bred ladies the way he pursued Mary Smith or he would quickly end up married, which, at twenty-two, he had considered akin to a slow, rotting death. So no matter how prettily Miss Aylsbury had thrown herself at him, Lucas had managed to sidestep her.

If Lucas had only known what a slow, rotting death

really was, he would never have likened marriage to it. Eleven years at sea, the first three as a midshipman, saluting fifteen-year-olds as his superiors, had taught him perspective. The irony, Lucas thought, was that he had gained his perspective because of Miss Aylsbury's wounded feelings, rather than Mary Smith's bared breasts, which, he recalled, were not all that fine.

The family waited for him in the salon. Cecily broke into a large smile, her hand dangling toward her full cleavage as if to say, "Look at me." Honoria, sipping her sherry, contrived to look like she were being forced to drink distilled vinegar.

But Uncle Albert clapped him on the shoulder. "My dear boy, have you had a pleasant day?"

"Thank you, Uncle, I have." Lucas poured himself a sherry and leaned against the mantelpiece. "Until my steward came home and told me the news about town."

Honoria studied the wainscoting. Cecily's smile increased in magnitude. The cat, Lucas thought.

Uncle Albert said, "What is the gossip, my boy?"

"Dinner is served, my lord."

"We will be in presently, Masters."

"Very good, my lord." Masters bowed and closed the door.

"The gossip, Uncle, is that I murdered Edmund to, shall we say, gain access to my cousin Lady Worthington." Lucas realized from the way Uncle Albert's smile froze that he was using the same bark he would use to address a slackard sailor. "We all know that this rumor is completely untrue. Edmund and I ran around like brothers when we were younger, and marrying his widow would feel something like incest."

Cecily's smile dimmed, and her hand drooped below her cleavage. Thus encouraged, Lucas said, "There's no way I can refute this dreadful rumor, but I expect us as a *family* to treat the rumor for what it is, unsubstantiated, malicious gossip. I am not making an idle request. God knows I have contributed to this family's spicy character, but I'll not allow anything below-board to occur in this house. Is that understood?"

"The navy has matured you, Worthington. You are a different person," Honoria said.

He bowed, although disliking her patronizing tone. "Aye. Now, shall we go in to dinner?" He offered his arm to Cecily as the highest ranked woman there.

She took his arm gingerly. "You are cruel, Worthington," she hissed.

"I am what Fortune has made me," he replied softly, and wondered what else mocking Fortune had in store for him. It was looking less and less likely, however, Lucas thought with a stab of regret, that it would be a pair of passionate blue eyes.

Chapter 4

A shaft of sunlight flooded Penelope's study, raising the sudden smell of warm dust. Penelope looked up from her household account books in surprise and beheld the Oriental rug glowing in rich red and blue. It had stormed for five days straight. Knowing how high expectations were that this harvest would make amends for the past two years, Penelope had added her prayers to the servants' that the rain did not damage the crops so near to harvest. It would strain all the community's resources to provide and accept charity through a third winter.

She walked to the French windows. Big gray and white clouds parted grandly to allow the sun to stream down. Penelope opened the doors and breathed in cool air. Returning to the desk, she blew out the lamp she had been using and set aside her letters. Lady Howath had written wondering whether they should cancel the Harvest Festival because of the rumors about Lord Worthington. Penelope had in turn written to her, Mrs. Simons, and Mrs. Tipplethwaite, a local institution, that she could not see the point, and she wanted her letters delivered immediately.

Penelope threw open the study door and came nose to nose with Masters. She gasped in surprise. Masters started, then tugged on his coattails and said, "Excuse me, Miss Lindon."

"Excuse *me,* Masters. The sunshine has infected me, I fear."

Masters nodded. "I have come to ask your advice on a matter of some delicacy."

"Of course," Penelope murmured and motioned for him to come in. She stood with the sunshine bathing her back in warmth while Masters directed his gaze somewhere just over her left shoulder.

"My brother has requested me to ask you to intervene in a matter concerning one of Lord Worthington's tenants."

"Oh dear," Penelope said sympathetically. The two Masters brothers were very good friends, but they did not comment upon the running of each other's households unless in need of desperate advice. "What's the problem?"

"A Mrs. Bagley. Her thatch has given way in the rain."

"The same Mrs. Bagley who lost her husband in the mill fire last year? Then why does she not apply to Lord Worthington?"

Masters cleared his throat. "I am told she had a bad experience with the late Lord Worthington. She has heard the gossip in town and fears the new Lord Worthington is, ah . . . "

"Cut from the same cloth?" Penelope suggested delicately.

Masters turned his full gaze on her, said, "Exactly so, Miss Lindon," and looked away again. "My brother has tried to use his authority within the household to persuade her to appeal to Lord Worthington—but with no result."

"Lord Worthington has no steward?"

"Lord Worthington has, apparently, been working the books himself." Masters's tone was a ringing reflection of his elder brother's freezing disapproval. "There is also this man Jarvis. My brother says the household is unsure of his position."

To create such ambiguity was to fly in the face of an unwritten code centuries old. Penelope imagined the consternation at Wildoaks. "What an awful situation!"

"I felt certain you would understand, Miss."

Penelope sighed, considered her options. "Well, if the mountain will not go to Mahomet . . . "

"Miss Lindon?"

Penelope shook her head. "Never mind me, Masters. Ask the stables to hitch the low phaeton, will you please? I shall discuss this matter directly with Lord Worthington. And would you please arrange to have these letters delivered?"

Although she had not been in Wildoaks in more than five years, Penelope had remembered its main hall as a tasteful space. Certainly she would not have thought the green-and-purple striped sofas along a far wall tasteful. She pitied the parlor maid dusting the large Chinese vase tucked into an alcove at the base of the imposing marble staircase. The maid had many more statuettes and paintings to go.

"Miss Lindon," said her Masters's elder brother, bowing. He was a stouter version of her Masters, with a little less hair, but he held his long nose at exactly the same proud angle.

"I would like to see Lord Worthington, please, Masters."

Masters inclined his head. "I will see if he is available."

Masters appeared from a door near one of the garish sofas and escorted Penelope to the room beyond it. Lord Worthington stood behind a large desk at the far end of the room. He looked as if he had just shrugged on his blue coat. From the numerous account books, ledgers and loose sheets of paper spread out over the desk, it also looked as if the books were giving him trouble. His spiky hair told a history of frustration.

Nonetheless, he was still the most handsome man Penelope could remember seeing, including Gerald. His disarray only seemed to add to his charm by making him human and attainable. Goodness, Penelope thought, I must control these thoughts.

He came forward. "Miss Lindon, what a wonderful surprise. Do come in. Masters, some refreshment for Miss Lindon."

"I am sorry, my lord, for disturbing you. You appear to have your hands full."

"Don't apologize, Miss Lindon. I'm attempting to piece together these estate books my cousin left me, and I cannot seem to make sense of them, so an interruption is welcome."

"Are they so much different from a ship's accounts?"

"Immensely. Please sit down. Over here, next to the window, away from this mess. You are comfortable? Good. Yes, these books are much different from the *Atlantia's* accounts. There, my problems started and stopped at her hull. I didn't much care how supplies came to the docks—that was a lieutenant's or purser's responsibility—nor what happened to it once it left my ship."

"You make it sound very easy, my lord."

"There were other challenges, Miss Lindon, but I did not have to keep track of income and outflow of money from various estates and holdings, some of which are more mysterious than sea monsters and St. Elmo's fire." He smiled disarmingly. "But you didn't come to listen to my troubles. What can I do for you?"

"It has come to my attention, my lord," Penelope said carefully, "that one of your tenants needs her thatch replaced."

"I'm surprised it hasn't come to my attention," he replied just as carefully, but the twinkle in his eyes vanished.

"My lord, may I speak frankly?"

"I will be disappointed if you do not."

Penelope glanced out the window for a moment so she could think how to begin. Looking at Lord Worthington distracted her. She found herself wondering what he had looked like in naval uniform, pacing the deck of a ship in heaving seas, ordering his men into battle. Doubtless he would be swift and decisive, and above all, masterful. She almost shivered.

"Although I am reluctant to say so," she said, "your cousin is not well missed. However, the circumstances surrounding his death . . . well, they have disturbed the whole community."

"You're telling me my tenants don't trust me."

He sounded matter-of-fact, but Penelope said quickly, "I don't think it is as bad as that, my lord. I suspect that they have become unused to trusting Lords Worthington before you came because of your cousin's character, now because of, well . . . "

"*My* character."

"My lord—"

He held up a hand. "I've heard the rumors, Miss Lindon. If my tenants don't trust me, then I have a definite course to lay in. I can begin by getting the name and direction of this tenant and seeing to it personally that her thatch is repaired. This afternoon, in fact."

"Her name is Mrs. Bagley, and she lives east of the river near the small bend."

"Very good. Thank you for telling me, Miss Lindon, and for being so frank."

" 'Tis nothing, my lord, but . . . perhaps you would wish to bring Lady Worthington with you?"

"Lady Worthington? Whatever for?" he asked,

frowning. "Besides, she's told me that she does not visit 'the peasants.'"

Penelope bit back a flicker of anger. "Mrs. Bagley is a widow, my lord."

Lord Worthington ran a tanned hand over his equally tanned face. "A young, comely widow too, no doubt."

"Yes, she is. In fact," Penelope said with a slight smile, "she's reputed to be the most attractive woman, barring Lady Worthington, on Wildoaks property."

"You needn't be amused," he said, some good humor returning, "for if she has the repute you claim, I'm certain there are bets in town about when I might uncover her."

Penelope could not help starting, for she had been thinking of just such bets.

He shook his head against the hand on which he propped it. "I see I have a long way to go. Well, since I cannot induce Lady Worthington to join me, would you lend me countenance, ma'am?"

"I have my phaeton if you wish to depart without delay."

"Miss Lindon, you're a woman after my own heart. If you'll excuse me for a few minutes, I'll make sure no one mistakes me for his lordship's secretary." Lord Worthington rose and strode to the doorway just as Masters came back. "Ah, good. Serve Miss Lindon, Masters, and pass the word for Jarvis." He rocked back on his boot heels, put a finger to his lips and said, "Please *summon* Jarvis and tell him to get his horse."

"Very good, my lord."

Penelope sipped tea and ate warm apple cake while waiting for him to return. She studied the littered desk, and, for the first time, seriously doubted whether Lucas Pargetter had murdered his cousin. Womanizer he might be—one need only consider the wickedly engaging smile that had melted her heart—but dissembler, well, she was none too sure. He could be a better actor than

Kean, but he appeared truly frustrated by the estate books.

When Lord Worthington returned, he did not appear flashy—a gold ring on his right hand was his only decoration—but the excellent cut of his brown coat and tan trousers ensured that no one would mistake this man for his lordship's secretary. Indeed, no one could mistake him for less than magnificent. Penelope hoped she did not blush at the thought and nodded to Jarvis, who followed, also dressed conservatively.

"It's good to see you again, Jarvis."

"Miss," he said.

"Shall we?" Lord Worthington asked.

Penelope took Lord Worthington's proffered arm. He could not be a murderer, she told herself. For how could he be when he made her whole hand tingle at one light touch?

Jarvis swung himself up on Red. Lord Worthington handed her into the phaeton. "Where is your groom?"

"You are looking at her," Penelope said, picking up the reins from their holder. "Do you prefer to drive yourself?"

"Not in the face of so direct a challenge, Miss Lindon."

Penelope blushed. "I did not intend—"

Lord Worthington chuckled and climbed in. "Don't worry, Miss Lindon. 'Tis only fitting that I give over the reins to you. This's your ship, not mine. Not yet, anyway."

Penelope was not sure how to take his comment, so she started her horse with a light flick of the reins. When they arrived at Mrs. Bagley's cottage, Lord Worthington said, "You're an excellent driver. How long have you been about it?"

"Papa insisted we all learn when we were quite young. That's Chad, Helen, and myself. Helen was the twins' mother. Ah, there's little Johnnie Bagley."

The tow-headed boy took one look at them and ran

back inside the cottage, screaming for his mother. Penelope chuckled and took Lord Worthington's hand to get down from the phaeton. At his touch, her gloved hand tingled again, and the feeling made her shiver. She glanced at her hand and him briefly, puzzled. She thought Lord Worthington might ask her what was wrong, but Mrs. Bagley's appearing at the cottage door carrying a baby on a generous hip distracted him. Fear and worry had obscured the widow's pretty features somewhat, but her famous hair glowed like a second sun. Johnnie reappeared from behind her plain blue skirt.

"Miss Lindon?" she asked, looking from Jarvis to Lord Worthington as if deciding which of them would eat her first.

"Good afternoon, Mrs. Bagley. Please permit me to introduce Lord Worthington to you. When he heard of your trouble he asked me to introduce him so you can tell him what needs doing."

The breezy speech seemed to reassure Mrs. Bagley. She curtsied very low, considering the child she carried. "Milord."

"Mrs. Bagley, my pleasure. This's Jarvis, my steward. May we come in and look at the damage to your roof?"

Mrs. Bagley pursed her lips and looked as if she were about to cry. She shifted the baby to the other hip.

"It's rained hard the last five days. His lordship will excuse the damp," Penelope said with a speaking look at him.

Mrs. Bagley hesitated. Lord Worthington smiled disarmingly. Then she said, "Come in, ma'am, milord. I have some cider left."

"That will be lovely, Mrs. Bagley," Penelope said, thinking, *You rogue,* in Lord Worthington's direction.

The hole in the thatch made the far half of the cottage as bright as outdoors. A large spot darkened the floorboards, spreading out from a puddle. Mrs. Bagley had pulled her furniture to the shaded side of the cottage's main room, making the space appear dark and cluttered. A dank odor engulfed them.

Mrs. Bagley grimaced, put the baby down in a crib next to the fire. She offered Penelope a chair at the table. Johnnie darted to a shadowy corner. Lord Worthington and Jarvis wandered about the place, pointing out different spots on the floor and along the roof and talking quietly between themselves.

"Does this trapdoor lead to a root cellar?" Lord Worthington asked.

"Yes, milord. And 'tis flooded." Mrs. Bagley's eyes moistened.

"Once it's dry, it should be no problem to restock. 'Tis just harvest time, after all," Lord Worthington said. "Why, your apple tree must have the most beautiful apples on Wildoaks."

Mrs. Bagley managed a tentative smile, then poured out the cider. Penelope marveled that Lord Worthington had noticed the apple tree outside in addition to noticing Mrs. Bagley.

"Do you have an attic?"

"Yes, milord. 'Tis up those stairs. The boys sleep there."

At Lord Worthington's signal, Jarvis climbed the stairs. Lord Worthington took a seat at the small table. It creaked under his weight. Although he smiled at her, Penelope read anger in the stiff set of his broad shoulders.

Jarvis loped down the stairs. "Worse up there, Cap'n."

"Here is the cider, milord, Miss Lindon, Mr. Jarvis?"

"Thank you, Mrs. Bagley," Penelope said, accepting for all of them.

"Join us," said Lord Worthington when it appeared that Mrs. Bagley would stand near the fire.

Mrs. Bagley looked to Penelope, who nodded. When Mrs. Bagley sat down, fingers curled around her cup, Lord Worthington asked, "How long has Mr. Bagley been gone?"

"Over a year, milord. He died in the mill fire."

"I'm very sorry." He took a sip, as though pausing to consider how to proceed. "You knew the thatch was weak?"

Mrs. Bagley's lips worked, and she glanced away toward the dark corner where Johnnie crouched.

"My lord," Penelope protested.

Lord Worthington turned his intent look upon Penelope. "I have every intention of repairing the roof, Miss Lindon, but it would've been far easier to repair before it got to this state. I'd like to know why it did."

Penelope stood. Lord Worthington and Jarvis also stood. "May I see you outside for a moment, my lord?"

Without a word, he followed her outside. "Miss Lindon—"

Penelope rounded on him, blinking in the sun and whispering angrily, "That poor woman asked your cousin to fix her thatch last winter, and what did it get her but a slip on the shoulder."

Lord Worthington looked taken aback and angry. "You might have mentioned that, Miss Lindon."

"Why do you think the woman is so frightened? Can you not see what is plain before you?"

His lip curled. "I thought it my sterling reputation."

"That and your cousin's."

They regarded each other for a long, tense moment. His jaw twitched. "If there is nothing else, shall we go back inside?"

Penelope inclined her head and went back in. They sat down at the table. Jarvis glanced carefully from one to the other, and Penelope hoped he could not discern her flushed cheeks.

Lord Worthington smiled at Mrs. Bagley, and Penelope seethed. "Mrs. Bagley, I will have someone repairing your roof, attic and cellar within the afternoon, and since my cousin neglected to fix it, I cannot permit you to suffer any hardship because of it. Will you and the children be able to stay here?"

Mrs. Bagley glanced at Penelope. Penelope relaxed her lips enough to smile in reassurance. Mrs. Bagley appeared to melt into her chair. "Thank you, milord. We are grateful. 'Twill be no inconvenience for us."

"Good. In future, ma'am, if you should have any difficulties, send for Jarvis here." He stood. "Thank you for the cider."

Mrs. Bagley curtsied and escorted them the few steps to the door. Once outside, Lord Worthington instructed Jarvis to ride back to Wildoaks and arrange for a carpenter.

"Make sure he replaces every damaged board. Inspect it personally."

"Aye aye, Cap'n." Jarvis mounted Red and was off.

Penelope climbed into her phaeton, Lord Worthington catching her arm to assist her at the last moment. She glanced at him coolly. "Thank you."

He climbed up with a lithe, graceful pull against the side. Penelope started her horse. They rode for several miles through the quiet countryside, but the coolness of lush trees overhanging the road interspersed with warm views of bowing grain fields and glimpses of tidy cottages did nothing to make Penelope feel more peaceful.

Lord Worthington pointed to a bank of trees at the roadside. "Would you stop for a moment?"

She pulled over into the shade, her heart pounding. Her horse snorted and stamped, sending a scattering of pebbles toward the wheels. She was alone with a notorious womanizer. What could she expect from him? More to the point, she thought, feeling her palms become damp, what did she want from him?

Lord Worthington took off his beaver, ran a hand through his thick blond hair. Penelope wondered if he knew the gesture likewise ruffled her nerves. He replaced the hat, and Penelope braced herself to have to say something quelling.

"I apologize, Miss Lindon, for becoming angry. You were trying to spare Mrs. Bagley embarrassment, and I appreciate that. I didn't know my cousin had such a reputation."

All amazement, Penelope found refuge in being sharp. "When I said, my lord, that there were few who would miss your cousin, I was referring to the numerous farmers and millworkers whose wives, sisters, and daughters have been more or less fair game. And then, of course, to those good women themselves."

He smiled faintly. "That was a shot below the waterline."

Penelope blushed. "Forgive me."

"Don't be sorry. I'm glad to have someone tell me what I need to know. But, you haven't said you accept my apology."

"I do." She watched herself twist the slack reins.

Lord Worthington laughed, surprising her. "It's ironic, Miss Lindon, that I never suspected my cousin of being a randy old goat because he sent me down for a similar reason."

"I have heard, my lord, that the difference between you and your cousin was his discretion."

He cocked a brow. "Ah, more gossip? I shall have to beg you for information more often. You're certainly awake on all suits. The question of discretion is a sore point indeed. But there is another difference between me and my cousin: I may have been caught, but I never forced myself on any woman."

Penelope flushed, but from pain, not embarrassment. Lady Drucilla had told Penelope that Gerald had not thought he was forcing her, only taking what was offered him by circumstances.

"My speech is too plain. Forgive me. Look, even that jay in the oak is scolding me. He knows I should not be speaking to a lady this way. I never have, either." He stroked his jaw thoughtfully. "I am convinced it's good for me, so I'll tell you a secret. I'm glad I was indiscreet those eleven years ago, because I cannot think what a useless fribble I would be today if Edmund had not sent me down. You are smiling. What are you thinking of?"

"I pictured you in a striped scarlet waistcoat with a purple coat," she said.

He laughed. "Miss Lindon, you are the first person here to make me laugh. I know I asked once before, but hope I may now consider you a friend."

Although pleased, Penelope's earlier wariness rose to the fore. "My lord, I do not think—"

"Are you worried about my reputation?" he asked lightly, although that serious look was in his eyes again.

"No, my lord," she said, not sure she was telling the truth, but wanting to be kind. "Even if you had no particular reputation, it would not be proper. It would cause talk."

He compressed his lips, and she thought he would argue. Then he said, "I respect your instincts, Miss Lindon. As a secret friend, then, would you tell me something?"

Secret friend, indeed! But there was her voice, saying, "If it is in my power, my lord."

"Have my other tenants been neglected like Mrs. Bagley?"

"Yes, my lord."

He sighed. "I suspected so. I cannot tell you how angry I was to see that woman's thatch. Had I let my ship deteriorate to the same point, I would have sunk her just taking her out of port. How can someone be so careless with people's lives?"

"It was not carelessness. I heard reports that your cousin refused repairs because he thought his tenants lazy."

"I'm sure Edmund made no secret of his opinion."

"No, my lord, he did not."

Lord Worthington shook his head. "I'm only surprised no one murdered him a long time ago."

"I know they do not miss him, but you cannot believe one of the tenants—" Penelope began, aghast.

"I don't know what to think, except that if a tenant had done such a thing, I feel certain he would've bashed in my cousin's head, not poisoned him."

Penelope shuddered, and Lord Worthington covered her hand with his. "Forgive me, Miss Lindon. Truly my tongue does run away with me when I'm with you. Now, I suggest you get me back to Wildoaks. I think I'll make plans to visit each of my tenants and see what I can do."

Penelope removed her hand. "I think that an excellent plan, my lord."

The smile on his face showed he had fully comprehended why she had taken her hand back. "Could you do me another favor, Miss Lindon? When we are not burdened with others, could you call me 'Captain' instead of 'my lord'?"

It seemed a small thing. "If you wish it, Captain."

Chapter 5

Penelope poured tea into gold-rimmed cups and fretted inwardly. Since Lord Worthington had come into the county, she felt as if she were participating in an endless tea party with her neighbors. The Crimpin ladies, Mrs. Simons, and Lady Howath had descended upon her mother and found Lady Lindon receiving.

Penelope appreciated the distraction for her mother's sake; it was good for Lady Lindon to come up for air from one of her novels. Penelope found it difficult, however, to watch Lucia Crimpin toss her curls about and say sugary things.

Chad crossed the entrance hall in front of the open drawing room door. He smiled and set his hand upon the oaken molding as if he would come in and greet her. Penelope widened her eyes and tilted her head slightly, holding up the teapot. Chad's eyes widened in response, then he grinned, bowed with a flourish, and was off. Penelope envied him.

"So, then, ladies, we are agreed," Lady Howath said, accepting her cup of tea. "Even after what Lord Worthington did yesterday, you could not persuade me to cancel the Harvest Festival. You are very eloquent, Miss Lindon."

Penelope suppressed her frown. She little liked Lady Howath's digs on any day of the week. She liked them less today.

Then her mother asked, "Why, what happened yesterday?"

The four visitors straightened as though one hand had pulled strings in their backs. "Do you mean you have not heard?" asked Lady Howath. "Yesterday, Worthington ordered a complete thatch for the Bagley widow's cottage, and he is paying for it."

Lady Lindon looked perplexed. "But that was kind of him."

Bless you, Mother, Penelope thought.

"Mrs. Bagley is a very comely widow," Mrs. Crimpin said. "And, he not only paid for it, but he also ordered his butler to send out two weeks' provisions for the woman and her children from the Wildoaks pantry."

Had Penelope received this information from Chad, or maybe even Masters, she would have whistled her surprise and amazement at such extreme generosity.

"Oh dear," her mother said again, but glanced at Penelope to assess the full egregiousness of Lord Worthington's actions.

Penelope, however, had to remain forcibly bland.

"Yes," Lady Howath said, "it appears he has not changed, despite eleven years at sea."

"Perhaps because of them," Mrs. Crimpin said sleekly.

Penelope thought of the papers on Lord Worthington's desk, the anger he had kept carefully controlled while he surveyed the damage to the cottage, and said, "Lady Howath, Lord Worthington did not strike me as a man who planned an assignation."

Lady Howath smiled indulgently. "You have never been married, Miss Lindon, so you do not know what all men are capable of. Doubtless he has learned your story and feels some obligation to protect you from embarrassment."

Despite Lady Howath's attempt at tact, Penelope felt heat creep into her cheeks. She found the conversation embarrassing, and wanted it ended immediately, not only because of the way it reflected her neighbors' judgments of her character and worth, but because it roused a strange sympathy in her for Lord Worthington. Why was she letting the matter bother her so?

She was flustered enough to say, "Perhaps he is genuinely trying to change his reputation."

"Then he has quite the job ahead of himself," Mrs. Crimpin said. "The Four Corners might have forgiven him his reputation for womanizing now he is Worthington had it not been for this suspicion of murder."

"How does that relate to his previous reputation?" Penelope asked. She sipped her tea, displeased with herself for being forward thrice in the same conversation.

"He admitted to Sir William that he met Lady Worthington on his last visit to Derbyshire some two years ago," said Lady Howath easily. "Given his reputation, the implication is—"

"I understand the implication, my lady. But he has been gone from here for eleven years, taken on a new life. Will no one believe that people change?" Penelope asked.

"My dear," began Lady Howath.

"There is no reason to believe people change," said Mrs. Simons, vehemently, "because they do not." She paused, seemed to listen to something, smiled. "More tea, please, Miss Lindon?"

Everyone stared at Mrs. Simons. Then Lady Lindon said, "Mrs. Simons asked for more tea, Penelope."

Mrs. Simons handed over her teacup. Penelope filled it.

Then Lady Howath shook her head and said, "No. If he is turning his attention to the tenants so quickly, I wonder if that other speculation is not too far from the mark."

Penelope opened her mouth to begin a seething protest.

Masters at the door saved her from an indiscretion. "Excuse me, Miss Lindon, there's a matter requiring your attention."

"Go right ahead, dear," her mother said when Penelope looked for approval. "I am certain you can handle it. She manages everything here so nicely, I have not to lift a finger."

Lady Howath smiled with a trace of pity. Penelope did not know to whom Lady Howath directed it.

"In the kitchen, ma'am," Masters said.

Penelope preceded him, walking so quickly her skirts cut about her, annoying her. In the kitchen, Chad leaned against the cutting block munching a biscuit and talking to Jarvis, who stood erect, hands clasped loosely behind him.

"Look who's here," Chad said gaily. "Didn't I tell you, Jarvis, that my sister'd be happy to see you? We've saved her from those old gossips."

"And you must go right back up there and see what they are saying, Chad."

"Egad, give over. You must be joking." Chad looked as if Penelope had proposed he dip himself in hot oil.

"They're saying some awful things about Lord Worthington, and I cannot very well go back and sit down. Go be your charming self, Chadwick, or should I say, Ul—"

"I'm off," he said before she could finish saying his given name of Ulysses, of which he was excessively embarrassed. "You owe me one for this, Penny." He nodded to Jarvis and left.

"Sit down, please, Jarvis," said Penelope, indicating the long servants' table tucked away in a nook near the outside kitchen door. "Please tell Lord Worthington that his kindness to Mrs. Bagley is raising some more ugly rumors in town."

"For repairing her thatch, Miss?" He raised his brows, clearly not understanding such a reaction.

"No, for sending out all those provisions." When Jarvis pursed his lips, Penelope added, "They will soon be saying he has singled out Mrs. Bagley for her beauty, and if he has not changed, why, 'tis as likely as anything he could murder his cousin for the estate and get Lady Worthington or any other woman on Wildoaks as a prize."

"Cap'n never wanted any of it, Miss." More than a tint of anger colored Jarvis's words.

"That may be, but it's a hard thing for people around here to believe. But what did you want to see me about?"

"Cap'n sent me to give you this." Jarvis half snorted as he drew a package wrapped in cotton from his coat pocket and proffered it. "To thank you for your help with Mrs. Bagley."

"It is not necessary to thank me in such a way," Penelope protested. "Indeed, I cannot accept a gift from Lord Worthington." Heavens, she thought, what would Lady Howath and Mrs. Crimpin make of that!

"Cap'n said 'tis for your two sloops."

Penelope could not scruple to refuse a gift for the twins, nor could anyone look askance at such a gift. With a little shrug, she took the package and found two perfect wooden tops each the size of her hand inside the soft cotton. "How wonderful. Wherever did Lord Worthington find them?"

"Carved 'em himself."

"Himself?" Penelope marveled at their smoothness and balance. It seemed to her that the wood itself was warm, but perhaps she was only flushed from the warmth of the kitchen.

"Ship cap'ns often take up pass-the-times, just like us regular folk."

Penelope rested her chin on her fist. Jarvis was almost talkative. "I hadn't thought there would be time for him."

"A mort of it. Fifteen minutes of action, fifteen days of ho-hum."

Chad breezed into the kitchen. He pulled Cook's
apron strings as he passed the stove, earning an exasperated glance. "It's lovely in there. From the way they
talk, the county should put every comely female under
lock and key." He smiled. "At least the last Worthington
took 'em by force. They're all afraid this one will
merely have to crook his finger."

Penelope started. Could Chad be right? Would Lord
Worthington only have to crook his finger? Even Penelope had felt his charm. Felt? she thought. Been so
overwhelmed she had forgotten herself, was more like it.

"What's the matter, Penny?"

Penelope brought herself back to business and smiled
grimly. "Lord Worthington will only make matters
worse when he starts these visits to his tenants."

"How?" asked Jarvis.

"They will think," said Chad, matching Penelope's
smile, "that he is doing some more reconnaissance."

"Excuse me a moment, Mr. Marston," Lucas said as
Jarvis entered his study. Marston the Younger's mouth
instantly closed, and he ran his finger down a column of
closely written figures in the large account book he held
as though he might find some backbone in the straight
column.

"What did she say?"

"She was not entirely happy about it, but she agrees
to accompany you provided her brother ride with you
too, Cap'n."

Lucas stroked his chin, felt in its roughness the hours
he had had away from his razor that morning, hours spent
poring over accounts and numbers. "A fair strategy." He
saw it clearly. If she had brought along another woman,
she would have shown the county she did not trust him to
behave, even with someone who wore half-mourning for

a fiancé. With Chad along, no one could accuse him of doing anything but ask Miss Lindon's advice while visiting honest people. And he needed Miss Lindon to strike the proper balance between attending to his tenants' needs and not compromising himself in their eyes and the eyes of his peers.

But her reluctance to go with him hurt. He covered that disturbing thought by saying, "Trust Miss Lindon to be awake on all suits. Master Chad is enthusiastic, I expect."

"Aye, Cap'n," Jarvis said dryly, causing Lucas to laugh. He imagined himself at eighteen and wondered what his reaction would have been had he been asked to spend many afternoons visiting tenants with an older sister.

"Thank you, Jarvis."

"Aye, Cap'n." Jarvis bowed to Marston and left.

Lucas rocked back in his leather chair. At least she was coming. He should remember how he had learned to be happy with little things when he had first been cashiered into the navy. Her coming was the only little thing he had to look forward to. Certainly nothing in the accounts brought happiness.

"So you agree with me that something's wrong here, sir?"

Marston closed the big book. "I haven't a merchant's facility for figures, my lord, but some of these transactions do appear unusual."

"Can you track them?"

"I can certainly try, my lord. But—"

"What is it, Mr. Marston? Speak up, man."

Marston cleared his throat. "When my father received your message requesting immediate attention, he informed me of certain conditions surrounding your late cousin's estate."

"Certain conditions?"

"Yes, ah . . . yes, my lord."

"You want to tell me what these conditions are?"

"Well, my lord, I cannot, that is—"

"Mr. Marston," Lucas said, rising, "I suspect my cousin of embezzling funds from his own estate. My cousin was certainly perverse, but I have difficulty believing he would do such a thing for his own amusement."

His color high, Marston said, "My father told me he performed certain transactions for the late Lord Worthington, but did not tell me what they were. He said they were performed in confidence, but were quite legal and aboveboard."

"Aboveboard, you say?" Lucas wondered whether Marston had used the phrase to be amusing. He paced around the desk, forcing Marston to crane his neck to keep track of him. "I prefer to be the judge of what's aboveboard or not. Is there anything in my cousin's will forbidding my knowledge of these transactions?"

"No—that is, not to my knowledge, my lord."

Lucas sat on the desk's edge, not two feet from Marston's chair, and leaned toward him. "Then when you go back to London, tell Mr. Marston Senior that I want to know what these transactions were all about, or this Marquess of Worthington will start exercising his title. You will inform me immediately of the outcome. Is that perfectly clear?"

Marston gulped. "Yes, my lord."

"Good." He rang the call bell and turned his attention back to the papers on his desk. "Masters will show you to a room so you will be well rested for your journey tomorrow."

Alone at last, Lucas poured himself some Madeira from the carved sideboard and looked around the study. His cabin on the *Atlantia* would have fit into one quarter or less of this dark-paneled, book-lined room, and had contained his bed, his desk, all his charts, a few books, two stern chasers, and a dining table. Here, a few comfortable leather chairs, divans, and reading tables scattered casually about broke up the space but did not overwhelm it.

He stroked the crystal snifter, took another sip of the rich wine. Occasionally, while harassing the French in the Mediterranean, he had captured a ship carrying wine such as this, but those instances were few and far between. Now he had both the wine and the room to pace about, not just the twenty-one feet of ship's quarterdeck he enjoyed as its captain. He also felt more trapped, more confined than he had since Edmund had sent him down.

Edmund had doctored his own account books for some mysterious reason. If Lucas could discover that reason, he might discover who murdered Edmund. He would not stand for any opposition in his quest, because until he found out the murderer, he would have no peace in his landlocked ship.

At least he had allies. Jarvis, of course, would ever be a loyal aide, and Lucas had improved the morale of the household servants by officially naming him as steward. Jarvis had immediately dismissed some incompetents and required higher standards of everyone.

And there was Miss Lindon. He picked up the politely worded letter Jarvis had given him: her thank you for the tops.

Under her cool brunette head and spinster cap resided the strategic power of an admiral. Lucas thought of women as calculating, but not strategically sharp. Miss Lindon was an exception. He would use her calm, quick thinking as his rudder. She also made him laugh, which could stand him in good stead through the coming weeks.

He wondered how Miss Lindon had earned her reputation for shyness. Although she occasionally lowered her gaze to her hands, he suspected she was hiding her feelings. Certainly she had not been shy with him; had anyone else seen her eyes snapping, her color agreeably high, he would have disputed the appellation "shy."

It was a shame she wasted herself on the memory of some soldier when she had so much to offer. Though not in her first blush, her oval face showed delicacy of mind, her slim figure proclaimed her as active, and her easy acceptance of things must make her attractive to any man.

What had Cecily said the soldier's name was? Gerald DeVine? Lucas felt annoyed as he thought of this man DeVine, rushing off to war and destroying two lives in his lust for glory. Lucas had known many such men during his navy years. The fools thirsted for battle, tasted the guns' smoke with the same relish as a dinner at Carlton House, and then lay scattered over the deck, maimed and killed. Had those delicious moments of anticipation been worth their deaths?

Miss Lindon needed to get beyond Derbyshire, someplace where she could meet a man who would make her forget her dead soldier. Lucas decided he would puzzle out a way to do that as his thanks for her help.

Three days later, Penelope put one weary foot on the staircase. They had been to five tenants that afternoon, five each the two days previous. Watching the women curtsey, the men doff their hats, keeping up small, polite chatter and trying to alleviate their embarrassment and nervousness had all worn her down. She wanted the solace of a bath and a quiet night.

The drawing room door opened, and her mother's lace-capped head popped out. "Oh, Penelope, do come in for a moment."

Resigned, Penelope followed her. She wondered dimly what small detail of household management had gone awry while she had been out. Four ladies sat in the drawing room: Lady Howath, Mrs. Simons, Mrs.

Tipplethwaite, and a younger woman dressed in the very height of fashion who looked like a pretty version of Lady Howath. They regarded her with unswerving interest, even the meek Mrs. Simons. With a sinking feeling, Penelope realized she was about to be pumped for information.

"Penelope, this is Lady Bodsmead, Lady Howath's sister. My lady, my daughter Penelope."

Penelope made polite noises and learned that Lady Bodsmead was from Norfolk and visiting for four weeks with her sister.

"The ladies are all anxious to hear about the progress Lord Worthington makes with his tenants," her mother said.

Penelope would not have wagered so much as a shilling to the contrary. She immediately upbraided herself for the thought, said, "Lord Worthington has a good affinity for the tenants."

"Could you be more plain, please, Miss Lindon?" Lady Howath asked.

"Lord Worthington has put them at their ease, my lady, and done quite a bit of good. He's given orders for thatches, innumerable floors, livestock, and seed."

"Yes," Mrs. Simons said, "good Christian work."

"And you accompany him, Miss Lindon?" Lady Bodsmead asked.

"Yes, my lady. As does my brother."

Lady Bodsmead tipped her head. "That's generous of you."

"Not at all, my lady. My father's tenants and Lord Worthington's tenants are all related, have been for centuries. Helping his tenants helps ours."

"I had not thought of that," Lady Bodsmead said, and Penelope thought that even if she resented Lady Howath, she could like the sister. "And what is your brother's interest?"

"He's my father's heir, my lady."

"Penelope and Chadwick spend a lot of time in each other's company," her mother added gratuitously.

"I enjoyed our brother's company," Lady Bodsmead said. "He was always lively and full of fun. Unfortunately, he was killed at Salamanca."

A dreadful silence descended, and everyone except Lady Bodsmead looked to Penelope, who blushed and looked out the window. The worst thing about maintaining her deception, she thought, was when she needed to be conspicuous about it.

"Oh, dear, what did I say?"

"Miss Lindon's fiancé was killed at Salamanca," her sister said.

"My dear, I am so sorry."

"Please don't apologize, my lady. You could not know."

Lady Bodsmead smiled kindly at her, then turned her gaze back to the other women. "Your new marquess was also in the Peninsula at that time, you know. Only he was offshore."

"Oh?" Mrs. Tipplethwaite asked. "Do tell."

"Bodsmead's youngest brother is in the navy. He spoke highly of Captain Pargetter, only he was Lieutenant Pargetter at the time."

"Oh?" Mrs. Tipplethwaite said again.

"I don't remember all the details, but my brother-in-law said that Lord Worthington's captain had put him in charge of a captured French frigate and ordered him to return her to the fleet south, near Gibraltar. With but a small crew aboard, Lord Worthington sank another French frigate and used it to capture a ship of the line. His superiors were quite pleased, especially his captain, who benefitted by extra prize money."

"It sounds thrilling," Lady Lindon said.

"Just like a novel," Lady Bodsmead said. Penelope groaned inwardly. What mischief would her mother get into now that she thought she had a real-life hero in the neighborhood?

Lady Bodsmead continued, "I must admit I'm surprised to find everyone so suspicious of him. From all I hear, he has no reason to covet a position that would take him from a glorious career, nor should he need to prove his courage."

"I do not think, my lady," Mrs. Tipplethwaite said, "that courage has any relevance here. Poisoning is not courageous."

"Just so, ma'am," Lady Bodsmead said, "which is why I do not believe Lord Worthington would do such a thing." She glanced at Penelope. Penelope detected exasperation there, and it was all she could do not to smile. At last, someone else doubted Lord Worthington's guilt, and Penelope felt some weight she had not known she carried lift.

"But Lord Worthington also has a sense of humor," Mrs. Simons said.

"Miss Lindon would know more about that than we do," Mrs. Tipplethwaite said.

With the ladies' eyes on her, Penelope replied cautiously, "It is true he does not appear to take himself seriously. He laughs at my brother's jokes."

"What does a sense of humor have to do with it?" Lady Howath asked.

"It would be a humorous act to leave Lord Worthington stretched out on a picnic blanket," Mrs. Simons said.

Penelope shuddered, and noticed Lady Bodsmead and her mother shudder too. Lady Howath and Mrs. Tipplethwaite raised their delicately plucked brows.

"Only if 'tis malicious humor," Penelope said, and instantly bit her tongue.

"I quite agree," Lady Bodsmead said, coming to her rescue. "From what you told me, Maria, Lord Worthington has demonstrated poor judgment, not malice, and even that poor judgment during his youth. Now, Mrs. Simons, you have obviously thought about this matter, and you are a vicar's wife, knowledgeable about human nature. Do you think a person could change so much?"

Mrs. Simons glanced from side to side before answering, and Penelope remembered her strange remark before. "No, my lady," she said quietly. "I do not think people change."

"There, then," Lady Bodsmead said, smiling, "it follows that Lord Worthington is innocent of his cousin's murder."

"You are being simple-headed, Kitty," Lady Howath said. "Mrs. Simons's opinion, while worthy, cannot exonerate anyone."

Mrs. Simons glanced at her gloved hands, folded in her lap. The sisters glared at each other until Lady Bodsmead said, "You're right, of course, but I should still like to meet the man my brother-in-law spoke so highly of. Did you not say there is a harvest festival coming up?"

Talk centered on the harvest festival until the ladies stood to take their leave. Lady Bodsmead pressed Penelope's hand, and, while her sister spoke to Lady Lindon, said, "I hope we may meet frequently. You have honest opinions, but don't worry, I won't burden Maria with them."

Penelope smiled back. She had not had a friend but Chad in over five years, not since Lady Drucilla had left. She thought of Lord Worthington, murder, her twins, and her neighbors, and feared she would have need of a good one.

The open barouche bounced along the road, Lucas's driver stolidly avoiding potholes without so much as a twitch of his broad back. Chad Lindon crossed his legs and asked, "That was the last one for today, right, Penny?"

"The last one," Miss Lindon said with a smile. She looked quite fetching with the sunlight setting her cream parasol to glowing and lighting her fair complexion. Why, it made one want to touch her skin to see if she were real.

"You are quite free until tomorrow at one o'clock, brother mine."

"Wasn't what I was aiming at a'tall," Chad protested. "Good for me. Be viscount someday, need to know this stuff." He grimaced. "If I survive Papa's next hunt."

"I had heard your father was neck or nothing," Lucas said.

"Yes," Miss Lindon said. "He has left us for the Quorn. He will return in a month or two with a party of gentlemen who think of nothing other than the brush they chased that day."

"And regale you with tall tales over dinner?"

She smiled. "Each of those stories is quite true."

"Penny, how can you speak such fribble?"

"I suspect your sister is being facetious."

"'Course she is. She likes it when I'm credulous."

Miss Lindon laughed, a light sound like bells. "Thank you, brother, for indulging me."

"Your servant."

Miss Lindon's affectionate glance at her brother stirred pangs of jealousy within Lucas. He had never been as close to anyone as Miss Lindon and her brother were. He envied them. Scarlet fever had robbed him of his older sister, his only playmate, when he was eight. He had been as close to his parents as a young man could be, but they had died in a carriage accident when he was only thirteen. After that, he had been sent to Wildoaks. Honoria and Edmund were both selfish beasts as children and been no company for him, Drucilla too young and a girl, and of course his aunt Lady Worthington did not regard the folk of the town adequate company for him.

"Thank you for indulging *me,* on these visits," Lucas said. "I don't know how I would go on without your sister."

She blushed. "I am certain you would do fine, my lord."

"Fine, perhaps, but not well. So for now I regard it as a new adventure, and, I must admit, I like riding again."

"You should look at our hacks," said Chad. "Doubtless you've not had time to purchase a good one for yourself. Father will not allow bad horseflesh in his stable."

"Please do, my lord," Miss Lindon said. "Papa would consider it an honor."

They talked about horses until they reached Lindon Hall. Chad jumped down with all the vigor of his eighteen years. He held up a hand for his sister, but Lucas waved him away and climbed down to assist her himself. When she was safely down, he kissed her slender hand.

"Thank you, Miss Lindon. You make a worthy admiral, even disguised as a first lieutenant."

She blushed, setting his heart thumping.

"'Scuse me, Penny, Worthington," said Chad, and loped off.

Lucas and Miss Lindon walked toward the house, along a path bordered by low-branched apple trees heavy with fruit. "I meant what I said, you know."

"Captain?"

"The secret to strategy is either to have the information you need to make good decisions, or to be lucky. Well, these past two weeks, I've been lucky, and every day proves it to me."

Miss Lindon shook her head. "I still don't understand."

"I asked you to help me because you showed such compassion for Mrs. Bagley, and I figured you knew the county. Do you know that you not only know the county, the county knows you? Do you know that they follow your advice like the word of Gospel?"

Miss Lindon's jaw dropped. "I had no idea."

"Jarvis told me that everyone he talks to says the same thing. They admire you for arranging so many things—the Harvest Festival comes to mind—for running Lindon Hall, for raising your sister's children. I couldn't have chosen a better ambassador. But, I must say . . . I'm concerned for you."

"Captain?"

"Do you enjoy yourself, Miss Lindon?"

"That seems an unlikely question coming from a marquess and former ship's captain, my lord," she said sharply.

Lucas smiled. "From a ship's captain, perhaps. The sea tamed the rogue but didn't drown him, and you haven't answered the question."

"The question's impertinent, my lord." She took several deep breaths and looked away from him, toward Lindon Hall.

Lucas ducked his head, but only for a moment. "Perhaps it is. But I owe you a debt, and providing you with some diversion seems to be the only gift I can give you. You have a merry wit, Miss Lindon, when you relax. Let me give you the chance to use it. As you said, the hunt will be upon us soon. I could have a house party and invite gentlemen and—"

Miss Lindon became whitely rigid. "No. I will not. Not after Lieutenant DeVine."

"Miss Lindon—"

Miss Lindon turned her back on him. "Thank you for your offer, my lord, but you must see that socializing with you like that would cause talk."

"What kind of talk are you particularly worried about, Miss Lindon?" he asked, his voice dangerously even.

"Your being associated with a former rake or a potential murderer?"

Her back twitched. "I doubted your being a murderer when I saw how unhappy you were about the account books."

Lucas felt as if he had taken a full broadside. "You doubted? Did nothing make you certain?"

She looked straight at him. "I do not wish to discuss this subject."

"I would discuss it. And I want your honest answer."

Miss Lindon's face set mutinously. "You must admit it looks strange. Oh, not for the reasons Lady Howath and Mrs. Tipplethwaite give, and although you do not seem the, the—"

"The murderous type?" he asked.

"The murderous type, if you will have it that way. But I know you have killed men before. Why would killing your cousin be so different?"

"Different?" he asked.

Chin up she said, "I will not be yelled at, not by anyone."

Lucas grasped her by her slim shoulders, felt their fragility. "Yes," he said in a low, tight voice, "I have killed men. I killed them with bayonet, sword, pistol, and cannon. I don't regret it. Every one of them would have killed me if he could. But I did not murder my cousin. I had no reason to. I did not want to be here. For years I hated this place. Do you understand? Do you believe me?"

White-faced, she said, "You are scaring me. Let me go!"

"Tell me why you don't believe me. I must know."

"Penny," came Chad Lindon's voice from around a corner apple tree, "are you all right?" Chad rounded the tree, saw Lucas's hands on his sister. "Did you trip?"

Lucas released her.

"Lord Worthington was just leaving," Miss Lindon said.

Chad's knowing gaze had taken in the tension between them. He put an arm around his sister's waist. "Good day, my lord."

Lucas bowed. There was nothing else to do. He strode away, heard Chad say, "What the devil was that all about?"

Lucas wished he knew. Something had taken hold of him, and he did not know how to make it right.

Chapter 6

When Penelope came into the breakfast room the next morning, she could tell Chad was still annoyed at her for not telling him what Worthington had been doing with his hands on her shoulders. He said good morning gruffly and handed her the paper, though, just like every morning.

Penelope did not know why she did not want to speak of the matter. She had always depended on Chad. But there was something about Lord Worthington that tied her tongue.

"Excuse me, Miss Lindon," Masters said from the doorway. "Mr. Jarvis is here with a note for you."

Dread settled over Penelope, dread and anger.

Chad frowned. "The note, Masters?"

"Mr. Jarvis says he must hand it to Miss Lindon."

Chad frowned even more. "Well, then, show him up here."

"Very good, sir."

When Masters had left, Chad said, "Now are you going to tell me what's to do?"

"No."

Chad frowned and thumped his open palm rhythmically against the table edge until Penelope glared at him.

Jarvis came in. "Good morning, ma'am, sir," he said, nodding, his expression even more grave and respectful than his dark brown coat and trousers. He met Penelope's gaze briefly, and she realized Jarvis knew what had happened.

"Cap'n asked me to bring back an immediate reply." He handed the note to Penelope.

She broke the red wax seal. She did not know what to expect, and the anticipation made her clumsy.

My dear Miss Lindon,

I can make no excuses for my deplorable conduct yesterday, but it is my greatest hope that you will accept my apologies. I am so sorry to have wronged you, not only because of the indignity you suffered, but because I fear I have lost the respect of someone whose respect I cherish.

I do not importune you to say whether you believe me capable of murdering my cousin. I have lost the right to ask you anything so personal. I inquire only if you can forgive my behavior yesterday. I would understand completely if you cannot.

If you can, however, would you consent to meet me at noon on the hill that overlooks the freight road and borders Lindon Hall and Wildoaks? With or without your forgiveness, I remain,

> *Your most humble, obedient servant,*
> *Worthington*

Penelope read the letter again, surprised by his vehemence. But although flattered, she could not forget her anger.

She had no fear for her safety today, nor had she on previous days. She knew that if she broke with him, she, who had been his most conspicuous supporter, he might never regain his credibility with the county. She wanted to be fair, and yet she could no longer convince herself that she owed him her consideration.

But all of her thinking, all of her cautioning herself came flowing back to one thought—she was mad, for she wanted to see him again, talk to him.

"Well?" Chad said.

"Tell Lord Worthington 'yes.' "

Jarvis nodded. "If you will excuse me, ma'am, sir."

Penelope folded the letter, placed it in her sleeve, and poured herself another cup of tea.

"Well?"

She had avoided telling him long enough. Now, hopefully, there would be a resolution. "Lord Worthington said something yesterday he regrets and wishes to apologize."

"How much does he regret it?" Chad asked, eyes narrowing.

"Quite a bit. 'Tis nothing you need worry about, though," Penelope added quickly.

He stood and leaned against the table, rested a hand on her shoulder. "Are you sure, Penny?"

"No, not really, but I will let you know when I am. Fair?"

"Fair." Chad sat back down. "But you ride Minerva in case you need to leave quickly, all right?"

Penelope nodded.

"I have errands to run in town today before Father returns. Do you need anything?"

"Yes." Penelope smiled ruefully. "But I cannot think what it is."

Lucas stood in the shade atop a hill bisected by a stone wall separating Wildoaks from Lindon. Below him, on the Wildoaks side, ran the road into town. Lucas could hear the occasional trap moving along it, but he looked down toward Lindon Hall, waiting for Miss Lindon.

She appeared on horseback, coming through a copse

of trees. From the distance, Lucas could tell her mauve habit was as formal as his black coat, gray trousers, and striped white-and-gray waistcoat. His Hessians gleamed even in the shade, and his cravat was tied in the intricate Mathematical. They had both needed their armor, apparently.

But as she came closer, he could see her cheeks were flushed, and somehow she had lost some pins from her hair. A few dusky curls trailed below her hat around her face and neck. She bit her lip.

In that moment, Lucas realized Penelope Lindon was beautiful. He must have been at sea too long, he mused, for him to forget how to recognize a beautiful woman. Or was it that her beauty was neither a coarse thing such as he had taken advantage of in his youth, nor the blatant beauty of his cousin's wife. Miss Lindon possessed a profounder beauty, a glimmer that began inside her and had to work its way out.

And in that moment, Lucas knew why he had angered her so. Some part of him had recognized his attraction to her and been afraid. After all, what sort of reprobate would try to seduce a woman who mourned a fiancé and helped him solve a thorny issue with his tenants?

He would.

Lord, he thought, disgusted. He had wondered if being back home would undo him and it certainly looked as if it would. What drove him to mischief here? Maliciousness? Boredom?

It had to stop. He would not hurt anybody else, certainly not Miss Lindon.

"My lord," she said.

"Thank you for meeting me," he said, and put out an arm to help her down from her horse.

She grasped it as she swung down, and her gaze met his. Lucas was sorely tempted to kiss her, and that would never do for an apology. She blushed, and Lucas berated himself for letting even a mote of his feelings show.

"I am glad you came," he said, and busied himself tethering her horse.

"Why did you choose this place?" Miss Lindon asked, going over to the wall and looking down at the road.

"I did not want to embarrass you by meeting you at Lindon Hall, and I always liked this place as a boy."

"So did Chad and I. We liked watching the passage on the road. Presently the twelve-twenty mail coach will come through."

"I have not seen the mail express coach since returning to England," he said, admiring the cut of her profile against the blue sky. Somehow she became more and more beautiful each time he glanced at her. He looked down at the road, hoping to distract himself.

A light barouche appeared, and Lucas recognized the driver's livery as his own. The plumed black hat on the passenger was so extreme it could only belong to Cecily.

"My cousin goes to town."

A rider appeared at the crossroad. He looked at first as though he intended to head away from town, then changed his mind. He trotted quickly behind Cecily's barouche.

"Who is that?"

"Mr. Simons," Miss Lindon replied. "The vicar. You met him at Lindon Hall."

"Mr. Simons. Of course."

The driver pulled up and the vicar stopped alongside Cecily's barouche.

"I do hope nothing's wrong."

"Something is," Lucas said.

"Oh! Look."

The vicar drew back suddenly, making his horse dance.

Cecily flung a hand at her driver, who started the matching bays smartly, leaving the vicar in a trail of dust.

"I wonder what that was about," Miss Lindon said. "I cannot imagine what they might have had a disagreement about."

"Lady Worthington does not take to sermons."

Miss Lindon bit her lip again. "I know few people who do."

There were many things he could have said. He rejected them all. "I have packed some food, Miss Lindon. Would you be willing to lunch with me, or would the association disconcert you?"

"No," she said. "That would be lovely."

She watched while he spread a patterned blanket under the ash tree and pulled a wicker picnic basket from deeper shade. He invited her to sit with one sweep of his arm.

Curling her legs under her, she sat down on one corner of the blanket, plucked at some blue-purple wildflowers growing in the long grass. Lucas pulled a bottle of wine, two glasses, and packets wrapped in paper and cloth from the basket. "Will you take some wine with me?"

She nodded. He uncorked the bottle, filled two glasses, held them out for her to choose. He drank from the one she left him, then set the glass down and opened the packets to reveal pâté and cheese, vegetable salad, roasted chicken, crusty bread, and raspberries with cream. "Miss Lindon, I find myself at a loss for words. I cannot think of anything I might say that will make you feel comfortable with me again, but I could not let the matter lie without trying to apologize."

"Do you know what it is like, to be at someone else's mercy, every day of your life?" she asked.

Lucas was taken aback. "Yes. When I first sailed, there was a midshipman, younger than I, a slackard, a bully, and my superior. Weekly he arranged for me to be caught in some lapse of discipline, and weekly I was punished for it. It's been some time since then, but I remember how it felt."

"Then you know how I felt yesterday."

"That was difficult for you to say. I asked you before for your honesty, and you have kept all your promises. Will you let me make one to you?"

When she nodded, he held out his hand. "I will never raise this hand to you in violence. Will you take it as my bond?"

She hesitated, then took his hand. He almost caught his breath at how trusting she was. He promised himself he would keep her safe. Even if it meant keeping her safe from himself.

He said, "You are my one true friend in Derbyshire, Miss Lindon, and I value your friendship deeply. Do you believe me?"

"I believe you, and I too, value our *friendship.*"

He smiled, although he found himself wishing he saw the slightest blush on her cheeks. "You are honest. Good. Now will you eat something?"

"Only if you will accept my apology for doubting you. Worse, for expressing that doubt. I should not have. I have a wretched temper sometimes."

"You have nothing to apologize for. I was being very forward. Indeed, I should have expected you to cut me dead and refuse to visit any more of my tenants."

Her gaze dropped to her wineglass resting on her skirts.

"You may still refuse. I do not apologize to retain someone who has given of herself for my gain." When she said nothing, Lucas put a hand under her chin and lifted it. To his horror, her eyes were bright with tears. "Miss Lindon!"

"I shall not cry, my lord. Not really, I promise. I did not

think you apologized for that reason. It's just that you make me feel grateful to you. You are more considerate than anyone knows, and I haven't found that in . . . well, in a long time."

"Since your fiancé left?" Lucas asked.

She looked startled.

"I am not the only person our Four Corners gossips about. From all accounts, your Mr. DeVine was all that was considerate. I am sorry he did not come back to you."

Again she looked down, and he wished and feared she would say something about her fiancé. He could never compete with a paragon. Instead she said, "You are very kind."

"You have been alone a long time. That is why I had thought to invite gentlemen here. Someone else should know you for the good woman you are. But I shall not presume again, I promise."

"That would also be kind." She raised her glass, smiled a little sadly. "To our better understanding."

He touched his glass to hers. The light clink sounded like a portent to Lucas. Something had happened, and he was not sure what it was.

"What was it like?" she asked. "Being in battle?"

To any other woman, Lucas would have made an excuse and changed the subject. But he thought she thought of her fiancé, so he told her a story. Not a victory, that day. He did not want her to think him bragging.

She listened intently, not asking questions, the dappled shade stroking her body as Lucas wished to do. When he had finished, she let him serve them both their lunch.

"When you have had a chance to eat," she said, "would you tell me another story? I have heard rumors of your taking French frigates and ships of the line. Are they true?"

"Regrettably, some rumors about me are all too true." Lucas heard the bitterness in his tone, chided himself for it. "I do not mean to—"

"We are putting aside our Four Corners rumors right now. Would you tell me the story?"

They ate. He talked, she was mostly silent. When their plates were long abandoned on the blanket, she held her hand up to the brim of her hat, gauging the sun.

"Do you need to return to Lindon Hall?"

"I should see to my twins, yes."

"I've enjoyed myself, Miss Lindon. You're a good listener. Have you enjoyed yourself?" Her answer was important to him.

"Yes." She stood, brushed off her skirts. "It is ironic, I think, that I have felt safer with you, a notorious rake, than I have with anyone else these past five years. Thank you."

Lucas wanted to take her in his arms and kiss every inch of her, feel the sun warm on her skin. He remembered his promise to himself, and said, "I am very glad."

Chapter 7

Penelope sat in her study's window seat, her feet curled into the cushions underneath her. She stared out at the rain, which had come up suddenly and lashed the house, preventing her from seeing farther than the hedges immediately outside. She also held a book on her lap, but could not remember its title. She and Lord Worthington had finished their visits the day before. After five straight days in Lord Worthington's company, Penelope knew herself dangerously close to falling in love.

She did not know how it had happened, what had prompted the desire she felt to have his attention, talk to him, have him merely take her hand on whatever flimsy excuse he could find. Penelope chided herself with his reputation, told herself that by falling in love with him, she was committing the most common sin of young women in Derbyshire.

Penelope tried to tell herself Lord Worthington was just like Lieutenant DeVine. For all his pretty apology and scrupulous attention to her this past week, had he not proved he was like Gerald? Had Lady Drucilla come to her immediately with her story, would Gerald have made her as pretty an apology? She would never know, and, not knowing, she admitted she did not trust her judgment.

And yet, Penelope did not feel the same way about Lord Worthington as she had about her fiancé. For the lieutenant, she had felt a pleasing fancy, a surge of pride to see the faces of those around her admire them, she in her debutante's gown, he in his scarlet regimentals. When she was with Lord Worthington, she felt her heart expand every time he looked at her, a thrill of happiness looking at him, a surge of tingling that led to a blushing anxiety whenever he touched her.

Was there something intrinsically different about Lord Worthington that her feelings reflected?

Penelope shook her head. It never mattered. She could not entertain such feelings because she could not act on them without endangering her care of her twins. So it was just as well he thought she should meet more gentlemen. Not, of course, because Penelope actually wanted to, but because it implied he was not interested in her himself. Penelope's pride told her it was as well that he believed her still in love with Gerald.

Someone was knocking on the door. "Come in," she said.

Masters entered and bowed. "My pardon, ma'am, I know you said you were not to be disturbed, but there is a Lady Bodsmead who has arrived calling for you."

"Good Heavens. Is there a fire in the drawing room?"

"No, ma'am. We were not expecting callers, and Lady Lindon retired with the headache. I put Lady Bodsmead in the morning room. It was still warm in there."

"Well," Penelope said, setting her book aside and stepping down from the window seat, "there's nothing for it, Masters. Show her in here, and bring up tea. Doubtless she's cold."

A moment later Masters ushered Lady Bodsmead in. Lady Bodsmead's pretty sky blue pelisse and white walking gown were both splashed with water, and the feathers in her matching bonnet were wilted, but her pretty face was as cheerful as Penelope remembered.

"Hello, Lady Bodsmead, please, come near the fire."

Penelope indicated a slender but comfortable chair she had pulled close. "It's a terrible afternoon. You must be chilled."

"Thank you, Miss Lindon. It is a terrible afternoon, and doubtless you were not expecting company, but I wanted to talk to you without my sister around. Maria is a good woman, for all her love of gossip, but I had the feeling you would not speak freely in front of her. This's the first afternoon I could safely get away by myself, and expect you to be here as well. You must call me Kitty. We are, after all, practically coeval."

Penelope blinked a little at this speech.

"Oh dear, I have overwhelmed you. Maria says I am forever doing that. She was so relieved when I found my dear Bodsmead, for he is someone who can match me word for word, although she complains, by letter, mind you, after every visit with us, that she could not get a word in edgewise."

Penelope laughed. She could well imagine how disgruntled Lady Howath would be if she could not be the master of conversation. Masters entered and left the silver tea service.

"How did you meet Lord Bodsmead?" she asked, pouring tea for her guest.

"Oh," Kitty said, waving her free hand, "during my Season. Of course, he was only the Honorable Arthur Ghent at that point. He was also bosom friend to the young duke my sister and parents wanted me to marry."

Kitty told her all the machinations she and her Arthur had gone through to be together during that long season in such a way that Penelope could not stop laughing for a minute.

"I miss him terribly, but Maria had want of my company for a while, so here I am, and, I must admit, it's quite exciting here, what with the whole countryside buzzing about your Lord Worthington."

Penelope stiffened. "He is not my Lord Worthington."

"Of course not," Kitty said hurriedly. " 'Twas only a manner of speech. But you must admit, Maria's neighbor—oh, I forget the woman's name, but she was the stolid-looking one."

"Mrs. Crimpin."

"Yes, Mrs. Crimpin. You must admit she was correct when she said you and your brother must know him the best of anyone around here. How go your visits?"

"We visited the last ones yesterday."

"Are you glad they're over?"

"Yes," Penelope said, "but I shall not resent them a moment if he regains the respect of his tenants."

Chad came in and said hello. Then, "Yes, thank God no more visits. I could not drink another cup of cider."

Kitty laughed, then sobered. "Do you think they shall work, these visits? Will his tenants remain suspicious of him?"

"For womanizing, or for murder?" Chad asked. When Penelope glared at him, he added, "They're separate issues, Pen!"

Penelope sighed. "He is right. I wish only there were some way to prove he was not involved, something definite."

"Maria mentioned something to me about a sketch."

Chad stood up. "We haven't looked at it in a while, Penny. Let's haul it out and see if anything occurs, hmm?"

Penelope agreed, although she did not know what good it would do. Chad went to fetch it.

Masters entered. "Lord Worthington is without, ma'am."

Kitty smiled. Penelope said, "Show him in, Masters."

As Lord Worthington strode into the room, Penelope lamented her choice of a plain, high-necked navy dress that did little for her complexion and less to brighten the mood of the wet day. His alert hazel eyes immediately sought Penelope's.

He smiled wryly and bowed, thrilling Penelope. "I'm sorry to make such a puddle on your study floor, Miss Lindon. Will you forgive me?" Despite the removal of his greatcoat, his buff trousers and bottle green coat were as splashed with water as Kitty's dress and pelisse had been.

"Of course," Penelope said, rising and extending her hand, which he bowed over while giving it a delicious squeeze. "You must permit me to introduce my friend, Lady Bodsmead. She is Lady Howath's sister, visiting from Norfolk."

"Your servant, my lady," he said, bowing over Kitty's hand.

"My pleasure, my lord."

"I wish we might get you some fresh clothes, my lord, but I fear we have nothing that big in the house."

"Quite all right, ma'am," he said, smiling so warmly at her that she blushed. " 'Tis my fault for walking in this cursed rain, and I'm accustomed to being wet."

They sat down, and Penelope passed him the cake plate. She was, out of all countenance, happy to see him, and she was sure Kitty read the pleasure on her face. She hoped only that Kitty would be discreet.

"You may know my husband's brother, Captain Jeremy Ghent."

"Why, yes, I do, the scoundrel. Whatever is he about?"

Kitty and Lord Worthington fell to talking about her brother-in-law and some vicissitudes of naval life. Penelope was content to listen, particularly since Lord Worthington glanced her way often as a way of including her in the conversation.

"Here it is," Chad said, rushing in, holding a paper

aloft. "Oh, Worthington, didn't see you." He glanced at
Penelope.

"Do not apologize." Lord Worthington rose. "Perhaps
I should excuse myself. I have interrupted you after all."

"No, you mistake the matter," Penelope said. "In fact,
you should be interested in this. It is the drawing I had
done, of your cousin, my lord. The one I mentioned.
Show him, Chad."

Lucas had not missed the speaking glance Chad had
given his sister, but he took the sketch and studied it.
Edmund was curled up as peaceful as anything. Had
Lucas thought he was looking at a sleeping man, he
would have laughed at her humorous depiction of his
windblown curls, the robin sitting on his leaf-covered
jacket, and the loosened end of his cravat tossed back
and over his shoulder. She had been well enough acquainted with Edmund to detail those ravages of nature
which he professed to loathe the most and which would
have caused him the most embarrassment.

With a few deft strokes, Miss Lindon had also captured the blanket on which Edmund lay, the riverbank,
and the surrounding dome of trees. She had used more
detail when drawing the lace-edged handkerchief he
held, the wine bottle, the two wide-mouthed glasses,
one overturned, the picnic hamper and its contents. His
cousin had feasted well that day. Inside the hamper were
a roast chicken, various packets, some undone, a loaf of
bread, and a jar of jam.

"This is very well done, Miss Lindon."

She blushed. "It is an amusement, Captain."

"Where was the poison?"

"In the jam," Chad said. "Put me off crumpets for a
week."

"So long?" Lucas asked quizzically. Chad grinned.

"Do you see anything that looks like it could be a clue?" Miss Lindon asked.

Lucas studied the picture again. "No." He released his pent-up breath. He did not know what he had expected. Had the sketch contained a clue, Sir William would have seen it.

Lady Bodsmead chewed her knuckles like someone half her age. "May I?"

Lucas handed her the sketch.

"Would you say that although your cousin lived most of the time in the country, he was a dandy?" Lady Bodsmead asked.

"Yes, he despised London, its dirt and chaos, but he always kept London manners."

"Then look here at this handkerchief," said Lady Bodsmead, pointing to the sketch. "It is lace-edged, but with a very narrow lace. To a dandy, an elaborate lace on his handkerchief is *de rigueur*. No dandy would carry such a plain handkerchief as this."

"A woman?"

"Possibly, my lord. Or a man with a sense of style but less ability to indulge it."

"I despise lace on my kerchiefs," Chad said. "Style or no."

Lucas smiled at him. "Me, too. Now Jarvis might have to serve witness that I have never had a lace-trimmed kerchief, should Sir William yet decide to arrest me."

Lady Bodsmead smiled ruefully. "My brother-in-law does consider you the most likely suspect, for you have motive and were seen near there. I have told him, respectfully of course, that he holds poppycock notions."

"No one else was seen near the river," Chad said.

"If it were someone from Wildoaks," Penelope said, "she or he would not have to be there. The poison could be placed in the jam before your cousin left, my lord."

"But who was his companion, then?" Chad asked.

"You assume he had one," Lucas said.

"Oh he had one," Miss Lindon said. "Even if that handkerchief were his, both wineglasses contained dregs. I remember that clearly because I looked round for some companion while I was sketching. Indeed, now that you mention that the poison could have been placed there before, I hope the person he met was the murderer. Otherwise we have someone who is willing to kill whomever stands in his way."

Chad frowned. Lady Bodsmead bit her knuckle.

"You are welcome to the sketch, my lord. Perhaps it will reveal something to you later when you look on it fresh."

Miss Lindon rolled it up and handed it to him. Lucas realized he had been pacing as though on his quarter-deck. What must they think of him? Then he thought about the suspicions Miss Lindon had of him such a short time ago. Did she trust him now, he asked himself with a rush of happiness, if only of not being a murderer? He wished they were alone so he could ask her, could take her in his arms and ask her what she thought.

"No, Miss Lindon," Lucas said, "I wish you would keep it. The way the wind blows now, it might not be safe at Wildoaks, and it is the only clue we have."

"If you wish it," she said in her restrained way.

"Forgive my pacing about. I often did it aboard ship."

"My other brother-in-law does much the same thing, my lord," Lady Bodsmead said. "Tell me, does no one on a naval vessel carry on a conversation standing still?"

"Not so you would notice," he said.

"Your pacing does not offend, my lord," Miss Lindon said.

He smiled at her and received one in return, one

that lit her face, stabbing him with a reminder of how beautiful she was.

Lucas excused himself shortly after, claiming estate business. In truth, he wanted nothing more than to go to ground, someplace far away from his confused feelings toward Miss Lindon. That he was confused he had no doubt, for one moment he wanted to protect her, another moment he relied on her calm strength, another moment he wanted to pull her supple curves against his chest and kiss her senseless.

Lucas slowed his bay gelding to a peaceful trot, but took in little of the now, sunny day. His thoughts were all on Miss Lindon. She did not resemble any other woman, and he did not know how to interpret her reactions to him. She seemed to enjoy their friendship, but she never presumed on him. She had also rebuffed his advances, a novel experience.

Again Lucas thought about Lieutenant the Honorable Gerald DeVine. What sort of man inspired such devotion? Then Lucas shook his head. If he were interested in Miss Lindon, he would not let any dead paragon stand in his way.

If he were interested. He was not truly interested in a woman who belonged to some other realm, some fairyland where men and women could co-exist without feeling attraction for each other, was he? Especially when she pulled him into it with her. He found himself treating her alternately as though she were a delicate piece of priceless porcelain and a hard ball of India rubber. The dichotomy left him feeling restless.

Restlessness, and its matching glove, boredom, had long been the root of his sins. At least when in the navy, he could endeavor to find some enterprise—the cutting out of an enemy entrenched upon an island or the elimination of a pirate—but what was there of the like here in landlocked Derbyshire? He had done all he could to solve his tenant problems, and he could not probe further into his cousin's death. He was like to be accused of making up evidence.

The only alternative he could think of was to go to London, but whom did he know in London?

Generally annoyed, he nevertheless said to his Masters as he handed the butler his hat and cloak, "Your brother sends his felicitations, Masters."

"Thank you, my lord. Mr. Jarvis waits in your study."

Lucas nodded, stood for a moment watching Masters retreat across the parquet floor with his hat, cloak, walking stick, and gloves. Did he in fact own the items, he wondered, or did the butlers of the world merely pass them around amongst themselves, knowing that *they* truly owned them?

Lucas shook his head to clear such thoughts and proceeded into the study. Jarvis stood up from a leather chair in front of the desk. One brow lifted, he handed Lucas a letter.

"I recognized the writing, Cap'n. 'Tis from Cap'n Barnes."

Lucas broke the seal. As he scanned the letter, he could not help his grin. Here was a way out, at least for a time. Barnes had been a fifth lieutenant on his first ship, and they had kept up through the years. Other than Jarvis, Lucas considered Matt Barnes his closest friend. He smacked the letter against his palm.

"The rogue is in London, Jarvis, on re-fitting for two months. He entreats me to visit him there and relieve his boredom. Ring for Masters." When he came, Lucas asked, "Is there staff in residence at Worthington House? I thought I saw salaries in the account books."

"Yes, my lord."

"Send a note to them immediately. I will leave for London at first light tomorrow. I want the house opened for a guest."

"Very good, my lord."

"You mean to have the cap'n stay with you, Cap'n?"

"I do. This blasted title should do someone some good."

Chapter 8

Penelope sat in Kitty's pretty blue sitting room, where, she explained, they could be private before tea. Swanning might not be the size of Lindon Hall or Wildoaks and Lady Howath might be a shocking gossip, but she had a pleasant eye for decorating.

"I am so glad you came," Kitty said. "How are your twins?"

"I am settling them with their first governess and thought to let her take their measure."

"It was very brave of you to take over their raising. I would not have had the courage."

Penelope blushed. "It was not courage. I wanted them. I always wanted children. I do not think I could have given them back then. I could not give them up now."

"Where is their father?"

"Somewhere around the Mediterranean. He left England shortly after Helen's death and has been home only once. The twins visit his mother Lady Eversleigh once a year, but she is too old to give them the love and attention they need. I did not want to see them raised only by nurses and governesses." Chaddie and Helen and I, Penelope thought, were too much alone.

"Arthur and I have not had much success with children," Kitty said wistfully. "I miscarried twice, and the doctors told me to rest before trying again." She wiggled forward on her chaise longue. "But I think I am increasing again."

"How wonderful! The best of luck, Kitty."

"Thank you. That is partly why I came here when Maria asked me. If I had stayed around Arthur, he would have worried himself—and me—to death. Now, hopefully, I will make it through the worst of the scary beginning time before he need even know."

"Have you told your sister?"

"No, you are my only confidante. Maria would write to Arthur. She is so proper about such things, and has no patience for people who do not conform to social niceties. In her world, a wife tells her husband immediately so as to avoid any possibility of intrigue."

"Who could think so of you?"

Kitty smiled. "Yes, for me the world spins because of Arthur. It has since the moment I met him."

"I envy you that," Penelope said, surprising herself. "He sounds like a good man, someone who cherishes you."

Kitty's eyebrows rose. "But I had thought . . . oh, excuse me if I am incorrect or too forward, I had thought you remained unwed from choice, because you mourn your fiancé. If you were looking for someone to cherish you, I am certain there are many men who would, and gladly. Why, Lord Worthington—"

"Is a neighbor, nothing more. I am happy as I am. I do not know what made me speak so. I suppose we all sometimes wonder at having a different situation in life."

Kitty eyed her shrewdly. "Something has upset you."

Penelope bit her lip.

"Oh, please," said Kitty, leaning forward and touching Penelope's hand, "do not think that I ask merely to pry. It is just that I have enjoyed your company here so much. I hate to see you upset."

Penelope hesitated. She had considered confiding in Chad, but doubtless he would either worry or laugh off her concern. Lady Drucilla had been dead these four years, poor girl. Penelope was out of practice speaking so candidly to another woman. "I received a letter from Lady Eversleigh this morning."

"She is not ill, I trust?"

"No. She has received *a report of a most alarming nature.* She did not say from where. She writes that rumor has it that I am shortly to become—or already am—the latest target of the attentions of one Lucas Pargetter, now Lord Worthington."

"Good heavens, why should she care whether the gentleman pursues you or not?"

"She said, *You are certainly acquainted with this man's reputation, my dear Penelope, and the notion that he has sought out your company fills me with alarm, for I fear that not even a woman of your caliber can withstand him for long.* She added that she was quite in sympathy with me, for she met him when he was much younger, she a woman of more than fifty years, and even she felt herself flattered by his charm. *He made me feel no more than twenty-five, my dear,* she said."

Kitty frowned. "That sounds a friendly warning from someone who lives far away and has not met him recently."

"That was her first paragraph. Her next few wandered around a bit, but the gist of it was that she always had reservations about my taking care of the twins. My allowing my name to be linked to Worthington's shows a distinct lack of propriety. Such a deficiency, should it result in anything unpleasant—she did not use the word *scandal,* thank God—would force her to write to Eversleigh. There is no accounting for what he might do. He could ignore the whole matter. He certainly has to date. He could also remove the twins from my care."

"Oh, my dear," said Kitty, her words muffled by the hand she held over her mouth.

"I am at a loss, Kitty. Has Lord Worthington's attention to me been compromising?"

"You would know best about whether his attentions have been compromising," said Kitty, tossing her curls decidedly.

"Apparently not," Penelope replied, "or I would not have considered Chad and all those tenants sufficient chaperones."

Kitty sighed, chewed her knuckles. Then she brightened. "You need a proposal of marriage."

Penelope's mouth felt odd of a sudden, as though she had swallowed salt water. "I have told you—"

"Not to accept. Just so you, or maybe I," Kitty said with a sly smile, "can say you had one and rejected it. That would prove to your Four Corners and your twins' grandmother that Worthington never intended you as food for scandal."

"That's a lovely idea," said Penelope, trying to laugh off Kitty's mad suggestion and hoping her suddenly racing heart did not betray her by making her voice catch and quiver. "Now all I need to do is pin down a man who's known to revel in compromising situations and wrest a proposal of marriage from him. Oh, Kitty, I do not think I can count on any such thing."

Kitty regarded her soberly. "Lord Worthington esteems you, Penelope. I am sure of it."

"Lord Worthington has held many women in esteem. He has proposed marriage to none of them."

"He has admired many, but esteemed? No, I do not think so."

"I refuse to speculate on Lord Worthington's feelings," said Penelope, trying to sound convincing. "You are right, a proposal would be the very thing. My refusal would raise my cachet, but I do not think it wise to count on such a thing. Why, he has been in London these two weeks now. You cannot think that an indication of his esteem for me."

Kitty frowned. "I have wondered at that."

Penelope's heart constricted, for she too had spent many hours together wondering at Lord Worthington's sudden trip to London. "Believe me, my best course of action is to limit all intercourse with him to the barest of neighborly contact."

Kitty arched her brows, skeptical. "Well, you know best. I will not press you." From the hall, a bell sounded. Kitty brightened. "Shall we go into the drawing room for tea?"

Penelope assented, and they left the sitting room. The murmur of feminine voices penetrated the hallway. Lady Howath had company. With a sigh, Penelope stopped before the grandfather clock to collect herself.

Across the hall, a footman opened the drawing room door for a maid bearing a tea tray. Lady Howath's voice rang into the hall. "It seems he has quite taken up with a Miss Barnes, sister to a friend from the navy. He was seen eight times in her presence last week alone, and has given no indication he will return to Wildoaks any time soon."

Penelope froze and looked to Kitty, who nodded. "I heard it this morning," she whispered. "I had not told you because I place no confidence in Maria's source, who often misinterprets. And I really think," she began, but stopped to hear what Mrs. Crimpin was saying in her nasal voice.

"I feel quite sorry for our Miss Lindon."

Penelope caught her breath.

"Poor thing, she must be finally realizing that Worthington was only toying with her, as he has with so many others."

"Penelope—" Kitty said, and took her arm to draw her away. Penelope stood firm.

"Yes, I quite agree," Mrs. Tipplethwaite added. "It is tragic, really. Steadfast for so many years only to have the indiscretion to fall in love with such a one as him."

"Do you really think it love, or merely that she is tired of running her mother's house?" Lady Howath asked.

"Who can ever be certain in matters of the heart?" Mrs. Tipplethwaite asked rhetorically. "But knowing her romantical disposition, I suspect it would have to be love which overcomes her. On day-to-day matters, she has too much sense to enter into anything so fraught with mischief as becoming the acknowledged object of a womanizer."

"I am still glad you convinced me of the rightness of writing to Lady Eversleigh," said Lady Howath. "Perhaps she can warn Miss Lindon in a way we cannot."

There was a chorus of consenting hopes. Penelope felt rigid with shock and anger. That they had dared to insinuate themselves in to her life like this! Did they not understand what writing that letter might do to her?

Kitty realized it. Her face was so pale, Penelope thought she might swoon.

But there was more.

"Was not her late fiancé similar in temperament to Lord Worthington?" Miss Crimpin asked.

"I do *not* know where you received that intelligence, Lucia," her mother said. "Gerald DeVine was a bit rough around the edges, but he was not a womanizer."

"Would you excuse me, Kitty?" Penelope whispered.

Kitty nodded and escorted her to the door. "May I call on you sometime?"

"I will be happy to see you." Penelope rushed from the house. The September air, which she had thought crisp and refreshing, now felt like daggers of cold piercing her lungs. Her heart racing, she fretted, pacing back and forth along the graveled drive until the groom brought her phaeton around. Only when she was a mile down the road did she pull over onto a broad verge and give in to her tears.

The purple curtain fringed in gold fell for intermission, and the houselights came up. Lucas sighed quietly, then smiled at the thin, pale young woman who sat next to him.

"Some refreshment, Miss Barnes?"

"Thank you, my lord, no."

They settled into silence. Lucas watched the men in the pit jostle each other as they went visiting or collecting drinks, heard their raucous calls to Cyprians in the boxes above.

A black-haired beauty in the box across from his tried to catch his eye. She fanned herself coquettishly, flirted with her eyelashes, leaned forward to show off handsome cleavage framed by a ruby red dress, and even tried to studiously ignore him.

Her attempts amused Lucas, but did not interest him. "Do you see any of your friends, tonight, Miss Barnes?" he asked, trying to do his duty by her. Matt had been shocked to see how ill she looked when she had arrived from Cambridgeshire, and his dismay had cut Lucas to the quick. When Matt asked Lucas to show her some of London's calm amusements while Matt re-fitted his ship, Lucas could not refuse. In the two weeks he had escorted her, she had developed some color, but it was a fleeting thing.

He could not help but compare her lack of passion to Miss Lindon's overabundance. He suspected Miss Barnes had never helped birth a babe, or visited sick tenants, or run the gamut of public sentiment. It was ugly work, some of the things Miss Lindon did, and somehow it had not touched her with its bitterness. He admired her for that.

"You are thinking of her again, are you not, my lord?"

Lucas blinked. "I beg your pardon, Miss Barnes?"

"You are thinking of the woman."

"What woman?" he asked, but unbidden, he saw Miss Lindon's soft face framed by her walnut curls blowing in a light southwester, each hand holding a bright-eyed, wayward twin.

"The woman you are in love with. The woman I can never compete with. Tell me about her so that I might know her and know how to please you. Please, Captain, my lord, I beg you."

She rose to her feet and approached him, arms outstretched. Mindful of the eyes all around, Lucas grasped her shoulders. "You are overset, Miss Barnes, you are ill. We must get you home at once." He motioned to her middle-aged companion, who sat in the shadows and had not said a word to him all evening.

"No, no, I am not ill. I want to love you."

She was attracting attention, so without further argument, he picked her up. She nestled her head against his shoulder, attached an arm around his neck, and they were off.

"She cried when I left her at the hotel, sobbed really. I had to stay until the companion administered laudanum."

"Damn," Matt Barnes said, pacing in front of the great marble fireplace in Worthington House's main drawing room. "I am so sorry. She seemed so quiet when it was us three."

"She has been quiet. She took me by surprise tonight."

"She must not be completely over her illness. Perhaps she misunderstood my asking you to escort her about London. What started it?"

"She accused me of thinking about another woman."

"Were you?" Matt asked bluntly.

"You were my superior by some three years, but I no longer hold His Majesty's commission."

Matt bowed. "Your pardon, my lord."

"Oh, don't cut up stiff with me." Lucas poured two brandies, pressed one into his friend's hand. "Sit down, will you. I want to wear down my carpet for a bit."

Matt obliged him, and Lucas took up pacing. "Has she some place to go where she can get the real rest she needs?"

"Possibly. My brother's widow and children live in Kent. I'll write her immediately."

"I'd offer you Wildoaks, but she'd misunderstand the offer. So would the rest of the county." He rubbed his face, thinking of Miss Lindon. She had trusted him so far, but what would she think of that?

"I'd never consider asking you."

"Why ever not?" Lucas asked, rounding on him.

"For the reasons you gave. Look, Worthington, I trusted you with Clarice so I cannot say that I give much credence to your reputation, even though it was whispered to me several times in the last two weeks by well-wishers. But I'm convinced others might. Having her chaperoned in London is one thing, the country quite another. Besides, I agree with you. She'd take it wrong."

Lucas paced with renewed vigor. "Do you understand what it is like to know that everyone questions your motives whenever you have any interaction with a woman? It is damned maddening."

"Surely no one says so to your face?"

Lucas shook his head. "No, but they are kind enough to suspect me of murdering my cousin because of his lady wife. Lady? Now there's a misplaced appellation."

"There's not a scrap of evidence."

"And that's why it is so blasted annoying. There *is* no evidence, and yet they want to suspect me."

"What you need, Worthington, is a local guide. Someone who can tell you whose ears need to hear what."

"I have one already. Trouble is, she's female, a spinster who lives on property adjoining Wildoaks. She helped me get on with people when I arrived in Derbyshire. She's steadfast, loyal, and intelligent."

"Your local tabbies will gossip about you and her, now."

"If they do not already." Lucas frowned. "She should have been safe from them." At Matt's blank look he added, "She mourns a fiancé killed at Salamanca."

Matt whistled. " 'Where forty thousand perished in forty minutes.' You do have a task ahead of you, don't you? I'd rather attempt to elude two seventy-fours with land to my lee."

"What do you mean, a task? Miss Lindon is not a task."

"Peace, Worthington. All I meant was that, if you decide to make Wildoaks your home, you will need to be scrupulous in your lack of attention to anyone. It won't be easy, either. Why, you're deuced handsome covered in cannon smoke and grime. Cleaned up, all you need do is smile at 'em and away they're swooning. It'd be amusing if my sister weren't living proof."

"I'm sorry about your sister, Barnes."

"Nothing you could do."

Lucas did not like that. Not at all, and not just about Miss Barnes. London had turned into another place where he could do nothing. Lucas realized he had retreated to the open ocean. And now he had to replace metaphorical food and provisions, but from where? To achieve what end? Just sustaining the body did not satisfy. Something needed to be done for his soul.

"Would it be easier for your sister if I returned to Wildoaks? Ordinarily I would not abandon a guest, but . . ."

"I do not know. In truth, I do not know. It shall be a watch and wait sort of enterprise. At least I have something to occupy myself while I do."

"I have not asked you how your outfitting goes."

They discussed the trials of outfitting a ship and getting experienced sailors, and the absurd whims of admirals who insisted the process be done from a captain's own pockets.

The clock chimed twice. "I think I will turn in," Barnes said.

Lucas bade him good night. When he was alone, he cursed himself under his breath. Even if he were to discover some end to put his hand to, the only person he could turn to for understanding was the one person he should most avoid.

Chapter 9

Penelope stepped off the road to let the vehicle she heard behind her pass. Instead, the barouche pulled up.

"Penelope, how are you?" Kitty asked. Lady Howath smiled slightly. "Maria and I are going to town, do you go that way?"

"Yes, I have some errands."

"Then do join us."

"Thank you." Penelope settled herself in the barouche next to Kitty. "'Tis a fine day to be outside."

"Yes, it is," Kitty said. "I love it when the trees just begin to turn."

"I have heard that Lord Worthington returned yesterday," Lady Howath said. "Do you know, Miss Lindon?"

Kitty's eyes widened alarmingly, but Penelope said, "No, my lady. I would have no reason to know." Her calm voice belied her thumping heart. He was back! Now every moment she would wonder what she would do if she saw him suddenly. She planned to ignore him entirely, but some rational part of her teased her she would probably do no such thing.

"Pity." Lady Howath sniffed.

Kitty found Penelope's hand where it rested half under her skirt and squeezed it.

"I do not know why you say so, my lady. Surely the comings and goings of a bachelor like Lord Worthington should be of no interest to a spinster like me."

Lady Howath stared at her as though she were glimpsing some strange creature who had popped from the woods. "Why, I meant only that I would have liked to know for certain."

"Does Sir William seek him then? Is there new evidence?"

Lady Howath frowned. "No, there is no new evidence."

"That is a shame."

"Why? Do you want him accused?"

"My lady, my wants are irrelevant, but evidence can exonerate one while convicting another."

Lady Howath looked like something had bitten her. Penelope said, "What do you do in town, Kitty?"

They found they had several errands in common. Kitty proposed they separate from Lady Howath and meet later for tea, to which suggestion Lady Howath regally assented.

"I must apologize for Maria twice now," Kitty said as they strolled to the milliner's shop, "for I have not been able to apologize for your overhearing that dreadful conversation three days ago."

"I beg you, give it no mind." Penelope could not say without acute embarrassment that she had passed the last three days in a flurry of activity designed to make her forget her pain, both at his defection and her neighbors' perception of it. Her linens had never been so well accounted, her books so well balanced, her preparations for winter so far advanced. "Besides, it is not your responsibility to apologize for her. That you do not approve her behavior is enough for me."

"You certainly put her in her place."

Penelope blushed. "I had no wish to put her in her place, but I am so tired of meek and mild."

"What do you mean, Penelope?" Kitty asked.

"Nothing," Penelope said quickly. "Look at that

bonnet, Kitty. How does it compare with what they wear in London?"

The conversation turned to fashion, and the ladies spent the afternoon pleasantly trying on hats, deliberating laces, selecting a carved ivory pipe for Lord Bodsmead, and visiting a woodworkers shop.

"Gracious," Kitty said, checking the watch in her reticule, "it is past four o'clock, and Maria will doubtless be pacing the private parlor of the Red Rose waiting for us. I am quite lost."

Penelope turned them in the right direction and off they set, chatting merrily about their purchases. A cool, smart breeze whipped Penelope's skirts against her.

"It is just round this corner."

They turned it and ran straight into Lord Worthington. For some reason, Penelope had thought his three weeks in London would have changed him. Instead she saw the same smile on his same dashing features, the same gray greatcoat he had worn when inspecting her drawing, the same broad chest to which she had desired to be pressed.

He doffed his hat, and the wind ruffled his blond hair like greedy fingers. "Why, hello. Miss Lindon, Lady Bodsmead, how do you both do? I hope I have not overset you."

"Not at all, my lord," Kitty said coolly. "We are sorry we were rushing. We are late meeting my sister Lady Howath."

"Of course. How has it been here these past weeks?"

He caught her eye, and Penelope looked away down the street to where a boy was receiving a tip for holding a horse, a fleck of gold tossed in the air. She could not speak. If she spoke, she would never stop speaking, and that she must not do.

"Quiet," Kitty said. "How was your trip from London?"

"Fair, thank you, my lady. I am happy to be home."

"If you will excuse us, my lord, we must meet my sister."

"Of course. Miss Lindon, you are quite well?"

She nodded, smiled, but felt her face's tightness.

"And your two sloops?"

"Also well, my lord."

Penelope and Kitty curtsied, they passed him, and it was over. Why then did her knees tremble, her face feel so cold?

A servant sprang out to open the Red Rose's door for them. Penelope looked back down the street, driven by some incorrigible impulse. He stood, hat in hand, looking at her.

She went quickly through the door.

"Penelope, you are pale. Are you faint?"

"No. No, I am fine, thank you. I just . . . could not speak."

"Can you face Maria?"

Penelope took a deep breath. "As always."

Lucas spent the next three days trying to find himself in Miss Lindon's company. He did not understand her reaction to him when he had seen her in town. Her pale face, averted eyes, but above all, her silence had unnerved him, then cut him worse than any saber or bayonet.

He had ached to comfort her. Then, when she had turned to look back at him, he had exercised his utmost restraint to avoid running after her, so poignant had she appeared.

So he wandered about the countryside, and drove himself into town. No Miss Lindon. He went so far as to contemplate inviting himself to tea. Then he remembered his promise to himself and went out for another walk, marveling at how a country spinster had captured his emotions. Was it that one moment she was quiet and grave, her face the calm of the deep ocean, and the next moment she was passionate, then vulnerable, then guarded? Or was it that he sometimes imagined a spark of attraction for him in her eyes? Did she trust him, or only make a pretense of it?

Trust him or no, he burned to know what had made her pale at his presence. Where was the cool head that had enabled him to wrest vessels and fortresses from enemies? Surely storming a fortress was easier to manage than understanding one woman?

As he approached Wildoaks, his thoughts no less ordered than they had been when he had left, Jarvis came out to him.

"There's news, Cap'n," Jarvis said.

Lucas scowled at him. "What is it?"

"While you were out, Cap'n, Mr. Marston arrived from London and brought the elder Mr. Marston with him."

"Why did they not inform me they were coming?"

"The old gentleman says they did."

"And the message got lost on the way to Derbyshire," Lucas said contemptuously. He rubbed his face. "Very well. Are the Misters Marston available for consultation?"

"They await your convenience, sir."

Lucas went inside, irritated that the Marstons, *père et fils,* were distracting him, and even more irritated at his own irritation. He wanted the information they had for him, had asked for it to be delivered promptly.

"Mr. Marston, good day. And Mr. Marston, how do you do?"

Marston the Elder wore his white hair brushed back from a generous forehead. He compressed his long, mobile mouth as though to relax spelled certain doom for the secrets he carried. His bearing was erect as an admiral's.

"My lord marquess," he said crisply, and bowed.

"Please be seated," Lucas said, waving them into

chairs clustered near the large window. The garden had begun to turn, and Lucas found sitting near the window relaxing.

The Marstons settled themselves, the elder with great dignity, the younger with much fidgeting about his coat.

"Before we begin, my lord, I would request that Lady Worthington be present."

"Why?"

Marston the Elder blinked. "It is her late husband's estate we are discussing."

"As it is my estate now, I think I have sufficient authority to hear your information." As Marston the Elder blinked rapidly again, Lucas said, "Very well." He pulled the bell and asked Masters to let Lady Worthington know her presence was requested in the study on business.

While they waited for Cecily, Lucas attempted polite conversation about their trip from London. Marston the Younger made no comment unless his father did, and the old man determined to take his time being gracious.

The sun had dipped into the room by the time Cecily deigned to grace the study. She had cultivated an air of intense sadness. Lucas coughed to hide his derision, then assisted her to a chair with cool solicitude.

He explained Mr. Marston's desire to have her present.

"Of course," she murmured. She tilted her head at Marston the Younger, and that gentleman began to flush under his collar.

"If you please, Mr. Marston."

Marston the Elder cleared his throat. "You asked about anomalous entries in your late cousin's accounts. I have to tell you, my lord, that I am uncomfortable speaking about personal transactions your late cousin asked me to perform."

"So I have been told. Proceed, sir."

"Really, Worthington," Cecily said. "There is no cause to be rude to Mr. Marston."

"Madam," Lucas said coldly, folding his arms, "from what my poor arithmetic can decipher, in the last twelvemonth your late husband bled some forty thousand pounds from this estate. He seems to have paid it in five thousand pound intervals into a bank in London and named Mr. Marston Senior as its executor.

"That account, in turn, has come up dry. I found a draft on the estate bank in London that Edmund had not yet dispatched, also for five thousand pounds, which makes me suspect this strange custom would have continued for some time."

"You are correct in that, my lord."

"The estate must have required repair," Cecily said.

"Edmund ordered no repairs to any tenant property in the last two years, and there are no entries in the account books for materials or labor. Edmund paid taxes last year from selling Penharrow."

"Penharrow?"

"The Worthington house on the Cornish coast," he explained. "What I want to know is what happened to that forty thousand pounds. Mr. Marston?"

"Your late cousin, my lord, asked me to disburse the funds to various organizations. I have here a list of their names and the amounts paid them quarterly." He pulled a crisp sheet of vellum from his black bag and handed it to Lucas. Written in minute script, the list filled the page.

"Never tell me Edmund was a philanthropist," Lucas said.

A glimmer of amusement lightened Mr. Marston's gray eyes. "At first I thought so, and was puzzled. Your late cousin had never resembled the type of man who gives to charity. My next thought was to ascertain whether these names had anything in common."

Marston the Elder coughed delicately. "It behooves a good solicitor to anticipate his client's needs, my lord."

"Just so, Mr. Marston," Lucas said, thinking about Miss Lindon's assessment of his cousin as a worse womanizer than Lucas's reputation could afford. Had Edmund paid forty thousand a year for his *chère amie?* "And did they?"

"At first I thought not, my lord. A few entries here and there I successfully traced to a common source."

"And those were?"

"Legitimate businesses."

"I saw no record of income," Lucas said.

"Neither did I, my lord, and, given that your late cousin had gone to such pains to conceal his part in their continuing good fortunes, I doubted he would have made arrangements privately with these businesses to reinvest his income."

"What do you mean, Mr. Marston?" Cecily demanded.

"Quite simply, my lady, that the money disappeared."

"Forty thousand pounds?" she asked, and by the hard set to her mouth, Lucas thought she must be adding up ball gowns and jewels and determining how much her husband had deprived her of.

"Soon to be forty-five," Lucas added. "What next, sir?"

"You must understand, my lord, that I gathered this information quite slowly, and ceased my activities altogether upon realizing that my inquiries were receiving raised brows. Nothing unsettling, of course, but I did not think it in my client's best interest to draw attention to myself. Then, when your cousin died, my lord, I halted all plans for future inquiries and sent my son after you."

"You did not think these deposits strange enough to bring them forward in the hope they might shed some light on his death?" Lucas asked.

"They were his private business, my lord. Besides, he

died here, begging your pardon, my lady, not in London, where such things may be arranged, even for a lord."

"Hmm."

"When you told my son you wished to know about these transactions, I began my inquiries again. I am sorry, my lord. It took over a month to have results. These legitimate businesses I mentioned actually hide two operations, both again, quite legal, although morally distasteful."

Marston the Elder raised one brow at Cecily.

"You wanted her present, sir," Lucas said. "Tell all."

"Quite so. The first is a usury, run by a man named Higgins. Discreet inquiries revealed that he had held a twenty-five thousand pound note from your late cousin. The second is a company that operates ships for the slave trade."

Lucas compressed his lips. He had come across slavers often enough, and since his years as a midshipman, had hated seeing their broad-bottomed hulls. If to lee of one, the sight presaged the sound of cries and groans, the stink of rotting flesh and disease. That Edmund was involved with a slaving fleet made him almost regret not being his cousin's murderer.

"But slaving is illegal," Cecily protested.

"Not if you operate from a concern registered outside Britain that sells directly to the West Indies," Lucas said.

"You are quite correct, my lord," Marston the Elder said. "My apologies for being vague. The company I mentioned funneled funds to a company located off the Gold Coast."

"So what happened to that fifteen thousand pounds?" Cecily asked. "From all I hear, the slave trade is very lucrative."

Lucas grimaced at her avarice. "Not if the ships sink," he said. "There was a series of violent storms across the Atlantic last year. My ship suffered some damage from one. I would have sustained more, too, but for the training of my crew. Slavers are notoriously lax sailors."

Mr. Marston nodded. "Four ships backed by the company your cousin supported sank in last summer's gales. He lost some ten thousand pounds on the venture. The difference between that amount and the note from the usurer can be accounted for by the interest the usurer charged."

"Five thousand pounds interest?" Cecily asked, astounded.

"It is not an uncommon amount considering the principal."

"Whatever was it for?" she asked.

Marston the Younger sighed. His father frowned. "I asked my son to find out that very point, but he could discover nothing I did not know from conversations with your late cousin."

"And?" Lucas asked.

Marston the Elder pursed his lips. "His lordship was excessively closemouthed about the affair. He said nothing to me about it except that I was to disburse the money in the manner specified. Then one day, when I asked him whether he needed additional counsel to advise him," he cleared his throat, "he told me he had complete confidence in me. The secret to the note was safe, he said, in 'Penelope's work' and did not reside in any outside agency. Can you shed any light on this, my lady?"

Lucas was startled. Penelope's work? What in blazes did Miss Lindon have to do with his cousin's thirty thousand dollar payment to a London usurer? Had Miss Lindon been closer to his cousin than anyone, least of all him, suspected? If so, why did she say nothing? Had she been involved in his death?

"Penelope's work!" Cecily cried. "What has your precious Miss Lindon to do with such a sum?"

"You know a Penelope, my lord?"

"Yes, indeed he does," Cecily said. "The little trickster. She has everyone believing she is so pure and innocent. She was probably carrying on with Edmund for months, years maybe. Now she has moved on to you. What idiots men are."

"Madam," Lucas said softly, incensed, "we know next to nothing about what Edmund meant. I will beg you to contain your accusations until we can investigate."

"I will not stay quiet while you cover up her involvement in the loss of thirty thousand pounds," Cecily cried.

"You will be quiet. Nothing is proven," he said with a deadly calm.

Wide-eyed, Cecily kneaded her hands.

Marston the Elder coughed. "Is this the Miss Lindon of Lindon Hall near here?"

"It is."

"Yes, I agree that the matter should be handled with delicacy. Would you prefer me to make inquiries?"

"No, sir, I should not."

Cecily opened her mouth, then thought better of speaking.

"Very good, my lord."

"Can you tell me anything else about this affair?"

"I have told you all I know, my lord."

"Thank you for coming this long way, Mr. Marston, Mr. Marston," Lucas said, bowing to each in turn. "Please consider yourselves at home here tonight. If you would also be so kind as to remain here tomorrow until I can contact Miss Lindon and inquire into this matter? At that point, I may have an additional charge for you."

"Of course, my lord. We are at your disposal."

When the Marstons retired, Lucas turned to Cecily, who had sat silent. "Do we understand each other?" he asked.

She glared mutinously. "I understand that if I go against

your wishes, you will remind me of the funds you can cut off, the way you can restrict my movements."

"Quite true. You will say nothing about Miss Lindon to anyone. That includes the family, the maid, your friends and correspondents. You speak to no one."

She rose in high dudgeon. "You are more like Edmund than you think." She gathered up her skirts and swished from the room.

Lucas stared moodily after her. He did not give much credit to her remark, but it had disturbed him nonetheless. Above all, he hoped the parallel did not extend to courting Miss Lindon. He was repulsed by the thought of Edmund's carefully manicured, white hands touching her soft skin, her dusky hair, Edmund's wet lips kissing her soft ones. He could not bear to think further.

He rang the bell and asked Masters to summon Jarvis. While waiting for Jarvis, he penned a short note, sealed it, and wrote Miss Lindon's name on it. How much he wanted to see her, but how little under these circumstances.

"What have you been doing?"

"Dinner, Cap'n."

Lucas snorted. "Finish your dinner, then take this note to Miss Lindon. Wait for a reply."

"Aye aye, sir." Jarvis bowed and turned.

"And Jarvis?"

"Aye, sir?"

"Thank you."

Jarvis raised one brow, nodded. "Aye, sir."

The note, sealed with the Worthington acorn, rested on a silver tray. "Mr. Jarvis is in the kitchen, ma'am. He says he must wait for a reply," Masters said.

"Who is the note from, Penelope?" her mother asked.

"Lord Worthington, Mama."

"I have not seen him in so long. Where has he been?"

"Perhaps this note is an invitation," Chad suggested. He had the grace to flush when Penelope glared at him.

With shaky fingers, she broke the seal.

My dear Miss Lindon,
   A strange matter has presented itself to me, which I lay at your feet. Apparently my late cousin has paid a usurer some thirty thousand pounds. Yes, Miss Lindon, the discrepancies in the account books. My solicitor has told me that Edmund referred to the note's secret as safe in "Penelope's work." I hope you can assist me in clarifying this matter. I remain, humbly,

               Your most obedient servant,
               Worthington

Penelope frowned.

"Whatever is it, my dear?" her mother asked.

"Lord Worthington has been presented with a mystery, which, for some reason, he suspects I can solve."

"And can you?" Chad asked.

"No." Penelope drummed her fingers on the arm of her chair, a habit she usually demonstrated only when deep into the account books. "I would speak to Mr. Jarvis for a moment, Masters. You said he was in the kitchen? I will join him there. Please excuse me, Mama."

Her mother waved her off, saying, "Of course, my dear. How very strange this all is, Chad."

Note in hand, Penelope left the drawing room for the kitchen. Cook entertained Jarvis with a mug of cider. He rose from the kitchen table when he saw her, and doffed his felt cap. She motioned for him to join her at the far side of the kitchen.

"Ma'am?"

"What is this about, Mr. Jarvis?" Penelope realized she was angry, trembling-in-her-knees angry. What right did Lord Worthington have to keep involving her in his affairs? She had to end this strange sort of possession in which she thought about him constantly, wondered what he was about, doubted her own judgment for being attracted to another here-and-thereian.

"I beg your pardon, Miss, but I do not know. Cap'n asked me only to deliver the note and wait for a reply."

"Did Lord Worthington's solicitor pay him a call, or write him a letter recently?"

"They had a meeting late this afternoon, ma'am."

Penelope took a deep breath. "You have spent a lot of time in our kitchen waiting for replies from me for your master."

"Aye, ma'am," Jarvis said steadily.

"Would you please tell him . . . no, belay that."

Jarvis's cheek twitched, and Penelope blushed to realize what she had said.

"Excuse me, *disregard* that. I will write a note for you to return to him. Make yourself comfortable here until Masters brings it down to you."

"Aye aye, ma'am."

Her note was the most businesslike piece of correspondence Lucas ever remembered receiving, including his orders from the Admiralty.

Dear Lord Worthington,
    Regarding your reference to "Penelope's work": regrettably I can be of no help to you. The only drawing of your late cousin I ever did was the

unfortunate sketch you saw before you left for
London. I wish you well, and remain, sir,

                    Most sincerely yours,
                    Penelope Lindon

"Such a cold little note," he murmured. He crushed
the letter and threw it into the fire.

"Cap'n?" Jarvis asked.

"How did she seem?"

"Angry, Cap'n." Jarvis related their brief conversation.

"Thank you, Jarvis. Good night."

"Aye, sir."

Thank God for Jarvis, Lucas thought when he was
alone. Someone who did not question him constantly,
who did not look askance, who kept his opinions to
himself.

He watched the crumpled note catch fire with a sudden blaze before turning to ash.

What was going through her beautiful head? Had he
done something to upset her? She was not one to make
fits and starts. Confound her prideful keeping to herself.

He prowled over to the brandy decanter, poured himself a snifter. He tossed it down his throat. The rich
liquid prickled and burned. He poured himself another,
tossed it down too.

It was getting to be time to storm the fortress of Miss
Lindon's silence.

Chapter 10

But the next afternoon after dinner, the fortress came by. Lucas happened to be outside when her phaeton pulled up the drive. "Why, hello, Miss Lindon," Lucas said as a groom rushed forward to take her horses' bridles.

"Please pardon my dropping by so unexpectedly, my lord. I was out and thinking about the problem of 'Penelope's work.' Then it came to me."

"Would you come in, Miss Lindon?" Lucas asked.

"I should not," she said, casting her gaze down to her reins. "But I remembered that your cousin had attended Oxford, my lord. He would be familiar with the classics. I was named for the Penelope of the Odyssey, not for a relative."

"You think Edmund's reference is to that Penelope?"

"Perhaps. If you remember the story, Penelope would not believe Ulysses was dead, yet there were suitors pressing for her hand. She asked the suitors if they would give her time to complete a mourning tapestry before she accepted one of them." Her eyes suddenly glowing, she leaned toward him. "'Penelope's work' must be one of the tapestries you have in your great hall."

"By Jove, I think you've hit it."

Miss Lindon smiled, the only smile he had seen from her since coming back from London.

Lucas smiled back. Then, "Would you come with me to the great hall to look at these tapestries?" When she hesitated, he said, "Lady Honoria is at home. Would you like her company?"

"I should not like to disturb Lady Honoria." Miss Lindon gave him her hand to help her down. That small gesture of trust warmed Lucas clear through.

Lucas summoned Masters to bring Jarvis with footmen and lanterns. The great hall was notoriously dark even in full sunlight. They assembled there quickly. With Miss Lindon at his side, Lucas strolled up the hall, the heels of his boots ringing on the flagstones whenever he stepped off a Persian rug.

The large tapestries dominated the walls interspersed with narrow windows, which were a relic from the room's days as a keep. Whenever he walked through this room, Lucas thought about how little he would have liked to live here when it was Wildoaks's main hall. He prized the outdoors and the sunlight too highly, and hated having to light lamps and candles during the day.

"There," Miss Lindon cried, indicating a tapestry to his left. "A depiction of Scylla and Charybdis."

"So it is." Lucas took in the many-mouthed monster snapping at the small ship, the gaping whirlpool ready to snare it, stripping its masthead as it did, and killing men without thought or feeling. A sight guaranteed to send a thrill through any sailor, it affected Lucas strangely to stand next to Miss Lindon and feel it. He found himself wanting to set Miss Lindon behind him, so he might shield her from all harm.

But Lucas knew better than to indulge in the actions accompanying such thoughts. "Should we take it down, then?"

Miss Lindon blushed. "I had only thought as far as getting to the tapestries."

"Excuse me, Cap'n," said Jarvis. "I suspect anything his late lordship put in there would have settled to the bottom, or he'd have put it there to get a hold of it easily."

"An excellent idea." Lucas felt up and down the dusty, gruesome tapestry, but could discover nothing.

"Perhaps one of the others?" Miss Lindon asked.

"What are you looking for?" Cecily asked from the hall entrance.

Lucas explained.

"There's no reason it could not be another tapestry, my lord. Scylla and Charybdis seemed the obvious choice to start."

"You're quite right, Miss Lindon."

With the footmen holding lanterns in attendance, Lucas began to feel the backs and sides of each tapestry in turn. When he reached one midway along a wall, he felt a lump high up. He asked for a ladder, and tried to maneuver the lump toward the side where he might cut it out. It stuck fast, probably in a tangle of threads and fabric, and he did not have the leverage to wrest it out.

Lucas rubbed his hands together to rid himself of the dusty feel of the tapestry, saying, "We'll have to take it down."

This task occupied the footmen for a full quarter hour and raised enough dust for the footmen, Masters, Jarvis, Lucas, and Miss Lindon to be set to sneezing.

Even with her eyes watering, Miss Lindon looked irrepressibly lovely, and Lucas wanted nothing more than to pick her up and whirl her about as though she were Tina.

The tapestry spread on the floor, the dust settling, Lucas bent over the lump, began working it toward the side.

"Whatever is going on?" Honoria asked, her voice ringing through the hall. Uncle Albert stood next to her.

Lucas explained again.

"But you haven't said why this 'Penelope's work' is so important, my boy," Uncle Albert said.

"It seems Edmund had a note to a London usurer for

some twenty-five thousand pounds plus interest. He said the secret to it was contained in 'Penelope's work.'"

Uncle Albert blanched. "Did you say twenty-five thousand?"

"Thirty thousand with interest."

"Good Heavens," Miss Lindon said.

Honoria too was pale. She glanced at Uncle Albert, found him looking to her, then looked away, an exchange Lucas found extremely intriguing. "I always knew he was up to something," Honoria said, tilting up her chin. With that, she turned on her heel and left.

Lucas bent to re-apply himself to his task. The lump was a packet, he felt sure. He nudged and prodded it to the side.

"Do you have it yet, my boy?" Uncle Albert asked.

Lucas shook his head. "Your knife, Jarvis."

"Aye aye, sir." Jarvis handed him a long blade. Lucas made a small slit in the tapestry's side and cut several long, entangling threads. He squeezed out a packet of letters.

"What is it?" Uncle Albert asked, pressing close.

"What have you found?" Cecily asked, joining them.

"Letters." Lucas turned the letters over. Tied with a red ribbon, they were yellow and brittle. He slid the ribbon off carefully and unfolded them.

"'My darling Montgomery,'" he read aloud, "'I pine to see you again, my darling. Who could guess that my mother would be so cruel as to refuse your suit and forbid you the house?'"

Uncle Albert and Cecily sighed. Lucas noted their sudden loss of tension and scanned the rest of the yellowed page. "It goes on like this, regrettably with poor spelling, for the rest of the page and is signed, 'Your true heart, Rosemary Pargetter.' Didn't we have a relative by that name during the Restoration?"

"We certainly did," said Uncle Albert, cheerfully.
"She died young of some contagion, though."

"Do you think the letters have been here for over a
hundred and fifty years?" Miss Lindon asked.

" 'Tis likely," Lucas said.

"Poor girl," Cecily said, "pining for her lost love."

Miss Lindon flushed, and Lucas swallowed his desire
to throttle Cecily. He could not say anything to Miss Lindon without embarrassing her further, so he turned to
search the remaining tapestries. After another half hour,
he found nothing except more dust and the need for more
handkerchiefs. He dismissed Masters and the footmen.

"Well," said Cecily, "that ends that." With a swish of
her skirt, she left. Cocking an eyebrow in the direction
of Cecily's retreat, Jarvis waited for Lucas to nod
shortly, then followed Cecily out of the room. Jarvis,
thought Lucas with satisfaction, required no word from
him to think Cecily's behavior interesting enough to desire to keep watch over her.

"Is it time to dress for dinner?" Uncle Albert asked,
winking at him over Miss Lindon's shoulder.

Lucas had no idea what had gotten into the old man.
"Almost, sir."

"Then you must excuse me."

When Uncle Albert left, Lucas said, "As we are deserted, Miss Lindon, would you permit me to show you
out?"

At once a reserve covered her face, as sure and in-
scrutable as the scarves of a Muslim woman. "Thank
you, my lord."

The setting sun suddenly threw its red brilliance into
the hall. Lucas had never seen the sight before. Awash
in light, the very stones of the hall glowed, the tapestries
losing their texture and becoming frescoes. It was like
being transported to Italy, where the light had such a
tangible quality, one felt as if one could grasp a beam

and hold it close, and its beauty suspended the breath. Miss Lindon, too, was affected. Her lips parted, and her hand found his. He held it tightly.

Then, just as suddenly, the sun passed the far edge of the window's corner, leaving them in semidarkness. The land of Faery vanished. Miss Lindon shivered. Here was his chance to explain. Lucas ached to say any manner of tender things, but he knew he must go slowly.

He tucked her hand through his arm. "I'm glad you had time to visit today, Miss Lindon. I've missed our talks." She would have spoken, and from her frown he guessed it would be something repressive, too, so he rushed on. "I told my friend's sister of them all the while in London. She taxed me severely for mentioning you so often. I must admit her brother could have found a better escort for her."

"You were escorting a friend's sister?"

"Yes, he's a fellow captain."

"Did you see much of her, my lord?"

"Yes. Captain Barnes was busy re-fitting his ship, never an easy task. His sister was recuperating from illness."

"Oh, that is too bad."

Lucas led her from the hall. "Yes, it is, and unfortunately, even the mild exertion of attending the theaters caused her to suffer a relapse."

"It sounds as if you had a dull time, my lord. I am sorry."

"You're very kind." In the better-lighted foyer, Lucas sensed a softening.

"Will you, from time to time, indulge my whim for pleasurable conversation?" he asked softly.

Miss Lindon stiffened, although that inexorable politeness did not descend again. "When I am able. Good evening, my lord."

"Good evening, Miss Lindon."

Lucas shut the door after her and frowned. Had he made progress, or not?

Chad regarded her with exaggerated interest all through dinner, and Penelope thought she might scream with vexation. What was her brother about? Could he know about her conversation that afternoon with Lord Worthington? That was the only interesting thing that had happened since she had seen him yawning over the paper at breakfast.

Goodness, she thought suddenly, surely he has not found himself a young lady and is smitten, not three weeks before he goes to Oxford. It would be entirely too bad of him to moan about going to college.

Penelope visited the twins after dinner, hoping that Chad would follow her and tell her what he was about. He did not, and she spent an hour reading stories to the twins, but without her heart in it. The twins were also grouchy. They were not sure they liked their new schedule of lessons. Penelope promised them a long walk the next day if they would but go to sleep.

This promise set them giggling for some reason known only to each other. Then they pulled the covers over their heads. Penelope blew out their candles and bade them behave.

In her room, she set her candle on her nightstand and stretched. It had been a turbulent day, and if she could not be satisfied about what Chad was about, at least she could crawl under her own covers and think about what Lord Worthington had said to her.

"How are you, Penny?" asked Chad.

Penelope jumped. Chad climbed out of the settle near the fire and grinned.

"Did I startle you? I'm sorry."

"No, you are not," she said, angry. "What are you about, Chad Lindon?"

"Penny, I'm worried about you." He held her shoulders. "The least little thing sets you off. I wondered if there was anything wrong."

"What could possibly be wrong? The twins are fine, the Harvest Festival is soon over, the tenants are happy, the account books in order, and none of the staff has mutinied."

"And what about Captain Lord Worthington?"

Penelope folded her arms. "Why do you not just say what you came to say? All this wriggling about the point annoys me immensely."

Her brother blushed. "He's been back almost a week, and he has not called, nor have you seen him. Just that strange note."

"Am I supposed to expect such courtesies from him?"

"Dash it all, I think so. You've helped him time and again. He should be grateful, and I'm tempted to tell him so."

"Calm down, Chad. As a matter of fact, I saw Lord Worthington this afternoon." Penelope explained what had happened that afternoon at Wildoaks. When she reached the point at which Lady Honoria and Lord Albert had exchanged that pregnant glance, Chad whistled.

"There's definitely something going on there," he said.

"And with Lady Worthington, too," added Penelope. "I believe Lord Worthington is having Jarvis shadow her."

"Well, of us all, he must know best how to handle that. But I wish he would decide the best way to handle you."

"And what do you mean by that?" asked Penelope in her chilliest voice.

Chad sighed. "Look, Penny, don't poker up. I've not asked you about the Captain before because I respect your privacy."

"So do not ask me now," said she, hotly.

"He cares for you—greatly—if I'm not mistaken."

Penelope turned away. "I do not want to hear this."

"Why? Because you care for him, too? I know how you feel about men—"

"You may know how I feel but you cannot feel it yourself," she flared. "Nor could I feel how Lady Drucilla felt. But I understood the consequences of what happened to her."

"You're right." Chad bowed his head. "But the captain is a good man. Every man cannot be like Lieutenant DeVine. Do you think I am?"

"No, Chad, of course not." She gripped his hand. "And I agree with you—Lord Worthington is a good man. Unfortunately, though, he is capricious. I was too much in his company, and when he left for London, the gossips' tongues clacked."

"Come on, Penny, who cares about them?"

"I must. Lady Eversleigh has already written to me, remember?"

"To warn you about him possibly involving you in scandal."

"And that consideration still holds," Penelope said. "I cannot trust Lord Worthington to be steady, so I won't risk losing my freedom to do what I please by calling attention to myself that way. I've done enough of that already."

"So he went to London for a while, so what?" asked Chad. "I don't see that as caprice. Has a whisper of suspicion touched him about some low liaison? No. Has he done anything to you to make you . . . "

Penelope could not control her sudden indrawing of breath.

"What? Did he do something to you?" Chad demanded. "That time when you tripped—you had not?"

"I prefer not to talk about it," Penelope said quickly. "He apologized." She kneaded her hands.

Chad studied her while Penelope squirmed inside. If he said again that she compared Lord Worthington to Lieutenant DeVine, she would break out in tears, for Lord Worthington's trip to London had indeed reinforced her fear that she could never tell what a man was thinking. Even Gerald had smiled so pleasantly at her in the carriage on the way back from Wildoaks. If Lady Drucilla had not told her, Penelope would never have guessed he had tried to accost her in her own home.

Could she trust Lord Worthington not to hurt her again? And then, she wondered, even if she reached a point at which he did not actually hurt her, but merely put her down as the twins would some favorite toy, never to be used again, what would the consequences be? Dread fear washed through her.

Chad smiled, tried to lighten the conversation. "Well, I won't call him out, then."

"I'd consider it a favor," she replied solemnly.

"Done." They shook hands. Chad laughed, and Penelope forced herself to as well.

"Get you to bed, brother mine."

Chad nodded and rose. As he touched the doorknob, however, Penelope said, "It is interesting to have him in the Four Corners, but do not push us together, Chaddie, all right?"

Chad smiled slightly. "I promise."

Chapter 11

Penelope laughed with Timothy and Tina as the brisk wind whipped her hair from under her hat and twisted her skirts about her so she could barely walk. The afternoon sun shone brightly, although without much warmth, and turned the falling leaves into kaleidoscopes of color. The smell of autumn crisped the air.

She and the twins had wandered for miles, and it was a joy to be with them, Penelope thought. Content to remain close to her rather than exploring, the twins had told her any manner of stories about their new governess and the staff Penelope would never have experienced.

"What's up there?" Tina asked, pointing toward a hill.

Penelope recognized it as the spot where she and Lord Worthington had picnicked. She felt a strange reluctance to climb it again. Would it still feel different to her? Then a stubbornness drew her on. It had always been her place, her place to go when she had been younger and wanting to think things out. It would be hers again.

Tina tugged at her hand. Penelope smiled down at her. "Up there you can see all around. Would you like to go?"

"Yes, yes," they chorused. Timothy tugged her other hand. Laughing, Penelope started up the hill.

The view over the stone wall made her catch her breath. Even the twins were silent and still, looking around. The trees, nestled in hollows and hills, formed patchwork accents of color around fields golden with the fall harvest, all outlined by stone walls and dotted with cottages.

"Is this all Grandfather Lindon's land?" Timothy asked.

Penelope laughed. "No, our land ends here at this wall. *That* is Wildoaks."

"But we went the other way when we visited the people in the cottages. You said *that* was Wildoaks."

"Wildoaks is a big place, a grand place," said Penelope.

"You're too kind, Miss Lindon," said a voice.

Penelope jumped.

"Captain, Captain!" the twins cried.

Lord Worthington emerged from behind a tree on the other side of the stone wall. He was dressed casually, as he had been the first time Penelope had seen him, in loose shirt and dark trousers. His concession to the late September wind was a roomy hunter green coat, which he carried over his broad shoulder.

He leaned against the stone wall. "Are you happy to see me, brats?"

They giggled, then Timothy said, "How much land *do* you own, Captain?"

"A great amount," said he solemnly, although Penelope detected a twinkle in his eye. "And how are you, Miss Lindon?"

"Very well, thank you, my lord." She looked down to the grass at her feet, feeling greedy at the sight of him and knowing how dangerous such feelings were. Had she not told Chad the night before all the reasons why she must treat men, and particularly this man, with caution? Had she not made a decision to treat him with distance? Surely her resolution could last more than one sight of him, however handsome he appeared.

Concern flickered over Lord Worthington's face. Then

he smiled. "This place is such a good spot for gazing and thinking. Do you like it, brats?"

They chorused their assent.

"Well, you cannot see as well as you should, though, your being such bantlings." He reached over the wall, picked up Tina, and set her upon it, one arm firmly around her. "Now hold on to me, my lady, and look."

In turn, Timothy demanded to be put up onto the wall. Lord Worthington obliged him after safely replacing Tina. Penelope's heart ached to see Timothy stretch his arm around Lord Worthington's neck. The twins trusted him so completely. With a start, she realized she was jealous of them.

"Is something wrong, Miss Lindon?" Lord Worthington set Timothy down on Penelope's side of the stone wall.

"Not at all, my lord. Merely an uneven step."

"Will you come walking with us, Captain?" asked Timothy. "Please? Please?"

"I'd be pleased to, but it's up to your aunt."

Two pairs of blue eyes beseeched her. Penelope could not deny them, and was annoyed. "If we are not taking you away from something important, my lord."

"Then I will." He drew on his coat and vaulted the stone wall effortlessly, making Penelope's breath catch in her throat. Witty, charming, devilishly attractive, and strongly competent in every situation, all his traits shone from him here, next to nature, with her children.

The twins each grabbed one of his hands, Timothy first, then Tina, and pulled him along. With a ruefully amused smile, Lord Worthington allowed himself to be led. Penelope could do nothing but follow as they showed him the pine cones they had stacked earlier, the squirrel nest in the forest, the deer and fox tracks near the brook.

Along the way, Lord Worthington amused them by

picking them up in turn and spinning them about. Chad occasionally played with them, tossed them in the air, but he did not have the vigor Lord Worthington did. He was not as powerful a man, not yet, anyway, Penelope thought loyally. Still, Penelope smiled when they laughed and giggled.

When they reached the gardens at Lindon Hall, the twins ran toward the house and the promise of afternoon sweets. Penelope offered Lord Worthington refreshment as well. He declined, and Penelope castigated herself for being unable to decide if she was happy or not. She should be happy, for the less time they were together in company, the less gossip there could be. A chance meeting, Penelope told herself, that is all today was. A chance meeting. You are safe, the twins were with you, now is the time to give him no encouragement, to establish the pattern for the future.

"I will order the carriage for you, then, my lord."

"Thank you, but I prefer to walk. 'Tis only a few miles, and there are two hours of daylight left at least."

The garden was very quiet of a sudden. Only a moment ago, Penelope swore she could hear the thunking and clanking of pots and pans from the kitchen and the cheerful tinkle of bridles interspersed by low murmurs of encouragement from the grooms at the stables. Now there was only the gentle buzz of late afternoon, the smell of roses from the bushes surrounding them. Penelope touched one silky bloom of a late, purple rose, trying to think how to express herself. "Thank you, my lord, for being so kind to them."

Lord Worthington smiled, completely unnerving Penelope. "I remember how much I loved my father's doing to me just what I was doing with the twins. He would toss me in the air, talking all the while about how the next time he might just decide not to catch me. It made it all the more fun. I'd shriek and carry on, but I didn't have to worry. He never dropped me."

"Where did you grow up, my lord?"

"Cornwall, until I was eleven. Then I came here. I was something of a wild creature. Edmund's mother tried to tame me."

"But you weren't very tamable."

He grinned. "No, I was not." Lord Worthington became serious, fingered another bloom from Penelope's rose bush. "My aunt thought it unnatural that I should miss my parents for months after they died, that the thought of them gave me pain."

"I often wondered if you felt guilty."

"Because I wasn't in the carriage with them? Yes, for a long time I wished I had not feigned being sick that morning. I remember lying warm in bed, reading the tale I'd fallen asleep over the night before, and thinking how wonderful it was to avoid church, when our butler came to tell me."

He looked so sad Penelope impulsively touched his arm. Lord Worthington shook himself, mustered a smile. "I didn't tell you that to earn your sympathy."

"I did not think it, my lord." They locked gazes, and Penelope became aware of a new sound—the high throbbing of her heart as she held her breath. Lord Worthington, too, seemed transfixed. Penelope managed to look away.

Lord Worthington sighed, but not from exasperation. "I wanted to ask how often they see their father."

"Once, when they were three, when he returned briefly to England. They also see their grandmother at least once a year. My brother-in-law found it hard to be with them."

"He must have loved your sister very much."

"Not so very much," said Penelope, "if he can leave her children. I know they look like her—Helen was quite fair-haired and lovely—but I still think they would have been consolation to him."

He lifted her chin with a gentle hand. Mesmerized, she allowed him.

"You can seem so shy in company," he said. "But you're a strong woman, Penelope Lindon. So many in the world are weak."

"I am not strong." To her surprise and horror, Penelope felt tears prick her eyes.

Lord Worthington placed her hand on his arm, and they walked silently down the rose-lined path while she regained her composure, Penelope chastising herself for her emotion, for her foolishness. Surely crying before a man was no way to make him believe she was indifferent to him.

"I must leave you now. If I call again, will you see me?"

Penelope studied his face, its compassion, the understanding written in the crinkles at the corners of his eyes, his self-ironic smile. Yet underlying these, Penelope glimpsed desire. It was impossible, she thought, impossible for someone as splendid as Lord Worthington to desire her.

"Would you be like Gerald?" she whispered, surprising herself and him, and then surprising herself even more by adding, "I am sorry. Yes. Yes, I will see you, Captain."

Penelope hurried toward the house before he saw her truly lose her composure.

"Penelope, I thought you were going to do those birds in blue," said her mother.

Penelope glanced at her embroidery. She had done them in dark green, the same color as the coat Lord

Worthington had worn. She shook her head in self-disgust. "I made a mistake."

"I'll say," her brother said, bending over her shoulder. "Who will ever believe in green birds?"

She glared at him. He stuck out his tongue at her, and she at him.

"Children," protested Lady Lindon.

Chad and Penelope laughed.

"Chaddie can always put me in good humor, Mama, especially when he is obnoxious and does not act properly."

Chad stuck his tongue out at her again.

Lady Lindon shook her head. "I don't understand you two sometimes."

"Well, Mama, I do not understand us either, but I know one thing for certain, I shall be picking out these stitches for hours. I cannot face that tonight," she finished with asperity.

"Now you won't have to," Chad said, waving to Masters, who approached them with the coffee tray. "Masters is your *deus ex machina*. Well done, Masters."

That worthy butler permitted himself a brief smile as he bent to pour coffee for the ladies and port for Chad.

"Good," said Lady Lindon, "for I would like to know whether you found 'Penelope's work.' You were not about last night after dinner for me to ask you."

"We searched every tapestry in Wildoaks and found nothing of consequence, just some old letters from a Pargetter ancestress."

"Pity."

"I re-read the book in the Odyssey that talks about it, and tried to think of something that gets done every day and undone every night."

"Hmm," said Lady Lindon, tapping her book cover.

"Hunh?" asked Chad.

Penelope explained. "Penelope stitched her tapestry

during the day, then picked out the stitches at night so she would be no further along in the morning when the suitors pressed her for her hand. If there were something at Wildoaks that was done during the day and undone at night, we might look there."

"Ingenious, tricky woman," Chad said, smiling.

"Maybe too tricky," her mother said. "Do I not remember that you painted a picture of poor Lady Drucilla? That would be a Penelope's work. Our Penelope." She tipped her head. "Or am I remembering what I was reading at the time?"

"No, Mama, you are quite right. I painted a picture of Lady Drucilla. But she took it with her when she married."

Masters straightened. "Excuse me, ma'am, but she did not."

Penelope was astonished. "She did not? But she wrote me of putting it up on her bedchamber wall at Lord St. Alverrin's."

"Did your brother tell you about the picture, Masters?" Chad asked carefully.

Masters nodded. "That picture was the subject of quite a dust-up between Lady Drucilla and the late Lord Worthington." He nodded at Penelope. "Begging your pardon, ma'am, but it is likely Lady Drucilla did not wish to upset you by mentioning that she could not take the picture with her."

"Could not?" asked Penelope.

Masters looked chagrined. "His lordship her brother insisted she leave it behind. That is all I know of it."

Chad eyed Penelope, said, "Thank you, Masters. Thank you very much."

"I am sorry to be the bearer of such unpleasant news." Masters bowed and left.

"Well," said Penelope's mother. "That sounds like

it was quite the tempest, if Masters is so reluctant to repeat it."

"There were times when I wished Lord Worthington to Perdition for his treatment of Lady Drucilla," Penelope said, barely containing her anger.

"That is not something you want to say again," Chad said.

"No," added her mother, plucking at her sleeve in alarm. "No, you certainly do not."

Penelope took a deep breath and tried to contain her indignation, and her sense of loss. She missed Lady Drucilla, and she had liked the picture. "I shall not, but why would Lord Worthington forbid Lady Drucilla from taking her picture?"

Chad snorted. "Sounds like more of his petty torments."

"You must write Lord Worthington a note immediately," her mother said. "There may be a clue in the picture."

"I shall write him a note first thing in the morning."

"No, Penny, this is not something you can write a note about," Chad said grimly. "You have to go there. And I will come with you."

Lucas sat in the same place he had spent the predominant part of the night—in a wide chair looking out the study window. He had wrestled far into the night and again this afternoon with the question of how he could compete with a dead fiancé, and what was more, a dead fiancé who had died so heroically at Salamanca. Like the bragging male creature he was, he had already told Miss Lindon of some of his exploits. She had been impressed, but he did not think she was swayed to think of him in the same light as her fiancé.

She had wondered if he could be like the paragon. Did that imply there was some hope?

At table the night before, Cecily had commented on his distracted mood, wondering why the object of his pursuit had not succumbed to temptation.

"Perhaps the seawater has dissolved Worthington's legendary power over women?" she had said and giggled.

Lucas did not like her assumption that he must be concerned with a woman. He liked it less that her assumption was correct. But he said, evenly, "My dear Lady Worthington, why ever should that make the least difference to you? In fact, were I you, I should be happy. The sooner I marry, the easier it will be for people to call you the Dowager Lady Worthington. Presently, I doubt anyone mentions it to you."

Her mouth had set in an alarming line, and Uncle Albert had winked outrageously at him. Honoria, of course, pretended to be oblivious to such conversation.

Someone came into the study, approached his chair. Lucas recognized the interloper's stride from years of experience.

"Cap'n, 'tis Miss Lindon and her brother without."

Lucas frowned. What did Miss Lindon do here with her brother? Either of them separately he could find explanations for, but together? He rose, found himself surprisingly stiff. Lucas tried to push his dark thoughts away. He should, he knew, be happy to see Miss Lindon at all.

Lucas turned from the window. Jarvis stood with his hands clasped quietly behind his back, but one brow twitched upward.

"What's the to-do, Jarvis?"

Jarvis shrugged. "They seem excited, Cap'n."

"I'll join them in a moment."

Jarvis correctly took this comment as a dismissal. Lucas paced for five minutes, calming himself, before he joined the Lindons in the drawing room. "Good afternoon," he said warmly. "It's good to see you both."

Miss Lindon rose, requiring her brother to do the same. "And you," she replied politely. "My lord, I think we've finally discovered the secret of 'Penelope's work.'"

"There are no more tapestries in the place. I thought of that later, and found two more, but to no avail."

"'Penelope's work' may be a picture I painted for your cousin, Lady Drucilla Worthington," Miss Lindon said.

Lucas raised his brows. "You and Lady Drucilla were friends?"

Miss Lindon frowned. "Yes, my lord. We became friends about five years ago, shortly before her marriage."

"You sound surprised," Chad said.

"It's just that Lady Drucilla was . . . " he said. He was about to say rapacious, but he could not bring himself to. Lucas could still feel his shock when the cousin he had long regarded as a cute little girl had been presented to him during her Comeout. Lucas had been back in England awaiting orders while his old ship was paying off.

There had been nothing of the little girl left in Lady Drucilla, not in looks, certainly not in manner. She had attempted to force a kiss from him when they had walked upon the balcony. His presentation sword, attached to his uniform, had saved him by tangling itself in my lady's skirts and causing an audible rip. He had laughed to think that the navy had saved him. Lady Drucilla had slapped his face. Astonishing creature. He could not think of it without amazement.

What did it mean that Miss Lindon and Lady Drucilla had been friends? Did it merely show how kind Miss Lindon could be? Or did it prove how well Lady Drucilla could exercise her guile?

Lady Drucilla had died suddenly, as had her brother Edmund. Were those deaths related, even though they were separated by some five years? Was Miss Lindon a link between them? Lucas could not believe she was involved, but if she stayed and they investigated this painting, they might generate some disagreeable gossip.

Lucas had sworn to himself to protect her, but from himself. Could he protect her from troubles she had caused herself? Should he? Ah, he reflected with irony, the cup of command tastes as bitter here as it had at sea.

"It's just that Lady Drucilla was what, Worthington?" Chad asked, arms folded.

Now why, Lucas thought, did Chad seem antagonistic?

"My brother is in a very welter of anticipation," said Miss Lindon, glancing at him with a warning look that Lucas found extremely intriguing. "Excuse his bad manners."

"Of course." Lucas pulled the call bell. "I was about to say that from what I remember of my cousin Lady Drucilla, you and she share a different sensibility."

Miss Lindon frowned, but before she could ask him what he might mean, Masters appeared at the drawing room door. "My lord?"

"Masters, I understand that a picture Miss Lindon painted of Lady Drucilla remained here at Wildoaks."

"Yes, my lord," said Masters, surprised.

"We had the information from your brother," said Miss Lindon. "He would not have told us about it, Masters, were he not convinced it was important."

"Of course, Miss Lindon." Lucas's butler appeared to straighten, and Lucas was again impressed by the easy way she could make people comfortable, even when she was not.

"Where is it?" Lucas asked.

"In the first attic, my lord. It is among the things Mr. Jarvis cleared for you from your lordship's room."

"Worthington had it in his bedroom?" Lucas asked.

Chad and Miss Lindon's eyes widened.

Unhappy, Masters nodded.

"Have it brought here immediately." When Masters had bowed and departed, he asked, "What did you think the picture might tell us, Miss Lindon?"

"Papers from your cousin? The painting is not large, perhaps two feet by three." She shrugged. "I do not know."

"We are trying to help, Worthington," Chad said.

"I know that," Lucas said.

"Your cousin's murder is a delicate subject for everyone. Let us go gently."

"Chad, whatever do you mean by that?"

Chad crossed his arms. "The look Worthington here gave you when you told him Lady Dru was your friend had nothing gentle about it."

"My lord?" Miss Lindon asked, then compressed her lips and leaned toward her brother, closing ranks. Lucas cursed inside even as he admired Chad Lindon's nerve for standing up to someone who was his superior in age, rank, experience, and height.

"You are entirely correct that this subject should be treated gently." And Lucas breathed a sigh of relief that Masters returned with a footman bearing the covered painting. The footman put it down on a table and pulled the covering away.

Lucas remembered how impressed he had been with Miss Lindon's pencil rendition of Edmund's picnic. This picture showed equal facility with oils. She had captured a sweet expression on Lady Drucilla's face, nothing like the hungry stare Lady Drucilla had last treated Lucas to.

"An excellent picture, Miss Lindon," Lucas said.

"My lord," she said and curtsied, very formal.

Lucas cursed again, but there was little he could say before the footman and Masters. He felt around the back of the picture. "Ow!"

"What is the matter?" Miss Lindon asked.

Lucas held up a finger oozing a large spot of blood. "A nail." It hurt like the devil.

Miss Lindon gazed at his finger. Then, as her eyes met his, she blushed deeply. "Let me help."

Chad proffered a small handkerchief. Lucas accepted it. Miss Lindon ran her hands over the painting's back. "The backing could be lifted out here," she said, pointing to the lower left corner.

"There's no need, I don't think," Chad said, tilting his head. "There's faint writing on the backing. See? There."

Lucas leaned forward. "Move the picture around, John, so it's right side up."

The footman obliged, and faintly, in Edmund's handwriting, Lucas read, "In form I should be for that part of life when death is a close memory. But in function, I am far too heavy to serve. I hide your secrets, though, and with those I am filled." He shook his head. "It's a d— . . . it's a riddle."

Miss Lindon bit her lip.

Chad Lindon rocked back on his heels, said, "It appears, Worthington, that your cousin indulged in a spot of blackmail."

Chad was right. Lucas knew he was right, but whom Edmund had blackmailed remained the question. Until and unless he knew that, Lucas would not speculate.

"When is death a close memory?" Miss Lindon asked, tipping her head thoughtfully. "When one is in a graveyard? But there is nothing that is not heavy in a graveyard."

Lucas smiled at her. Her unswerving honesty convinced him that Lady Drucilla had fooled Miss Lindon into thinking her sweet and mild.

"At a funeral?" Chad said. "Eating the cold meats?"

Lucas thought of large platters, had no idea where a platter could be that was so large it could no longer hold anything. Then it came to him.

"John, put the picture down. All of you, come with me."

Chad and Miss Lindon exchanged glances, but they followed without demur, and the two servants followed them.

Lucas led them back to Wildoaks's grand entry hall, stood before the hideous Chinese vase in its alcove he had noted the first day he came home.

"Flowers," Miss Lindon said, "flowers for a funeral."

"But too heavy to serve," said Chad Lindon. "In more ways than one, I would say."

Lucas removed the vase's equally opulent lid, tilted the vase, and peered inside. The inside was white and gleamed faintly. "There's a packet down there. I'll turn it out."

With the footman John assisting him, Lucas tipped the vase over, and a vellum-wrapped package fell out onto the parquet floor. Miss Lindon retrieved it. As she handed it to him, her fingers grazed his. She quickly pulled back her hand, a blush stealing across her face.

Lucas, too, felt a tremor of feeling at her touch. He wanted to sweep her into his arms and carry her off to some deserted place despite the mystery he felt sure would unfold with the packet. Her brother pursed his lips. Lucas took the hint and broke open the ribbon binding the packet. Papers crinkled as he unfolded them.

Lucas glanced through the top note and sighed. When Chad Lindon had mentioned blackmail, he had been spot on the mark.

"Are you all right, Captain?" Miss Lindon asked. Her blue eyes brimmed with sympathy. He should have felt immensely reassured, particularly since she searched his face, not the covering note he held open. But he could not, not while the shocking questions raised by Edmund's letters remained unanswered.

"Masters, assemble the family in the study."

"Yes, my lord."

"We will excuse ourselves, then," said Miss Lindon.

"No, stay." He took a deep breath, but he could not meet Miss Lindon's eye. "If you would be so kind."

"Do you know who did the murder?" Chad Lindon asked, interested despite his earlier standoffish demeanor.

Lucas glanced over the note again. "I have certainly found motive enough for it."

Chapter 12

Lord Worthington led Penelope and Chad into the study, indicated they should sit down on a leather couch, one of a grouping in the multicolored shadow of the study's stained glass window. He excused himself. The study seemed cavernous from its weight of books. Penelope twitched a stray fold of her gray dress into place so she would not have to look around.

Chad, too, tugged at his cravat, then his burgundy-and-white striped waistcoat. Next, Penelope thought, he would also tug at his burgundy coat. He did, making her smile slightly.

"I dislike being here," Chad said, catching her smile.

"As do I."

"Then why are we? We've given Worthington his clues, we don't owe him any more. Nothing good can come of this meeting. It is certain to be embarrassing."

"He asked us to stay," Penelope said. She could remember how her shoulders had felt as Lord Worthington had held them in the garden, insisting she tell him how she could believe he was a murderer.

Chad made a face.

Penelope straightened her shoulders. "And like you, I want to know why Lord Worthington went all flinty over Lady Dru."

"Not flinty, Pen, wary. Wary Worthington. Who

would have thought I would be trading in Womanizing Worthington for Wary Worthington, hmm?"

"And when have you ever used such a sobriquet?" Penelope inquired with a frown.

Chad held up a hand. "Never once. I swear. Really."

"Chadwick Ul—"

Lord Worthington returned and set the sheaf of papers facedown on the table next to a leather chair set at an angle to their couch. He sat down as though steel encased his frame. Very much the captain in charge of hundreds of lives, Penelope thought. She felt such a perverse wave of tenderness for him that she looked out the window to the flowers and golden trees beyond.

Lady Honoria strode into the room, looking like an ascetic crow, her expression resolutely implacable. She barely glanced at Penelope and Chad. "You asked for me?"

Lord Worthington had stood when she entered. "There's some unpleasantness. Please sit down."

She grew pale at his brusque tone, yet otherwise seated herself with composure. Penelope felt a flicker of sympathy for the older woman, but she knew better than to show a sympathy that Lady Honoria would not appreciate.

Two men in identical black coats and trousers from a more antique age came next into the room. The younger one flushed when Lord Worthington introduced them as his solicitors. The older one bowed smartly over Penelope's hand.

Lady Worthington and Lord Albert arrived together, wearing such matching expressions of faint annoyance that made Penelope certain they had exchanged hostile words in the hallway.

"What's the to-do, my boy?"

Lord Worthington tapped the sheaf of papers twice with a heavy hand. Lord Albert blanched and sat down heavily, only to struggle up when he realized Lady Worthington yet stood.

"Why are they here?" Lady Worthington asked, pointing at Penelope and Chad.

"It has been implied that Miss Lindon might have had motive to do away with Edmund. She deserves to be present."

Penelope blinked. When had someone said something against her? And on what evidence?

"Miss Lindon and Mr. Lindon are also responsible for finding what we will discuss once you sit down."

Lady Worthington's eyes narrowed. She made no move to sit and relieve the gentlemen of standing, however, until Lord Worthington again asked her to be seated.

Pouting, she spread herself along a green leather sofa, her dress of deepest black looking as if a deep well had opened up on it. Penelope noticed she sat with her back to the afternoon light. Did she merely aim to sit in the most flattering light, or did she think some shadow might help obscure her expression?

The gentlemen sat down. They formed a strange, tense little circle, Penelope thought: she and Chad; the two Marstons; Lady Honoria and Lord Albert, her chin high, his being stroked by a long white hand; and Lord and Lady Worthington each sitting alone, she defiant, he implacable.

"I intend this conversation to be completely candid," said Lord Worthington coolly. "To that end, nothing said here will leave this room. Is that understood?"

Penelope nodded automatically, and noticed with amazement that everyone else did too. Generally, Lord Worthington was so easy, showed such a light touch in his dealings. Yet when he desired it, he could bend others to his will by its sheer force.

He continued. "Three days ago, Mr. Marston Senior told me the results of an investigation I ordered into some strange entries in the Wildoaks accounts. A quarter of the entries were traced to a legal, but distasteful business."

Chad raised his brows. Lady Honoria and Lord Albert did not register any feeling.

"The rest of the entries indicated payment to a London usurer. Mr. Marston could not tell me why Edmund was paying a usurer. He could, however, say that Edmund had told him the secret was in 'Penelope's work.' That's why we were searching through the tapestries day before yesterday. Today Miss Lindon thought of something else that might be considered 'Penelope's work'—a portrait she once painted of Lady Dru. It led us to that repugnant vase in the foyer, where I found these letters. Cousin, Uncle, I believe you have something to explain?"

Lady Honoria and Lord Albert exchanged a glance. Lady Worthington leaned forward eagerly.

Then Lord Albert straightened, stopped rubbing his chin, and said, "This mess begins with me. Three years ago, I took a trip to London. The details aren't important, except that I fell in with a Captain Sharp. He fleeced me of some fifteen thousand pounds at one sitting."

Penelope had heard of such things happening, but she had never met anyone who had been so foolish. Who would have thought that witty old Lord Albert would have entertained such a vice?

"I was forced to give this gentleman my vowels, if one can call such a one as he a gentleman. I was able to hold him off for over a year by paying him from my quarterly allowance."

He looked so dejected Penelope said, "How very difficult for you, to be sure."

Lord Albert smiled sadly. "Thank you for that kindness, Miss Lindon, but the difficult part was yet to come."

"Go on, Uncle," said Lord Worthington. He glanced at

Penelope, and she was pleased to see sympathy lurking beneath the steel.

"Eventually this man became demanding, and I was forced to contact a usurer. It wasn't a comfortable arrangement, but I got by until Edmund found out about it." Lord Albert broke off and stared at his buckled shoes. "Edmund could have paid the usurer off at once, but he chose not to."

"What did he demand in return?" asked Lord Worthington.

Lord Albert gazed steadily at his nephew. "This subject is barely fit for the ears of gentlemen. There are ladies here."

"Don't quibble, Uncle," Lord Worthington replied sternly.

Lord Albert grimaced and shifted his arms about as though his coat were itching him. "Edmund demanded I assist him keep his pursuits quiet. I'm sorry, m'dear," he said to Lady Worthington, who flushed, "but there it is."

"So you functioned as Edmund's lackey for over a year."

"Yes."

"Knowing his absurd habits," Lady Worthington snapped, "you had your hands full."

Lord Worthington said, "There's more. Go on."

"If you know that, Lucas," Lady Honoria asked, "why don't you just come out with it, instead of making him tell you?"

"It's long been my policy, Cousin, to ask men to speak for themselves, rather than rely on secondhand sources."

Lord Worthington spoke so levelly that Penelope felt a thrill of pride. Whatever he had been, whatever people thought of him, he had honor to spare.

"He's right, Honoria," Lord Albert said. "Yes, there's more to the story. I made the mistake of mentioning to

Edmund that Sir Harry Blackmun also paid the usurer. He owed some ten thousand pounds."

"My God, Honoria, do not tell me you maintain a *tendre* for that old roué?" Lady Worthington asked and cackled.

Penelope glanced sharply at Lady Honoria. The woman's face, although still pale, was proudly reserved. She seemed to be looking at some picture well to the left of Penelope's shoulder.

Lord Albert continued. "Edmund arranged to co-sign Sir Harry's note from the usurer with the proviso that he could withdraw at any point. The usurer agreed—he was assured of getting something back on his debt that way. Edmund set up the same payment scheme."

"Whatever for?" Lady Worthington asked. "Ten thousand pounds with interest! What did he think he was doing?"

"He wanted a hold over Honoria," Lord Worthington said. "There's a note in here." He tapped the sheaf of papers. "It says, 'Honoria will not disgrace the family if she knows I can toss her lover to the usurer whenever I please.'"

"It was no idle threat," Lord Albert said.

"Indeed not," put in the senior Marston. "Usurers are known to exact frightful recompense from those who fail their payments."

Lady Honoria swayed, then recovered her composure.

"When did he tell you about it?" Lord Worthington asked.

"Three weeks before he died," Lady Honoria said, the tremor in her voice a grim contrast to its cold tone.

"Why?"

"I had received a note from . . . from Sir Harry. He told me his debt was clear and we could be married immediately. Edmund never liked him. He said Sir Harry was a fortune hunter, and I believe he was responsible for setting his creditors upon him. He had to fly to the Continent, and would not permit me to marry him under those conditions."

"Edmund found out about the note?"

"Yes, I do not know how. He summoned me here to the study and told me about his arrangement with Sir Harry's creditor." She rounded on Lord Albert, her color suddenly high. "This is all your fault, Uncle. You made stupid mistakes, not once, but twice. How could you think my brother would not use that information? He was cruel, vile, the worst kind of hypocrite, making you carry on his *affaires d'amour* while he forbade me a legal marriage, a small bit of happiness."

Lord Albert hung his head.

"Where is Sir Harry now?" asked Lord Worthington.

"The Continent again," Honoria said defiantly. "How can he live here now that Edmund, his co-signer, is dead? He still owes five thousand pounds."

"How much of your quarterly allowance do you put toward his debt?" Lord Worthington asked.

"All but a hundred pounds."

"And you, Uncle, how much do you yet owe?"

"Three thousand," the old gentleman murmured.

"Mr. Marston, arrange to have my uncle's debt cancelled."

"Very good, my lord."

"Worthington," Lord Albert said with hope, "do you really mean it?"

"I have done it. I am head of this family, and I have always paid my debts."

"And Sir Harry?" Lady Honoria asked.

"Cousin, I do not quibble over what you do with your own money, nor will I prevent a marriage once it is possible. I do not, however, feel myself under obligation to promote the match. We can discuss the matter further at some other time."

Lips tight, Lady Honoria nodded. Penelope felt herself grow warm in sympathy for Lady Honoria, even though she thought Lord Worthington's actions fair.

"What I am interested in, however, is the timing of these events. You found out about Edmund's plans regarding Sir Harry three weeks before he died, and Uncle, since you still owed money, you were probably smoothing the way for him to the day he died. Am I correct?"

Uncle Albert nodded.

"You did not enjoy your servitude, as Miss Lindon has alluded to. And Lady Worthington has mentioned odd habits."

"He did not like to be out of doors. Carriages and horses had to be hidden, rooms ventilated, notes sent—"

"I have a fair idea," Lord Worthington said, holding up a hand. "Did you arrange the picnic the day of his death?"

"No." Uncle Albert shook his head. "That's what I don't understand about the business. Edmund loathed picnics."

"But how amusing a place to murder him," Lady Worthington said waspishly.

The word "murder" cast a pall over the group. Chad recrossed his legs, and the younger Marston coughed.

Lord Worthington frowned. "I do not agree with Lady Worthington's sentiments, Uncle, but that is, regrettably, the point at which I must aim. You both have motive."

"Surely you do not intend to make these matters public?" Lady Honoria asked, aghast. Penelope, too, was shocked that he might reveal such private business to Sir William Howath, who told his wife every little detail.

"'Twould not be my preference. At the moment, however, I am suspected of the crime, and I have no great desire to spend the rest of my life under doubt."

"You truly think we could murder him?" Lord Albert asked.

"Why not?" asked Lady Worthington, twining a slender finger through her pearl necklace. "You both hated him with a passion, and who wouldn't kill to rid themselves of a blackmailer? You both had access to the picnic basket."

Penelope gasped at the blunt and nasty rejoinder.

"If we are to speak of who hated him," said Lady Honoria, "we might speak also of you, Cecily."

Lady Worthington spluttered.

"He has notes in here on you, too, my lady." Lord Worthington again touched the sheaf of papers. "If what they say is true, I might have helped you murder him."

Lady Worthington blanched. "Whatever do you mean?"

Chad's upraised brows mirrored Penelope's amazement.

"Precisely what I said." Lord Worthington picked up the sheaf of papers. "It seems these papers are not only his blackmail records against his sister and uncle, but also against his wife, and one other. In them he mentions certain suspicions about you and describes what he asked you to do in consequence. One week before his death, there is an entry saying," he turned to the proper page and read, " 'Have told Cecily what I discovered. She flew into a rage, but I have her well in hand. She will not make a fool of me.' "

He glanced briefly at Penelope, and again she glimpsed his sadness at what he was doing. She tried to give him a slight smile, but was afraid it resembled a grimace.

"What have you to say, my lady?"

She fell back against the couch. "I feel faint."

Lady Honoria curled her lip. Penelope shared her disgust, then felt contrite. She did not know how she could have stood to have such information revealed in front of others.

"No," Lord Worthington said roughly, "you do not. Talk to me. I cannot protect anyone unless I understand."

Lady Worthington pushed herself up violently and spat, "Yes, I hated him. Hated him since the day we married. He carried on with any woman he could find and treated me with contempt. You remember, Honoria, how he tried to push me into visiting the tenants wearing a dress fit only for a governess. He said a lady should be humble, meek, and perform useful tasks. Useful! As if he did anything useful in his life.

"But I was not alone. Everyone else in the house hated him. Honoria, Uncle, the parlor maids—he tipped them about as if they belonged to a band of wild horses."

Lord Albert laughed bitterly. "It must have caused Edmund no end of satisfaction to think that if some footman were ever careless dusting that vase, all the stories would come out. We lived close to the precipice, didn't we?"

Lord Worthington nodded. "Did any of you think you were safe? Edmund was too volatile, too fond of his own way. You could not trust him to blackmail you peaceably, could you?"

"He reminded me of what might happen every chance he got," said Lady Honoria. "He told me about dark London alleys, people who get lost in them and never return. 'There are always the alleys, Honoria,' he would say."

The senior Marston sighed and shook his head.

"When did you and Uncle discover your common interest?"

"A week or so before he died," said Lord Albert. "We were at dinner. My lady Worthington had not come down. It was between the fish course and the ragout that he told us."

"I visited Uncle later," added Lady Honoria. "I wanted to talk about what we might do."

"Did you plan to murder Edmund?"

"No," said Lady Honoria.

Lord Albert shook his head.

"Did either of you talk to Lady Worthington about this?"

"Of course not." Lady Honoria flushed with indignation.

"Beggin' your pardon, my dear," Lord Albert said ironically to Lady Worthington, "we ruled out the possibility because we suspected you might add your own game."

Chad bit his lip, probably to keep from whistling at this sally, if Penelope knew her brother at all.

Lady Worthington glared at Lord Albert.

"Did you, my lady, consider murdering Edmund?"

"Of course I did." She tossed her head. "Unfortunately, someone beat me to it."

Another dead silence passed. Lady Honoria gazed at her hands, folded in her lap. Lord Albert fiddled with his watch, opening and closing its glass face. The junior Marston looked nauseous, the senior calm and resolute.

Lady Worthington glared at Lord Worthington. Penelope also noticed she had gathered up some of her black skirt in one delicate fist and was twisting it into hopeless wrinkles. With a flash of understanding, Penelope realized Lady Worthington probably had put up with the same kind of abuse as what Lady Drucilla had suffered under Gerald DeVine's hands. Penelope could not imagine living with someone like that, but she could imagine desperately wanting to kill a man who forced her to submit to physical indignities, who treated her without the least shred of respect or sympathy.

"May we go now?" asked Lady Honoria.

Lord Worthington raised his brows.

"I do not see what else there is to discuss," said Lady Honoria. "You have asked whether any of us murdered Edmund, and we have given our replies."

"You assume, Honoria," said Lord Albert, "that he trusts us to respond truthfully. Were I in his position, I would not."

"And what would you do, Worthington, should one of us prove a murderer?" Lady Honoria asked stiffly. "Would you turn a member of your family over to be hanged?"

Lord Worthington appeared frozen. Then he said, "'Twould not be my preference. However, I came into this title because someone committed a foul act. I feel that weight every day."

"You are cruel, Cousin," Lady Worthington said, narrowing her pretty eyes.

"You have said so before, my lady, and I beg to quibble. I am not cruel, I am practical. Eleven years at sea have taught me that one cannot let crime go unpunished, or it corrupts everyone connected to it. Like gangrene, it must be cut out."

Penelope winced. The image of Edmund Pargetter's blue face and staring eyes swam in front of her vision, blocking out the warm study. She shivered. Chad took her hand and squeezed it.

Lord Worthington glanced at her and compressed his lips. "Of course, there are ways to punish this crime other than through legal channels, and with a minimum of scandal. To do that, however, I need your continued cooperation."

"Ask whatever you want, my boy."

"Thank you, Uncle," said Lord Worthington. "I will start by asking you where you all were that day, from the morning on."

"But the doctor said the poison could have been put

in the preserves anytime," protested Lady Honoria. "There is no time that could be isolated."

"I suspect," said Lord Albert, "that Lucas is looking for actions that would indicate whether we knew about Edmund's picnic, or any contact we might have had with the kitchens."

"Correct."

"I knew about the picnic. Edmund asked me to talk to Cook about putting together a luncheon for two," Lord Albert said. "I realize that is a damning admission, but there 'tis."

"Uncle mentioned it to me the day of," said Lady Honoria.

"Did you know whom he was meeting?"

"No, my boy," Lord Albert said. "Nor where. I am sorry."

Lord Worthington rapped his chin with a knuckle. "You see, the most distressing part of this whole mess is that if one of you poisoned him, you knew you were likely to poison another person as well."

"How do you know that he was not meeting one of us and the poison given him during the picnic?" Lady Worthington asked.

"Why, you were out riding that afternoon, I believe," said Lady Honoria.

"Yes, I was," Lady Worthington flung back, rising from her graceful reclining position. "What of you, you holy cat? You disappeared for hours that afternoon with a headache. Humph. I remember your telling me not two days before that headaches were the sign of woman's weakness, and you never indulged."

Lady Honoria flushed a deep purple.

"That is enough," Lord Worthington said. "Sit down, both of you." When the women took their places, he continued, "I do not know whether he was meeting one of you. At first I was inclined to doubt it. He could easily meet any of you here with a minimum of fuss, and we all know how intensely lazy Edmund was.

"Then I reconsidered. Any meeting in the open can be risky. Perhaps, I thought, Edmund was trying to frighten the person he had summoned, or was planning some big announcement that someone wanted desperately not to happen. I'm not certain, but either way, the deed required forethought. It was done in cold blood by someone who said damn the consequences.

"So, then, during the afternoon, Lady Worthington, you were out riding, and Honoria, you had the headache. Can you fill in the rest of the day for me, please?"

They did so, mentioning routine tasks and activities. Penelope did not see any holes in their stories except for Lady Worthington's afternoon ride.

"What about your ride, Cecily? Where did you go? Did you see anyone riding in a hurry?"

Lady Worthington's eyes gleamed with a martial light, but she said smoothly, "I was nowhere near the river, and the only person I saw was the Reverend Simons. He was riding off to visit some sick old widow north of Wildoaks."

"He stopped to exchange pleasantries, then?"

"Oh, yes," Lady Worthington said, waving a hand, "he often does if I see him while out riding."

"And you, Miss Lindon," he said, startling Penelope, "did you see the vicar?"

"Why, no."

"About what time did you find Edmund?"

"Worthington—" Chad said.

Penelope put a hand on his arm. " 'Tis all right. It must have been between three o'clock and half past. I had put the twins down for a nap at half past two, then went immediately for a walk. That spot on the river is about two miles distance from Lindon Hall."

"Thank you, Miss Lindon." He smiled slightly at her before addressing the others. "It might interest you to know that the servants confirm your accounts of that day. I consider that a hopeful sign."

"You have been spying on us?" asked Lady Honoria, aghast. "What must they think of us?"

"Nothing more than what they do already," he responded dryly, "I'm sure. I asked Jarvis to make some inquiries. It took him a week to gather this information casually."

"Quite right, my boy."

Lord Worthington nodded. "Thank you, Uncle. Now I can think of nothing more I can ask you, and it is almost time to dress for dinner."

Lady Honoria stood, and the gentlemen did as well. "Cousin, may I hope that you will continue to be discreet?"

He bowed. "When I first heard the rumors in town and from my tenants, I asked us to behave as a family and keep our secrets within it. That is still my wish, and I will do all in my power to keep it that way."

Lady Honoria nodded and left the room.

"See you at dinner, my boy." Uncle Albert also left.

Lady Worthington stood. "You are despicable, worse than Edmund, and I don't care who hears me say it."

Lord Worthington bowed, smiling. "Thank you, my lady."

Her mouth tightened. With a swish of her flounced skirt, she strode from the room.

"I am sorry, Miss Lindon, gentlemen, that you had to hear this diatribe. Mr. Marston, do you have an idea of what I would ask of you?"

"My lord, I will investigate one Sir Harry Blackmun immediately. He might have thought you would be more sympathetic to his plight than was your late cousin."

"I knew I could count on you, sir. Also check into the

gossip columns for last year's Season. I find my cousin Lady Worthington too passionate on the subject of her husband's death, given the feelings she has expressed today. See if she had any beaux from last year, any consistent escorts. My cousin's papers do not mention a name, only that such a man existed. Please copy the papers for yourself, sir, before you leave tomorrow."

"I will see to it immediately, my lord. Pray excuse us."

Lord Worthington handed the senior Marston the sheaf. "Of course, sir, and thank you. You are welcome to join the family for dinner, or afterward in the drawing room, if you prefer."

"Thank you, my lord." The Marstons bowed and left.

"Thank you both for staying," Lord Worthington said.

Penelope stood. She felt horribly uncomfortable, but there was something she needed to know. That need, coupled with the reserve to him that at once frightened her and put her back up, compelled her to say, "I accepted your reason for us to stay before, my lord, but now that we have passed through the bottleneck, I do not think your reason sound."

Lord Worthington twitched an eyebrow, and Penelope flushed. "What I mean is, why did you really want us to stay?"

Lord Worthington sighed. "I am sorry you are as perplexed as I am. Let me see you out, for I know you must need to be home. I hope I may see you both soon?"

Penelope shook her head. "Do those letters mention me? Did your cousin think he had something to blackmail me with?"

Chad gasped.

Looking unhappy, Lord Worthington considered his answer. "The letters do mention you, but not as a target of his."

"Will you tell me what they say?"

He frowned. "It would do you little good. *Your*

reputation remains intact, Miss Lindon. Take that if nothing else from this sordid business."

She did not miss the emphasis he placed on her reputation. His reputation would remain tarnished, and Penelope was not certain she could trust him to determine what was best for her reputation and situation. "That does not satisfy, my lord."

"Admirals are never satisfied," he said with a small smile. "Even when they're dressed as lieutenants."

"I am no admiral," Penelope said, aware that he was trying to distract her as she blushed.

"Who among my family looked the likeliest murderer?" he said quickly.

"Lady Worthington," Penelope said without thinking, and put a hand over her mouth.

"A nice, tactical response. We share opinions. I wanted confirmation of mine." He looked grim. "That is why I asked you to stay."

Penelope recognized that she would get no more from him. Angry and unhappy, she said, "You are correct, my lord. It is time for us to leave."

His mouth twitched. Not a smile, not quite a grimace. He showed them to the door, bowed over her hand.

Outside, a groom pulled up Penelope's phaeton. They climbed in, and she took the reins. They were well down the winding drive before Chad whistled and said, "That has to be the most unpleasant afternoon I have ever spent. It even beats the dressing down Papa gave me last year for hacking about on one of his hunters."

"I kept seeing Lord Worthington's face—the previous one, that is—all blue and distorted. Ugh." She shivered.

Chad shook his head. "You are not going to fool me, you know. You are dying to know what those letters say, and you are madder than spit at Worthington for not telling you."

"Nonsense. I never spit."

Chad crossed his arms. "Fine, do not bother to tell me."

Penelope watched the mare's twitching ears and recalled Lord Worthington's rigid posture, the firm control in which he had kept his voice while speaking of such a gruesome subject. He had shown too much compassion to her and her twins before to be totally devoid of feeling. "I just want to know what he is thinking."

"Do you truly think he wanted your opinion?"

"Yes," she said, "I think he did." And I do not know what to think about that, she thought.

Chapter 13

A long weekend trapped with his relatives found Lucas no closer to understanding his family's opportunities for murder. Their motivations he sympathized with well enough, although he did not know just what Edmund had had on Cecily. She refused to speak about it, and neither Uncle Albert nor Cousin Honoria had any inkling.

Unfortunately, that left him confused, but with little to do other than brood over whether he should tell Miss Lindon the contents of Edmund's note as related to herself. Her disappointment and hurt had cut at him. Had he not tested himself against steel and cannon, he would have buckled under the weight of her feeling.

He told himself it would do her no good to tell her. The truthful part of him teased him, whispering, that she would only regard her fiancé as more of a paragon now.

Lucas picked up the top note, read it through for God-knows-what time, grimaced at Edmund's smug tone.

Congratulations on finding my little treasure trove of mail that has nothing white about it. You may wonder why I began the hunt with the portrait Miss Lindon painted of my sister. I thought it only fitting, since my sister's treatment of Miss Lindon gave me my first taste of blackmail. Subsequent in-

stances have had their own piquancy, but nothing is more sweetly satisfying than holding in thrall someone who tried to hold others in thrall.

I had long known that my dear sister had a naughty streak. How well I remember her amusement when the servants worked themselves up into a welter looking for something she had stolen from Mother or Honoria. The degree of suspicion and name-calling amused her highly.

As she grew up, her taste for mayhem changed. I am certain she arranged for at least one duel over her fair person, although all I could wrest from her was a tossing of her curls in my direction. As her brother, I was supposed to be immune from such attempts at persuasion.

Lucas paused, frowned as he frowned whenever he read that part. It was the *I was supposed* part that alarmed him. He shook his head. Both of them were gone.

But I saw her accost one Lieutenant Gerald DeVine, fiancé to Miss Lindon. I saw her with my own eyes.

Lieutenant DeVine had excused himself from the port. I was excusing myself a few minutes after. We were probably on the same errand. I do not know what Dru was doing in the hallway.

She laid her hand upon his arm. He appeared uncomfortable, pointed back toward the dining room. As I crept closer, I heard him say, 'Lady Drucilla, will you permit me to escort you back to the drawing room?' Her reply, fittingly enough, although totally lacking in any propriety—plucky girl—was that she hardly needed escorting in her own home.

Lieutenant DeVine appeared flustered, but he

*drew himself together, made a creditable bow, and
begged to be excused.*

*My sister laughed. The hall rang with it. She
took a hand and pushed Lieutenant DeVine into
the very alcove in which I later moved the Chinese
vase holding these letters. I heard him protest,
saying that he loved his fiancée very much, he was
looking forward to being completely uxorious.*

*I could not hear Dru's reply, but Lieutenant
DeVine next said, 'No!'*

*I walked around until I could see them. Dru was
kissing him with all the skill of a Covent Garden
gull.*

*You may imagine my shock. But there was more.
Lieutenant DeVine pried her fingers off his arms,
held her hands together in front of him. Very much
the military man fending off a guerrillera. I
thought it boded well for his chances on the Peninsula. It is too bad one can never tell how
much—or how little—skill may serve in war.*

Lucas grimaced.

*He backed away warily, in the sort of half
crouch a stalked animal will adopt, then went
back into the dining room.*

*I pounced on my dear sister, and, though our
conversation was too heated for me to repeat
verbatim, here are the salient points. At first Dru
claimed she had felt such a genuine attraction for
Lieutenant DeVine that she could not help herself.
Then she tried to convince me with a fierce shake
of her head that she had done it to ensure Lieutenant DeVine would be a suitable husband for
her friend Miss Lindon. That sat as easily with me
as spoiled fish. When she realized I would never*

believe such a faradiddle, she admitted she had done it completely out of spite. She had envied Miss Lindon her fine (imagine my shock!) fiancé and could see no reason why he should not prefer her to Miss Lindon.

I had seen my Dru betray herself at last. Never once, since she had put up her hair, had she said she wanted to do something just because she wanted it done. She had instead preferred to work subtly on other people, to my great amusement.

Of course I could not let this opportunity escape me. I informed my dear sister, in my best head of the family voice, that unless she wanted me telling her friend what she had done, she would start paying better attention to me. You may imagine my surprise when she agreed. For some reason, Miss Lindon's good impression of her mattered more than her defiance. I asked her once why that appeared to be so. She muttered some nonsense about Miss Lindon being the person she could have been had she not been born my sister.

And that, as they say, was that. Dear Dru never strayed, not even when I arranged to unload her on St. Alverrin. Perhaps she saw some opportunity there, so long as she were careful and prevented herself from giving him some bastard.

She was, however, extremely loathe to part with the portrait Miss Lindon had painted of her, so it gave me especial pleasure, first to refuse her demand, second to put the clue leading to my other little enterprises in it. It all started with Dru, after all.

No, Lucas decided. No good could come of his telling Miss Lindon. She would feel awful to know that a woman she had admired had tried to seduce her fiancé. She would feel worse to know that Lady Drucilla's transgression had pushed her into marriage with St. Alverrin, whose reputation for passionless possession was well known. Edmund could not have ended his sister's brushes with flirtation and seduction more effectively.

So, he thought again, annoying himself, so, there is no proof of anything, only more suspicion. The content of the letters—likely to become public whether he wished them to or not—would reinforce the Four Corners' suspicions of anyone named Worthington, not mitigate their current suspicions of him.

Lucas put the letters in a drawer, locked it, and paced around the desk. Perhaps a ride would knock some of the doldrums from him. He strode out of the study. But as he passed the drawing room door, he heard Cousin Honoria.

"Forgive me for being surprised to see you. You have not visited Wildoaks in some time."

It was not Lucas's usual habit to overlisten conversations, but these were not usual times, and the door was ajar.

"I am come as the lead member organizing the Harvest Festival this year." It was Lady Howath of all people, and she sounded like she was tasting something nasty.

"Has there been a problem?" Cousin Honoria asked smoothly.

"Of course not. I am here to speak to Worthington about whether he would take up his father's role in the festival."

His father's role? Lucas wondered. He did not remember his father having a role.

"I congratulate you, Lady Howath," said his cousin dryly. "Reaching the decision to ask Worthington to participate must have required some fortitude. I had heard there was some talk a while back about abandoning the festival altogether because of him and the events of my brother's unfortunate death."

This was news to Lucas. But unfortunate indeed!

"It is true that it was felt that neighborhood sentiment would not be so . . . neighborly . . . if he were taking an active role. Miss Lindon, however, argued that by not including him, we would be lending credence to these very rumors. The festival is, after all, for the common people. It is not up to us to impose our opinion on them."

Lucas almost snorted. Lady Howath was, if anything, the very person to inflict her opinion on anyone.

"I believe Worthington has found Miss Lindon very knowledgeable about local affairs."

That from Honoria was charity, Lucas thought, for Miss Lindon had witnessed her embarrassment.

"Miss Lindon," said Lady Howath with a sniff, "is too kind. Indeed, I fear for her. Her being so often at Worthington's side, with his reputation, has given rise to speculation. Unpleasant speculation, I must add."

Lucas held his temper.

"My dear Lady Howath, I would not have thought a woman of your discernment to place credence on a reputation made eleven years hence."

"It is not for me to concern myself, but I know Lady Eversleigh, naturally, would be."

Everything clicked into place for Lucas.

"I know for a fact that Lady Eversleigh has written to Miss Lindon warning her of the dangers of questionable associations."

Of course she had, Lucas thought with disgust. And here was the knot tying the whole mess together. Miss Lindon played it cool to keep her children—for they were her children by nurture, if not birth—and Lucas would be forever prevented from offering for her as long as the suspicion of murder hung about him. Were she ever asked to choose between himself and her twins, Lucas did not know what choice Miss Lindon might make.

Then it came to him. He wanted to offer for Miss Lindon. He wanted to marry her and keep her by his side forever. He would be happy to offer the twins a home. They were Miss Lindon's children, and anything of hers was welcome to anything of his.

"There is nothing questionable about Worthington," said Honoria. "I beg you, let me finish. Some people have the great misfortune to fail at whatever they try. Others have as great a misfortune: to succeed at whatever they try."

"My dear Lady Honoria, that is not a misfortune but—"

"It can be a great misfortune when one is not permitted the media to work on. It is like a painter or writer denied paper, paint, or ink. Worthington excelled in the navy because he had something he believed in to excel in. Before that, no one permitted him to touch anything. He took no hand in any estate. He was too active to become scholarly or contemplate the clergy. He will excel at managing Wildoaks for the same reason he excelled in the navy. Unless unfounded gossip drives him away."

Such praise from his austere cousin, and she among those who had sent him down in disgrace. Had she had such an opinion then? Had her motives been noble? Or had her trials over Sir Harry Blackmun made her more sympathetic and introspective?

"What are you saying exactly, Lady Honoria?"

His cousin sighed. "I am not without ears in town, although it has been years since I added my voice. Not since Edmund married. I know that you are the one who has perpetuated these rumors. I would also be willing to lay odds that it was you who let Lady Eversleigh know of his interest in Miss Lindon."

Lucas was doubly glad he was not in the room with them, for what he might say to Lady Howath.

"You do not deny it. That is as well, for then I would have to introduce subjects I am sure you do not want to hear to ensure your cooperation. I hope we understand each other."

"We understand each other well enough," Lady Howath said.

"Good. Then in the spirit of our new understanding, I shall ask you to refrain from blackening Worthington's name, and to leave Miss Lindon out of it. You had something you wished to say to Worthington, I think."

Quickly Lucas crept to the study and waited for the footman to ask if he could attend Lady Honoria.

In the drawing room Lucas bowed politely to Lady Howath. She looked a little pale, he thought. Good.

"You know the festival is a week from Sunday, my lord?"

He nodded. "Wildoaks will make its usual contribution, and I look forward to attending."

"Do you know that your father used to participate in the games and award prizes before he and your mother moved away?"

"No, I didn't. But it sounds like him."

"I and the others," said Lady Howath, "would like to know whether you would consider taking on his role."

"Does one of the others include Miss Lindon?" he asked.

Lady Howath glanced at his cousin. "Why, yes."

"Then I would be pleased to," said he. "She has been an invaluable source of advice for me here. I am yours to command. If you will excuse me, ladies?"

"Lady Howath has a pressing engagement, Worthington. Perhaps you could . . . ?"

"Of course. My lady?"

Lady Howath rose, and Lucas showed her the door.

Then he went back into the drawing room. Honoria was fanning herself.

He kissed her cheek. "Thank you, Cousin."

"Worthington, whatever are you about?"

"I heard what you said before."

His cousin blushed. "Have to defend my family, don't I? You were a scoundrel, Worthington. You may still be a scoundrel. But you are *our* scoundrel."

Lucas smiled, then he thought about what he had heard. "You think she wrote to the twins' grandmother."

"It was in her face."

Lucas paced. "You guessed that I care for Miss Lindon."

"Are you asking if I would betray your secrets—"

"No, Honoria. I'm asking how much of a secret it is."

Now she picked up her knitting, clicking the needles. "Your admiration is so little a secret as to be no secret at all. Your intentions, well, that is the thousand pound question."

"As much as that?" Lucas asked.

She smiled. "Others may take those odds. Uncle and I, we can afford ten pounds apiece. But I shall not tell you who has bet to what end."

Lucas smiled back. "I shall not ask. You will have to adjust your bets accordingly, however, for I intend to ask Miss Lindon to marry me."

"Indeed?" she asked, and he noticed that the rhythm of her needles increased. "And so what is the new uncertainty?"

"Whether she will have me."

Honoria looked like she was about to laugh in disbelief, then she frowned. His cousin, Lucas thought, was not unintelligent, merely cold. "An offer would affect those twins, and suspicion of murder likely does not rank high in Lady Eversleigh's book of desirable traits."

"Likely it does not."

"I am sorry, Worthington. I would do what I could. Regrettably that is not much."

Lucas tipped his head to indicate the chair Lady Howath had occupied. "You did something, and for that I am grateful."

"I did not murder Edmund, by the way. I detested him, but he was my brother. I do not think Uncle had anything to do with it, either. He is a born panderer. Only look how he has followed after you and your steward this weekend trying to weasel out your preferences. I think the difference between you and Edmund in his eyes is how difficult you make things for him."

Lucas frowned. "I am at a standstill, Cousin. There is nothing to be done I have not done."

Honoria pursed her lips. "At least Sir William Howath feels the same way. But you do not mention Lady Worthington."

"No," said Lucas. "I do not."

"I see. Well. I am reassured on that score, then."

Lucas bid his cousin goodbye, had his hand on the door, when she said, "I meant what I told Lady Howath about you, you know. I thought it when my mother and brother sent you into the navy. Indeed, I approved their choice, although for different reasons. They thought to punish. I thought it might be the making of you. I am glad you have proved me right."

Not too long ago, Penelope thought, the first sight of the silver tea tray would quiet Lady Howath and Mrs. Tipplethwaite for a moment. Now they did not so much as pause. Entertaining her neighbors was become so nerve-rackingly tedious. Penelope wished all the excitement would go away, that her life would return to its normal rhythm of taking care of the twins, her household, the tenants. And yet, a voice inside her whispered that she would be restless if her life returned to the way it had been before Lord Worthington came to Wildoaks.

Lord Worthington. Penelope had worried about him through the weekend, wondering how he fared in that house of relations who had motives for killing one Lord Worthington already. Penelope did not doubt that he could acquit himself in any threatening situation, but she could not imagine he felt easy.

Across the low table, Kitty caught Penelope's eye and winked, lifting Penelope's spirits. What would Kitty think if she knew where Penelope's thoughts were tending? Would she wonder how Penelope could think of another man after her own fiancé's betrayal? Would she wonder what possessed Penelope to keep giving her neighbors food for gossip when she had been warned by Lady Eversleigh against being conspicuous?

No, Penelope thought, Kitty would not wonder. Given her direct way of expressing herself, Kitty would ask a question. She would ask Penelope what she was looking for.

What *was* she looking for? Penelope wondered. Unbidden, the sight of Lord Worthington rose before her. She saw again the straining muscles of his arms as he vaulted over the wall, the sun bouncing off his bright hair, his easy smile. He had shared confidences with her. Penelope had wished to have that perfect afternoon go on for ever. She wished now that he were here to share this tedium, to say something quizzical that would make her laugh, to take her in his arms . . .

"Tea, Lady Howath?" asked Penelope breathlessly, to dispel the feelings she had conjured inside herself.

"Yes, my dear, thank you."

"I am glad Lord Worthington has agreed to participate in the festival," said Lady Lindon.

"As I was coming back from Wildoaks, I met the others coming from town. I thought we should share the information with Miss Lindon immediately, since it was on her insistence that we pursue the matter," said Lady Howath with a tone bordering on insolence.

Kitty looked quizzically at her.

"I thought it a good idea, too," said Mrs. Simons, then blushed.

"Come, Adella—" began Lady Howath.

The flustered woman shook her head, shaking loose a rather frizzled curl from under her bonnet. Did defiance cross her face as she patted down the curl? "I am as entitled to my opinion as you are to yours, my lady."

"Well, of course, but—"

"Of course you are," said Kitty. "I wish only that I could see just how Lord Worthington feels about the matter."

As if on cue, Masters appeared at the doorway and said, "Are you home to Lord Worthington, my lady?"

"Of course," said Lady Lindon. "Show him in directly."

Lady Howath and Mrs. Tipplethwaite exchanged glances. Penelope wished she could become smaller than Swift's Lilliputians and run scrambling for cover in the Persian carpet's fibers. She forced herself to look at the carpet, not at the door and so betray how eager she was to see him again.

Masters said, "My lord Worthington."

Penelope heard his booted footsteps.

"Lady Lindon, do forgive me for intruding on your party."

His deep voice sent thrills through her. Penelope looked up. Lord Worthington shifted his gaze past her mother's shoulder and caught hers for a breathless, spellbound moment.

"You're never an intruder, my lord," said her mother.

"You must also forgive my attire. My horse threw a shoe close to Lindon Hall."

"Naturally you came here. Quite sensible."

Lady Howath's eyes widened at this remark, and Penelope felt herself in sympathy with that lady for the first time since Lord Worthington had come to Derbyshire. Her mother never spoke of things as being sensible.

"Penelope, do pour Lord Worthington some tea. Doubtless he is parched from his ride." As Penelope hastened to pour tea, her mother continued, "Please, sir, sit down. You know Lady Howath and her sister Lady Bodsmead, and you have met Mrs. Simons, the vicar's wife, but perhaps you do not know Mrs. Tipplethwaite, who was away when I first introduced you to the Four Corners."

Lord Worthington performed the requisite bows to the ladies and sat down next to Lady Lindon. Penelope handed his teacup to Kitty, who passed it to Lord Worthington. Penelope was glad not to have to risk letting her hand touch his, or she knew she would not be able to contain her agitation from the probing gazes of Lady Howath and Mrs. Tipplethwaite.

What was wrong with her? She had controlled her public emotions with little effort when Gerald had first betrayed her. Why did she have such difficulties now, when the provocation for her to betray herself was so lessened? But was it? Staring at the carpet, Penelope realized the truth. It had been easy to mask her feelings about Gerald, to pretend to be his grieving fiancée—because she had never loved him.

Penelope loved Lord Worthington with an intensity she had not known herself capable of. He was kind and gentle and full of good humor. He was also powerful, capable, and the very sight of him made her feel dizzy and excited, to say nothing of how she felt when he touched her.

When had her feelings changed? When had she stopped thinking of him as a man like all other men? When had she no longer been so concerned that he would be like Gerald? When had she forgotten his reputation, forgotten that he was likely using her for his own ends?

She glanced up at him, only to find herself riveted by his gaze. Lord Worthington tilted his head slightly, smiled at her, then turned to nod at something Mrs. Tipplethwaite said. It was enough, Penelope thought, that one glance. They could communicate in one glance. She felt warmed to her bones.

But what was she going to do? If she continued associating with him with the frequency she wanted, her neighbors would not disregard his reputation. There would be talk, and possibly more letters from Lady Eversleigh. Penelope could not have that. Nor did Kitty's solution appear likely—Lord Worthington had given no intimation that he inclined to marriage.

Indeed, Penelope did not even know if she would marry him if he asked. For all Lord Worthington's excellent qualities, would he be willing to raise another man's children?

"Lady Howath was telling us you have agreed to take your father's old place at the festival," Lady Lindon said.

"I look forward to it," Lord Worthington said. "Lady Howath was very kind to come and tell me about it."

Lady Howath flushed. Penelope and Kitty looked to each other, brows raised. Then Lord Worthington smiled slightly, and Penelope had a sudden suspicion that something had happened to Lady Howath at Wildoaks.

But Lady Howath was never happier than when she was ordering someone about. "Mrs. Simons will ask the vicar to make the announcement this Sunday."

"Yes, I will," murmured Mrs. Simons.

"It'll be a grand time," Mrs. Tipplethwaite said. "Quite like when I was a girl. Do you know, my lord, I had the most terrible *tendre* for your father. Before I met Mr. Tipplethwaite, of course."

"No," he replied gravely, "I didn't know."

Penelope and Kitty exchanged smiles as the ladies stood.

"You must come see me soon," said Kitty, hugging Penelope, "before Bodsmead comes. He is to 'surprise' me by coming before the festival, but I discovered it from one of the underbutlers."

"I will. 'Tis a promise."

When the four ladies had departed, Lord Worthington rose and said, "Will you come for a walk with me, Miss Lindon, while I wait for my horse to be re-shod?"

"Yes, do go ahead, Penelope," her mother said.

Really, Penelope thought, her mother was become almost pushing. "I'll get my bonnet."

"And something warm," said he. "The air is cool."

A few minutes later they were strolling through the gardens on the way to the woods. Punctuated by birdsong and the sound of bells calling the menfolk home from the fields, the crisp, fragrant air exhilarated Penelope. Despite all the problems she saw ahead, she felt free outside and away from the gossips' eyes, with the person she had grown to love at her side.

"How are you, Captain?"

Lord Worthington stopped walking. "Miss Lindon, do you know you're the first person to ask me that question since Friday?"

"I'm sorry," she began, confused.

"No, no, don't be sorry. Be anything but sorry, I beg you." He held up his hands in mock distress.

"Well, then, answer the question. And don't think to spare my feelings. I suspect you've passed a most dreadful weekend and won't be fobbed off with light anecdotes of cozy family dinners." Her eyes widened at her own temerity.

Lord Worthington laughed, making her heart pound. "Miss Lindon, do you ever doubt why I've grown so dependent on you? You can be counted on to put things into proper order for me."

"I am . . . I'm not always like this, Captain."

"I hope you will always be like this with me." He searched her face, and Penelope forced herself to drop her gaze to the path. With a sigh, Lord Worthington continued, "Your suspicions are correct. It's been a dreadful weekend. Uncle has annoyed Jarvis with requests to know my habits so he might thank me for clearing his debt. He doesn't know how sorely tempted I am to forbid him from ever setting foot in London again. His unfortunate servitude to my late cousin was, I fear, the only thing that kept him from losing even more money."

He picked up a forked branch along the path and tossed it aside. It skidded along the newly fallen leaves, rustling them. "As for Honoria, well, I feel I know my cousin much better than I ever did, and for that I am thankful. She has appealed to me privately to cancel Sir Harry's bet. I denied her request. Do you think that wrong of me?"

Amazed and gratified that he wanted her opinion, Penelope replied truthfully, " 'Tis a hard decision, but a correct one, I think. Lady Honoria has been sadly treated by your cousin, but who can tell whether she's clung to Sir Harry merely because of your cousin's treatment? I think her making an honest sacrifice for him will show her whether she truly loves him. In the meantime, if you know any eligible *partis,* you might invite them to Wildoaks for a lengthy stay."

"As I once suggested for you."

"Yes," Penelope replied, trying to forget that day. "But your cousin's circumstances are quite different."

"I agree with you. Come, don't look so dumbfounded. We've been through much together since I proposed that scheme, and I am come to know you better. Besides, I should be quite jealous of any time you spent on some worthless fribble."

He said it so warmly Penelope blushed. "Captain—"

"I was thankful my horse had thrown a shoe when I saw who was in your drawing room, for it gave me an excellent excuse to be about here, but in truth you were my destination. Tell me, if you would, please, whether, that is . . . " He smiled with self-mockery. "I am making a hash of this."

Penelope bit her lip, her heart beating quicker. She desperately wanted to hear what he might say, and she wanted to cover her ears like the twins to avoid bad news.

"The thing I'm trying to say is, now that I appear to be taking a more active role in the festival, would you take it very much amiss if I did not offer to escort you?"

Whatever Penelope had expected him to say, it was not this. "It would be very strange if you *were* to escort me."

"Yes. That I realize. But that was not my question. Would you take it amiss if you did not have some offer to refuse? Even an offer that would be known to us two alone?"

They had walked down the path leading from the garden to the Home Woods. Penelope stopped under a giant spreading beech. "Lord Worthington, I do not expect anything from you."

He smiled. "No, I'm sorry, that answer will not pass muster. I must own the rightness of your desire to keep all deliberate contact between us quiet. You do not deserve to be painted the same dismal color as me and my family."

"Captain—"

With two fingers, he touched her face next to her eyes. "But your eyes, they tell me your mouth lies."

His expression, intent and tender, mesmerized Penelope. She made no protest when his lips covered hers. Then such sensation filled her she barely knew what to do or think. Exultation blossomed, her heart dashed down a lane strewn with flowers and sun-warmed berries. This heady feeling came from being kissed by someone you loved. She had not felt anything like it with Gerald. At last Penelope understood every poem she had read and puzzled over, castigating herself for being an unfeeling creature incapable of loving a man.

Lord Worthington drew back, making Penelope aware that she had taken hold of his strong arms. "I should not—"

"You are not like Gerald," she said, frowning.

He stepped back. "Deuce take it, Penelope, you know I am no paragon. I thought you had forgiven me my reputation." He set his shoulders and bowed. "I apologize for my heinous behavior and remove the offending article forthwith."

He would have turned and left her there. But that kiss had awakened the spirit Penelope had reined in for years. "Stop right there, my lord. I do not excuse you."

His brows rose, but he stayed.

"You are as quick to put the wrong interpretation on events as our neighbors. Are you not the one who has told me I am an admiral disguised as a lieutenant? Do you think I would let myself go into a position where I could be mistreated?"

His lips quirked. "So you do not think yourself mistreated, my lady admiral?"

"No," Penelope retorted. "One wonders how you achieved your reputation when you so mistake the woman you are with."

His expression appeared to kindle, then sharpen. He folded his arms. "You compared me to DeVine, and I know you have mourned his memory for five years. Who else but a paragon would merit such treatment? What else could I be but the loser in such a comparison?"

His honest words, so very much like a man, warmed

her. His honesty deserved hers. "I have had reasons for wearing my mourning that have nothing to do with Lieutenant DeVine."

"But the whole county believes it."

"That was our intention. Mine and Lady Drucilla's, I mean. When she told me how Gerald had treated her, I could not—"

"How DeVine had treated her?" Lord Worthington asked.

Penelope nodded, surprised by his surprise.

"How did she say DeVine treated her? Did she by any chance say he had accosted her after dinner one night at Wildoaks?"

Amazed, Penelope nodded.

He grimaced, laughed ruefully. "I did not anticipate this. I wonder if Edmund was not as correct in his actions regarding Drucilla as he was with our uncle."

Hands on hips, Penelope said, "How can you say such a thing? Lady Drucilla was a good friend to me. I was horrified by her brother marrying her off to that awful man."

Lord Worthington was shaking his head. "You don't know the true story. How could you?"

"The letters you found," Penelope said, putting it together. "Lady Drucilla lied to me?"

He took her hand. "She pursued your Lieutenant DeVine, backed him into that same alcove where Edmund secreted the letters. The poor man protested his love for you, and she would have none of it. Edmund overheard it all, and blackmailed her into marrying St. Alverrin. It was his first experience with blackmail. He found he liked it and commemorated his initiation by placing that clue in your portrait of Drucilla."

"But why marriage to St. Alverrin?"

"For reasons he kept to himself," Lord Worthington

said, his mouth tightening so that Penelope knew she would get no more from him.

"It is so incredible," Penelope said, staring into the woods, "almost as incredible as Gerald saying he loved me. He never said so. He never mentioned what had happened between him and Lady Drucilla. He kissed me only twice, once when we became engaged, once before he left for the Peninsula. The poor man."

She looked up at Worthington, saw a muscle twitching in his jaw. "Oh, Captain, that is why you did not want me to know what was in those letters."

"Yes. It's not very pretty, the Worthington jealousy."

The Penelope who had walked out that afternoon would have blushed and suggested they return to the house. But the Penelope who had discovered herself to inspire Lord Worthington's passion said, "If you would like, I shall take it as a compliment."

He smiled. "You are absurd." Then he sobered. "I came here to assure you that I would do my best to protect you from gossip, and that I regard you."

"You said that already."

"Did I? Did I say that I wanted to marry you?"

Chapter 14

Penelope caught her breath, shook her head.

"I do. But I know I should not make you such an offer, not with this suspicion about me."

Penelope hung her head. "It does not matter."

He cupped her face with his hands, tipping her chin up. Those warm hazel eyes gazed into hers. "It matters a great deal. You are my anchor to this strange land I have found myself in again. Can you have failed to see it? I am in love with you, and those truthful eyes of yours say you are not indifferent to me."

Penelope's truthful eyes filled with tears. "I cannot marry you, not even were your cousin's murderer discovered."

He released her hand, stepped back. "What is this? You *are* still in love with DeVine."

Penelope shook her head. "No, no it is not that. I was never in love with Gerald. As I said, the mourning was Lady Drucilla's idea. A protection. So no one would think I wanted to marry. Especially not Eversleigh."

She found she could say no more, her throat felt so thick with tears. She covered her mouth with her hand.

He folded her shaking form to his, smoothing her hair. Every curve of her found its match in every hard angle of him. Somehow she had known she would fit like that, and the certainty made her ache all the more.

He said, "I *have* made a hash of this. Now we shall

be very plain with each other, hmm? Do I understand from what you have said that you and Eversleigh have an arrangement that you may take care of his children provided you not marry?"

Penelope nodded.

"Of all the damned things I have ever heard in my life!" He took her gently by the shoulders. "Look at me, Penelope. What Eversleigh has done to you is no better than what Edmund did to his family, do you understand?"

"No. No. No, Eversleigh is not blackmailing me. How can you say such a thing?"

"I have become something of an expert."

Penelope flinched.

Lord Worthington took a deep breath, began in a softer tone, "It is blackmail of the worst kind, first to take advantage of your generous nature—for I am certain you offered to raise those children—and then restrict you with your own love. By God, Edmund had it right again. He only blackmailed those who had things to hide. You have nothing to hide."

"I do now."

"I am not ashamed of my feelings for you."

Penelope smiled. "Nor I for you."

He would have taken her in his arms again, but Penelope stepped back. "I need to think. Please, will you let me think?"

"I can deny you nothing."

She shook her head. Together they walked back to the stables, found the head groomsman had finished the shoe for Lord Worthington's horse.

"Penny!" said Chad, striding up to them. "Here you are."

"Why are you bellowing for me, Chad Lindon?"

"Oh, Worthington. Nice to see you. Heard you'd been here. Thought you'd left."

"Do stop dropping your subjects, Chad," said Penelope, which earned her a frown from her brother.

"Mr. Lindon. As you see, I have not left."

"Yes," Chad said, glancing between them, "well. Penny, Miss Gregory has something she wishes to discuss with you. I said I would look for you. That must have been a quarter hour ago."

"Miss Gregory?" Lord Worthington asked.

"The twins' new governess. How did she appear, Chad?"

"I am not yet convinced Miss Gregory possesses any sensibilities whatsoever, but she seemed white about the lips."

Lord Worthington smiled, although Penelope glimpsed the strain in it. She tried to smile back, said, "I must go."

"Of course. Good day, Miss Lindon. Mr. Lindon."

"My lord." She did not want to watch him go. It was bad enough to hear Red's hooves recede on the gravel.

Chad was at her shoulder. "What's happened, Penny, and don't think I shall be fadged off with some inanity, such as you and Worthington were discussing the festival."

"As a point of fact, we did touch upon it." But at the word touch, Penelope recalled that searing kiss, and pretended to shoo a fly lest her brother see her face flame.

"Are you going to tell me what happened?"

"No. Do stop teasing me, Chad. I need to attend to Miss Gregory." And Penelope left her brother standing in the entry hall of the manor. She ran up the stairs as if the hounds of hell were pursuing her. There would be time to think, and relive each second and sensation of that wonderful kiss, later.

Jarvis's distinctive step came across Lucas's study floor. Next the reflection of Jarvis's head appeared in the stained glass window Lucas was staring at, although faintly, for the two candles he had kept did little to push back the night.

"You're not drunk, sir," said Jarvis, setting down his tray and decanter on the desk behind Lucas's chair.

"No, I am not drunk," Lucas said, glancing at the level of brandy in the decanter that had been on the desk. It was not far below the level of the one Jarvis had brought. "But thank you for the second decanter. I may decide to be drunk later."

"I won't take it back, then. 'Depend on it,' I said to that Masters, 'depend on it, with the face he had on when he came back from Lindon Hall, he ordered us all out because he wants to get on a powerful drunk.' I should hate to have them all look at me as someone who knows as little about you as they do. Sir."

Lucas's expression softened. "Take a perch, man."

Jarvis folded his arms and leaned against the broad desk.

"Do you remember the fort near San Marcos? Their lordships needed it taken, if only for forty-eight hours so supply lines could reach the 5th Foot?"

"Aye, sir. I remember. The hill it sat on would have made a pretty shot for the guns."

"When I learned that the fort had already fallen to rebels, I thought all my problems solved."

"I remember how angry you got, sir, when the rebels refused to open the road to our supply lines."

Lucas's mouth tightened as he remembered the guerrilla leader's suave, even ornate appearance. Don Miguel had bowed low and regretted to say that the 5th Foot was in such a tricky position that he hesitated to let supplies through lest they fall into the hands of Napoleon's forces instead.

Lucas had a standing order to give all aid to any enemy of Napoleon. In theory, that order should have trumped his most recent order to open the fort. But the notion of leaving the 5th in such difficulty galled him beyond bearing.

"I remember also what you said, about forgiveness being easier to get than permission."

And that was what Lucas had asked Don Miguel for, when he informed him he had sent his second lieutenant to the fort's magazine with a flint and orders to barricade himself in and light it should he not hear the proper password.

"He would blow himself to jelly," Don Miguel had said in horrified tones.

"He is an officer, *señor,* and of the opinion that if he must come into the fort this day without seeing his duty done to other Englishmen, he might as well be the first one blown straight to heaven."

"I shall write to Wellington, protesting this bizarre and reprehensible behavior, Captain."

Lucas had nodded. "You must do as you see best, *señor.* It is all we can ever do."

Now Lucas poured himself a drink and mulled his impulse to write Eversleigh and call his bluff. Like their lordships of the admiralty, Penelope would have to be asked her forgiveness. But like their lordships, she was likely to forgive him his rashness if it got her what she wanted.

Lucas recalled how stirring her lips had been beneath his, how her soft breath had brushed his cheek, how luminously her eyes had gleamed. Lucas felt close enough to touch what he wanted, just as he had those four years ago near the fort. And like incapacitating the fort, he found himself sticking over one crucial issue. Then it had been asking Deveril to get himself down into that magazine and hold it, explaining he would have to sit by himself in the dark for nerve-racking hours. Today it was—what else?—Edmund's blasted murder.

Were Lucas Eversleigh, he would laugh at the presumption of someone of Lucas's reputation, someone accused of his own cousin's murder, calling his bluff.

Or would he? Lucas thought suddenly, sitting up.

"Cap'n?"

"The fact of the matter, Jarvis, is that I know nothing of Eversleigh. I am judging him by myself, my standards. But there might be appeals to be made. He gave them up to begin with, after all."

Jarvis was shaking his head. "I have no idea what you're talking about, sir. Who's this Eversleigh?"

"Miss Lindon's brother-in-law. The twins' father." Lucas stood up, and Jarvis straightened. "Didn't you tell me there is to be a cockfight at The Green Duck tonight?"

"I may have mentioned it in passing."

"A keen young man such as Mr. Lindon would be likely to attend, don't you think?"

"Aye," said Jarvis, rubbing his chin. "Aye, he would."

Lucas clapped him on the shoulder. "Then why are we sitting in the dark like this, man? We could be drinking in society."

"Society. Aye, sir."

In the semiprivate back room of The Green Duck, Lucas drummed his fingers on a dark pine table. A glass of port stood before him, its ruby color ironically reminiscent of the dress Mary Smith had worn eleven years ago. What an idiot he had been, Lucas thought, smiling with not-so-gentle disgust at the place where he had earned his exile into the navy and later served to cast the suspicion of murder over him.

The locals in the front room had looked as suspiciously at him as commoners usually looked on gentlemen, but Lucas had been pleased that some of his tenants had nodded politely or touched their forelocks.

The proprietor had assured him the cockfight would begin promptly—"Or thar' abouts, me lord"—at eleven.

Lucas opened his pocket watch, which told him it was ten of eleven. If Lucas could not contrive to meet Chad Lindon unobtrusively and soon, he did not know what drastic measures would tempt him. You are become melodramatic in your advancing age, Lucas old boy, he told himself, and put the glass to his lips. Then he heard men coming into the pub speaking the distinctive bray of the English upper class. Lucas assumed his most indolent posture, hooking his arm over his chair back.

"My lord," said the proprietor, "there are several gentlemen without. Could I presume on your lordship to share this room with them?"

"Of course," Lucas said, pitching his voice to carry. "Please have another bottle brought in immediately."

Lucas stood to welcome Chad Lindon and the other new arrivals. He knew Viscount Balleagh from town, but there were two contemporaries of Chad Lindon's and an older, compact gentleman much closer to Lucas's age who wore sober brown. "Gentlemen, well met. Won't you join me?"

The others made convivial noises, and Lucas met Mr. Hewitt and Mr. Dubreque. Then Chad stood next to the older man, and said, "Worthington, this is Sir Roger Morley. Sir Roger arrived at the Hall this evening. Sir Roger, Lord Worthington, our new neighbor." Chad's neutral tone had put Lucas on the alarm, then, as Sir Roger bowed, Chad alarmed Lucas further by drawing his finger across his throat.

The younger gentlemen were full of talk about the coming fight. Such talk led the conversation until the serving girl arrived with a bottle and glasses. Then she became the focus of appreciative attention, as she was amply endowed in all the right places. Lucas's first thought was gratitude she did not appear closely related to Mary Smith.

Sir Roger did not enter into the flirting or nuzzling of the girl, nor did Lucas, but he watched in amusement as the others did. He smiled when Mr. Hewitt pushed the girl into Chad Lindon's lap. Chad's stammered apology had them all chuckling.

Lucas poured drinks all around, and shortly they were called away to the start of the fight. Lucas had hoped, during the course of it, that he would be able to take Chad aside and ask him what about Sir Roger had engendered such a warning. Sir Roger, however, seemed determined to remain near Chad.

So Lucas watched the fight with the same feigned indolence. The fight itself held little interest. Fortunately, due to the singular aggressiveness of one cock, it lasted a short duration, at which point everyone paid up or collected amidst a great deal of excited talk.

"You have lost, Lindon?" Sir Roger asked as Chad passed over some guineas.

"I had heard rumors Digby's bird was quite splendid, but I did not want to believe them."

"Did you bet, Worthington?"

Lucas smiled. "No, my pleasure was vicarious. Digby is a tenant." Digby caught Lucas's eye at that point across the pen, and Lucas nodded to him. Digby grinned and went back to collecting his part of the winnings.

"I hope you gentlemen will let me buy another bottle to celebrate," Lucas said.

"I was hoping you would say that, my lord," Sir Roger said.

It was no surprise to Lucas that soon he and Sir Roger were deep in conversation and discovering they had both been in the war, although Sir Roger had belonged to the 3rd Light Dragoons.

Then the proprietor was back, bowing and saying, "The Reverend Mr. Simons, gentlemen."

Mr. Simons looked surprised to see such a group of gentlemen, and when he spied not only Chad Lindon, but also Lucas, he frowned openly. The serving girl brought a fresh bottle. She glanced at Lucas appreciatively, and she may have nudged the vicar with her hip. Lucas could not tell, but Mr. Dubreque elbowed Mr. Hewitt and smiled.

"Vicar," Lucas said pleasantly, "do join us."

"Thank you, no."

"It is very late."

"The service of the cloth knows no regular hours."

"Only irregular men," joked Mr. Hewitt.

The vicar glanced askance at Mr. Hewitt, his expression disapproving. He looked even more disapprovingly at the girl, who fanned her lashes at him before swaying from the room.

"If you will not join us for a drink, will you not sit down?" Lucas asked. "I am sure that is why you yourself are here; you needed to rest before riding back to town."

"No. I was asked to meet someone here. But he is not here."

"Let us not keep you, then, sir."

"My lord," said the vicar. He bowed curtly and left.

Mr. Hewitt and Mr. Dubreque sniggered into their hands. Chad Lindon was trying not to smile. Sir Roger turned back to Lucas, poured them both a little more port. Neither of them had drunk much, Lucas thought wryly, despite attempts to force the other.

"A stiff-rumped man, your vicar," Sir Roger said.

"He is not known as the warm shoulder one cries upon," Lucas replied, "but he serves well enough for all that."

The younger men were beginning a song, raising their glasses high and then bringing them clunking down onto the table. Sir Roger smiled, leaned forward, and said, "I should very much like to clear up something between us, my lord."

Lucas realized from the sudden quicker beating of his heart that the words had made him stop breathing. "And what would that be, Sir Roger?"

"I should tell you what Lindon has been trying to tell you by force of will alone. My aunt sent me here to assess the lay of the land. You, specifically. It is a dreadful impertinence. Were I in your shoes, I would resent it. But there it is."

"Would your aunt happen to be Lady Eversleigh?"

"I have that honor. Should I ask how you guessed?"

"It has come to my attention that certain people have made it their business to think they needed to protect Miss Lindon from someone of my former reputation. They succeeded instead in frightening her, which I do not look upon with a friendly eye."

"The report frightened my aunt as well." Sir Roger took a sip of port. "She considered the present situation ideal, and would not like it disturbed."

"I can appreciate her feelings. Miss Lindon is beyond all measure an excellent woman."

Sir Roger's lips twitched. "You would have to say so, of course."

"Indeed, sir, I do not have to say anything at all. But what I do say, I mean."

Sir Roger smiled. "I plan to tell my aunt I do not consider you a danger to Miss Lindon. Do you know what decided me, Worthington? Believe it or not, 'twas the sight of that serving wench. You did not ignore her, nor did you size her up like a man with lust in his heart. No, your expression measured her for effect, much as I might have looked upon casks of spirits for tired soldiers."

Behind Sir Roger's shoulder, Chad was looking anxious even as he lifted his glass in a noisy toast with the others. Lucas nodded reassuringly, although he did not appreciate being patted on the head by Sir Roger Morley.

"Mr. Lindon is clearly on your side."

"Mr. Lindon is on his sister's side. Moreover he knows that I hold his sister in esteem and wish nothing unpleasant to happen to her. Or hers."

Sir Roger pursed his lips and nodded. Message received and understood, Lucas thought. Now, however, Lucas was done being the inquisitioned. He would try being the inquisitor. Lady Eversleigh's reconnaissance officer should know the lay of his home land.

So Lucas sipped his port for a few moments, then said, "Have you seen your cousin recently?"

Sir Roger swirled his port. "Eversleigh?"

"Yes."

"He is not often in England." He scratched his neck, a light rasping. "I do not know when he might return again. It is too bad, too, for Eversleigh could be a fine companion. He was a fine companion, before his wife died."

Lucas did not mistake what Sir Roger said as an answer to his question. Indeed, if Sir Roger told his lies so poorly, he must have been a joy to his sergeants major who could read a falsehood or evasion on a man's breath if necessary.

"Should he visit, I should enjoy meeting him."

"You are very kind, my lord," Sir Roger said. "I do not think it likely. Not anytime soon."

"Where did he last make his home?"

"Lisbon, I believe."

"Ah. Beautiful city. I had occasion to be there often."

"I did not, regrettably. I was more often in the field."

"It is the military life, Sir Roger. Doomed either to look at great expanses of ocean, or great expanses of fields, and precious little else."

"Do you know his grace the duke of Nowhere?" Chad Lindon said in a carrying voice. "Excellent fellow, but he never passes the port."

"I shall arrange for another bottle," Lucas said, standing. "Excuse me, Sir Roger." The younger gentlemen shouted a hurrah, and Lucas went to the doorway to signal the proprietor.

Standing by the front door, Jarvis caught his eye. He gestured sharply toward outside with his chin. Lucas nodded. He ordered more wine, excused himself from the party, then, whistling quietly, he stepped outside.

Jarvis waited for him by several wagons and traps and sleepy horses. "I just followed Lady Worthington here, sir. She came right from Wildoaks, trotted up here, went round the entire place. I think she would have gone on toward Lindon Hall and town, but she saw me and cantered off toward Wildoaks."

"Do you think she knew you were following her?"

"No, sir. I was off Red by the time she came round, looking like I'd come out of here. She just didn't want to be seen."

"Was she meeting someone, or looking for something?"

"She had nothing in her hands, sir."

Lucas swore softly. "We go back to Wildoaks. When we get there, you talk with Masters. I want all notes and mail coming in for Lady Worthington in your hands before she gets them. We take turns watching her. She's not to be out of sight."

"Aye, Cap'n."

Lucas rejoined the party in the back room, which was showing signs of breaking up.

"Sir Roger is sent by—" Chad said under his breath.

"I know," Lucas said. "How is your sister?"

"He came before dinner. Penny was not happy. No, happy must be the last word describing my sister tonight."

"Tell her . . . tell her not to worry."

"Just what are you about, Worthington?"

"Trust me." He clapped Chad on the shoulder. Chad did not have to feign his wince. Lucas raised his voice. "Next time, do not bet against Wildoaks, eh, sir?"

The sun, skimming the hills and lighting the dewy air, made Penelope squint as she directed the footmen to place Sir Roger's trunk upon his hired phaeton. He came down the steps of Lindon Hall and bowed low over Penelope's hand. "It was a pleasure seeing you, Miss Lindon. I wish I could have stayed longer."

"It was good of you to come all this way for such a short time," she replied, wishing she had known what he and Chad had been about the last night. But Chad remained sound abed.

"One does what one can with what one has. I have to go past Highland Grove. Shall I send along your best wishes to Lady Eversleigh?"

"Please," said Penelope.

"I shall tell her all is well with Master Timothy and Lady Christina. And yourself, of course."

"You're very kind," Penelope murmured, although she thought she must be dreaming.

"You do excellently by them, ma'am."

Penelope blushed, glanced away. It happened to be toward the sun, so she could shade her eyes with her hand. "Thank you. I love them both dearly."

Sir Roger bowed again, then he stepped into his phaeton. Penelope watched it until it passed down the drive.

Inside, Masters handed her a letter. "This has come for you from Wildoaks, ma'am."

"Thank you." Penelope recognized his handwriting.

My dear Miss Lindon,

I hope this note finds you bearing up under the burden of an unexpected guest. I happened to meet Sir Roger last night—you may ask your brother the circumstances—and we passed a pleasant evening conversing about what basis there is in present for my past reputation."

Penelope bit her lip. Poor Worthington. He would have hated that as much as she had hated being put on the spot by Sir Roger's sudden arrival. She had been discussing Timothy's desire to tickle his sister during their lessons with Miss Gregory when a footman brought news Sir Roger had come. Nothing was designed to make her feel more off center.

I believe I have allayed his apprehension, so I beg you to put any further thought of the matter from your head.

I would have liked to relate you more of the conversation in person, but I must apologize for not only appearing to ignore you, but ignoring you in fact. Jarvis and I are taking turns watching an interested party.

"Be careful, my captain," she whispered.

You are in my thoughts.
                                          Your most obt srvt,
                                          W

Which direction ran those thoughts, Penelope

wondered. She felt warm and cold together. She could not quite believe that Sir Roger would tell Lady Eversleigh that, considering Penelope's association with Worthington, she yet did well by the twins. It was almost incredible.

Penelope folded Lord Worthington's letter, tucked it closely into her sleeve, and went to the breakfast room. Her morning chocolate steaming before her, she stared out the window at the misty trees and hills beyond.

If she could marry, could Lord Worthington truly make her happy? It was so difficult to answer that question. He seemed to want sincerely to be a presence in her life and in the twins' lives. But sincerity, like the rich taste of the chocolate, could last only so long as its substance was there. Would he feel differently about her ten years from now when any claim she might have had to beauty was gone? As a surrogate father, how would he treat the twins on a day-to-day basis? Would he understand that they often landed themselves in the soup because they were curious rather than malicious? Was he one of those who believed in thrashing boys? Did he look on the twins as a skirmish to be won before he could take her, his battle prize, or could he truly love them?

All questions that yet needed answers. But there was one question Penelope needed to ask herself first. Did she want Lord Worthington to make her happy? Yes, Penelope thought. Yes, she wanted him to make her happy. She wanted to feel his strong arms around her. She wanted that feeling of being alive. She wanted his sense of humor and his force of command. She wanted to be part of a whole, completing him while he completed her.

Above all, Penelope wanted to be herself. She was tired of being meek and mild. She was tired of living a lie. She plucked at her gray dress, its color embarrassing her with its dishonesty. Penelope had donned it under false pretenses, based on a lie Lady Drucilla had told her. It was the lie of a lie.

Penelope went into her library, penned a short note.

Dear Lord Worthington,
I am glad you had opportunity to meet Sir Roger. He left this morning. Had he stayed longer, I would have introduced you to him.
I hope your other business proves fruitful, although I regret for your sake its necessity. I shall not feel ignored, no matter the circumstances.
Sincerely,
Penelope Lindon

She sent the note on its way, wondering what he would think when he read it. She pictured him in his library, its stained glass window casting glorious patterns of color.

Color, she thought, and she smiled.

Chapter 15

As Lucas ushered Cecily, Honoria, and Uncle Albert into church the morning of the Harvest Festival, he was convinced that the entire Four Corners was there. The church resounded with the noises of heels against the stone floor, coughing, and the light whispers of excited people. People stood in the back, along the walls, and above in the choir loft. Smiling parents held excited infants in their arms to make more room.

Lucas opened the well-worn door to the Worthington box and waited for his relatives to file in. The Howaths smiled politely from their box behind his. Lady Bodsmead's eyes were twinkling with high merriment, perhaps because of the handsome gentleman standing next to her. Lucas nodded to her, amused. Well, he would know later what made her so animated.

He glanced casually across the aisle to the Lindons' box, and caught his breath. The answer sat before him.

Penelope wore green. No mauve or lavender or gray, but a rich, glowing green the color of distant, sunshine-topped hills. Long green ribbons fluttered around her poke bonnet. When had she ordered it? What did it mean?

He caught Penelope's eye. She blushed and buried her nose in her prayer book, looking deliciously self-conscious. Her blush increased as Tina pointed at her aunt, and waved to Lucas. Did Penelope sense the smiles behind her, the pointing fingers the women held behind cupped hands just below their chins in a futile attempt at discretion?

"Did that little girl just wave to you?" asked Honoria.

Lucas turned away from the aisle toward Honoria. "Yes."

"Do you know her?"

"I do, indeed. She's Lady Christina Eversleigh."

"Oh." Honoria glanced over his shoulder. "Good gracious, is Miss Lindon in colors? She is taking quite a risk."

"I hope not," Lucas said. "I will make sure of that."

Honoria lifted her brows, but could not comment before the Reverend Simons called the packed church to order. Lucas hoped she had not heard the bravado in his words.

When Lucas next checked his watch, only a half hour had passed. Reverend Simons had read a mercifully short service. He closed his heavy prayer book with a thump against the pulpit, and surveyed the congregation from his vantage on the high carved pulpit. "Now let us all say a prayer that our festival pleases God and us."

A crowd of happy townspeople shortly separated his party from the Lindons in the church. He caught up to them outside on the small church green, even as he noticed that Cecily had managed to give them the slip in the crowd. Lucas had expected just such a maneuver. Jarvis was on the watch for her.

Lucas nodded to Chad Lindon, as Penelope was bent to listen to something Timothy told her. The fortyish woman with her hair pulled back in as severe a style as her dark dress must be Miss Gregory, Lucas thought.

Tina let go Penelope's hand and ran toward Lord Worthington, who swung her up into his arms. "Captain, Captain," she exclaimed, drawing indulgent and speculative glances of their neighbors and a frown from her governess.

"Why, what's this?" Lucas asked as though surprised to find a five-year-old in his arms. "A little dipper?"

Timothy also approached Lucas. "We have not seen you in some time, sir," he said gravely. "I hope you have been well."

Lucas set Tina down and bowed to Timothy. "I have been about my estate business. I do thank you for your concern."

Timothy grinned, throwing away any effect of gentlemanly reserve. "We want to see you ride and shoot." He pretended to point a pistol. "Boom! Boom!"

Lucas ruffled Timothy's hair, a gesture the boy accepted with another grin. He and Uncle Albert bowed to the ladies.

"I must apologize for the twins this morning, my lord," Penelope said, giving them a speaking glance. "I fear their excitement has overridden their better behavior."

Timothy made a face.

"Good morning," said Lady Lindon, nodding to include the whole party. "You look in fine fettle, my lord. Are you ready to enter the fray?"

"I have been advised where I should make my best showing," Lord Worthington said dryly.

"I am quite certain you will," said Lady Lindon with a smile that earned her a surprised expression from Penelope.

"Boom!" Timothy said. "I'll bet you're the best there is."

"Give your uncle Chad some credit. I'm told he's an excellent shot."

"I plan to put in a good showing," said Chad. "My lord."

"I hope you do."

"You must excuse me," Lady Lindon said. "I have to

join the cooking committee, although why anyone thinks I know anything about roasting animals is beyond me. Well, perhaps they will let me judge the baked goods. Your tenant Mrs. Smith, my lord, makes a divine shortbread." With that, Lady Lindon left them.

"What other events will you enter, Worthington?"

"I am also committed to the footrace and archery."

"We had planned to see some of the fair first," Honoria said. "Perhaps you would join us?"

"May we?" Tina said to Penelope, then announced to Lucas, "I want to see the puppets."

"Me too," added her twin.

"Children," Penelope said, "do not presume so on Lady Honoria, Lord Albert, and Lord Worthington."

"Come now, Miss Lindon," Uncle Albert said, " 'twill be no presumption unless the puppeteer has not learned the valuable trick of entertaining the more senior members of his audience too. And I have not had the pleasure of seeing a fair through such young eyes in . . . well, a long time."

His family, Lucas decided, was rallying nicely. He might wish his uncle would choose his own agenda, and not take up whatever other one was offered, but he had enough experience to know one could not have everything.

Looking at Penelope's vibrant expression, lighted by her beautiful green dress, though, he thought he might be close.

"The puppets it is, then," Lucas said. "Which way?"

Judging by the way Lord Worthington had smiled as he had approached them, Penelope decided her impulse to wear the green dress had been right. Nothing, she declared to herself, would mar a happy day. Worthington had induced, possibly even strong-armed, his family to do the inviting. The innocence of children more than met any potential awkwardness halfway. Not even Lady Howath approaching could dim Penelope's spirits. Indeed, she reveled in the attention she received. Sir Roger had been and gone. She could have this day.

"We know the way," said Timothy. "We will show you. Come on, Aunt Penny."

"A moment, Timothy," Penelope said. "First you must make your bow to Lady Howath and Lady Bodsmead. Tina, you, too."

The twins made creditable deference to the ladies, and everyone wished each other good morning.

"You look wonderful, Miss Lindon," Kitty said, loud enough to be heard above the general conversation of how fortunate they had all been to have it not rain. "Please let me make my husband known to you," Kitty said.

Lord Bodsmead was everything Kitty had described, and very pleasing in his manners, even to small children. "Did I hear your boy here say there was a puppet show he would like to see?" he asked, crouching down to Timothy's level.

"Indeed, sir, I did."

"Lady Howath," Lady Honoria said, "perhaps you, your sister and brother-in-law would care to join us? The Lindons have already accepted our invitation to head into the fair together."

"I shall accept for us all," Lord Bodsmead said, "for I love puppet shows, and I think I smell cinnamon buns."

There was nothing more to do than stroll toward the fair. Miss Gregory supervised the twins, and Lady Honoria took charge of Lady Howath. Uncle Albert engaged Chad in conversation about the shooting match later. Penelope wondered if he was taking tips on whom to place a side-bet. That left Bodsmead and Kitty and Penelope and Worthington to take up the rear.

"Very adroitly done," Penelope said in an undertone

to Worthington as Kitty pointed out some sights to Bodsmead.

"You look wonderful in green," Lord Worthington said. "It makes your eyes resemble the sea just before a storm."

"Captain—"

"All wild and dangerous and beautiful."

"My eyes are blue, not green."

"Who said I described their color?"

"Captain—"

"Why did you wear it, Penelope?"

"I wished to be myself." Saying the words was like burning every one of her lavender and gray dresses.

Lord Worthington smiled, a tender, relaxed smile. There was no hint of seduction in it, only a comfort and understanding that warmed Penelope as no hearth fire or sunny day ever had.

They followed the crowds of people through a town festooned with colorful placards. As the buildings thinned, a large green opened into a hollow. Bright tents created a solid phalanx at the green's edge, where an occasional tree, turned red or umber with autumn leaves, spilled shade. Each tent had a flag or banner flying. Laughter bubbled up from the people already walking around the tents, and rousing music played.

Beyond the tents and some tethered horses, another open green was dotted with pennants. Men were pulling large targets into a row for the archery and shooting.

" 'Tis a beautiful sight," said Lord Worthington.

"Well at least it is an organized one. No booth out of order, no fights yet, the targets going up on time."

"Practical woman," Lord Worthington said fondly. "You deserve a lot of credit for the work you have done."

Penelope wriggled her shoulders at the praise. "They

work hard, the yeomen and townsmen. They deserve a party."

"So I have always said as well," Lady Howath said.

Penelope nodded, then smiled when Kitty pulled a face.

A light wind brushed Penelope's face, bringing with it the tempting smell of roasting meat and sweet cinnamon.

"Sticky buns!" cried Timothy. He would have bolted down the hill but for Penelope's remonstrance.

Sticky buns in hand, given by a woman whose smile filled her large round face, they strolled off toward the puppet show.

"An overabundance of riches," Lord Worthington said, pointing to some brightly patterned shawls in one booth, a fine collection of silver bangles in another. Two townswomen debated the merits of the silver bangles, but broke off their discussion to watch Penelope and her party pass.

"What merchant do you visit yourself?" asked Worthington.

Spying an unholy, teasing glee in Chad's eyes, Penelope answered promptly, although she knew where the answer would lead. "There's a toy maker I visit every year for the twins. There's also a milliner I like."

"Then we must visit both. Aha. I believe we've found the puppet show."

The red-draped stage fronted by bales of hay nestled under a large oak with twisting, spreading branches. The "theater" was almost filled. Mothers and children already sitting on the hay bales talked and laughed with their friends, glancing curiously at the lords and ladies. Penelope could name each of them. Many she had sat with during a lying-in or a sickness.

They settled themselves on hay bales. Presently the small red curtain fringed with gold rolled back, and

Punch and Judy appeared on the stage, accompanied by several other colorful puppets. Penelope laughed almost as loudly as Lord Albert at the puppets' antics.

The show over, the adults stood together in the throng of mothers and children leaving the theater and smiled as the twins repeated lines from the play, then dissolved into giggles.

Chad checked his pocket watch. " 'Tis approaching eleven and the footrace, Worthington. The puppet show went on longer than I had thought."

Penelope took a small misstep on a wooden toy a child had dropped. Lord Worthington steadied her by taking her arm.

"Lead on, Mr. Lindon," said Lord Worthington, tucking Penelope's arm through his.

The party strolled past more merchant tents. Penelope smiled at women she recognized and wished them good morning. She did not care that they raised their brows at the picture she made. Penelope did, however, feel startled that she had come to feel so much so quickly. Her hand pressed against Lord Worthington's ribs, it was as if the last five and a half years had melted away. Would she, Penelope wondered, have felt this way if Lord Worthington had come home earlier?

"I wonder what my life would have been like if I had entered the merchant service," said Lord Worthington.

Penelope blinked to hear this sudden echo of her own thoughts, and Chad quirked a brow.

"Whatever do you mean, Worthington?" Lady Howath asked.

"Would I be like these merchants, bringing their goods to fairs, or, in my case, seaside markets? Only look at how that woman shows her yarns. See how she smoothes the skeins so the colors pick up the light? Would I have learned such skills?"

"Surely a captain would not bring goods into the market," said Chad.

"I doubt I would have been a captain by now if I had been on a merchanter. The navy gives you incentive to rise quickly. I was also extremely lucky."

"My brother is a captain, as you were, Worthington," Lord Bodsmead said. "He has mentioned you from time to time, and luck has never entered it."

"Bodsmead speaks nothing but the truth," Kitty said, and spoiled the effect by laughing.

"I protest, sir," Lord Worthington said. "Captain Ghent aside—for your lady has mentioned him to me— I must insist I was lucky, for I could not even climb a rigging. I thought I would surely have fallen straight into the ocean the first time my captain desired me to give him a report. And I am put in mind of my luck because of those good men there." Lord Worthington pointed to a carnival act that had set up at the outskirts of the fair. The performers had set up several ropes stretched tightly between two posts some ten feet above the ground.

Lord Worthington crouched down, pulling the twins close. "Look, now," he said, "do you see how the man on the rope keeps his foot straight? That is not the best way to do it. If you point your toes out, you have better balance. Remember that, children, the next time you climb a tree."

Penelope bit back the protective response that she did not intend the children to ever climb a tree.

"Is that so, sir?" inquired a man pleasantly. Penelope looked up to see a dark, middle-aged man dressed in sober brown except for his waistcoat, which was a brilliantly striped red and yellow. "How do you know so much of walking ropes?"

"He's a captain," said Timothy importantly.

Lord Worthington stood and bowed. "Former captain

of His Majesty's ship *Atlantia,* at your service. Although I must admit I have not tackled rigging since I made first lieutenant."

The dark man also bowed. "Giovanni, Captain." A speculative look came into Giovanni's dark face. "Would you, Captain, do a great favor to a poor entertainer?"

The Bodsmeads, Chad, Uncle Albert, and several townspeople and tenants overheard Giovanni's request and smiled, sharing a secret. Lady Howath and Lady Honoria had wandered a little away toward a tent. Lady Howath was deep in conversation with the merchant, a short, round man who resembled his soaps.

Lord Worthington smiled ruefully. "I would, sir, with pleasure, except that I am also—"

"Please, Captain," said Timothy.

"I think, Captain," said Penelope quickly, "that we would enjoy such a demonstration." Her glance flickered over to the smiling fairgoers, then back.

"Well, then, I would be delighted. Would you be so kind as to hold my coat?"

Timothy and Tina cheered. Penelope gladly accepted Lord Worthington's blue coat. Lord Worthington approached the ropes, then swung himself up easily.

"Are you sure this is a good idea, Penny?" Chad asked.

"Indeed," Kitty added. "Not quite what one expects from a marquess."

"Perhaps not," said Penelope, watching Lord Worthington steady himself before walking the rope, "but Lord Worthington still feels he must prove himself, and if his father was beloved by his tenants for participating in games of skill, what better game than this unplanned demonstration?"

Lady Howath and Lady Honoria rejoined them.

"Is all well?" Penelope asked Lady Howath.

"Everything seems to be in place," responded Lady Howath.

"My feelings exactly."

"But where has Worthington gone?" Lady Honoria asked.

"Yes, where?" Lady Howath asked. "Of course, he has gone on to run in the race. It is just starting."

"No," Penelope said and gestured toward the ropes and poles. Arms outstretched, Lord Worthington was walking the rope as surely as if he were on firm ground.

"Good heavens," said Lady Howath. She swept a hand over her face and dislodged her broad plumed hat. "Whatever is he doing?"

"Showing the performers a better way of walking the rope," said Bodsmead as Kitty caught Lady Howath's hat.

"He is quite splendid," Lady Honoria said. "Look at how the performers are watching him. We shall have quite a show soon."

Lord Worthington pivoted on the rope and saw them watching. He saluted them cheerfully. Reaching the post, he invited a performer to come up with him.

"I think we have our show now," said Chad.

A large crowd had gathered to watch Lord Worthington walk the rope. He smiled and gestured with his hand. Penelope could not help but smile.

Kitty said, "He looks at home up there."

A reluctant smile tugged at Lady Howath's mouth. "He certainly does. I never thought when I asked him to participate in the festival, that he would take me so literally."

Chad coughed to cover a laugh. Uncle Albert thumped him on the back.

Lord Worthington said something to the performer, who laughed heartily. Then Lord Worthington climbed down the pole. The crowd clapped and cheered. Lord

Worthington bowed modestly, then strode up to their group.

"That was terrific!" exclaimed Timothy. "Will you show me? Please?"

"Me too, me too," Tina said, hopping from foot to foot.

Lord Worthington glanced at Penelope. "Maybe, if you are good and your aunt says you may."

"We will talk about it later," Penelope said to allay further discussion here, although the idea of Lord Worthington teaching her twins to do such things did not frighten her as it would once have.

"Lady Howath, Miss Lindon, I must congratulate you again on the festival. I am having a marvelous time, and it looks as if my tenants are, also. Thank you."

Did Lady Howath blush? "Thank you, my lord. We did our humble best."

"You did look as if you were having a good time," said Kitty.

Lord Worthington grinned. "I have not had such fun in close on a year."

He held out his hand to Penelope. She gave him his coat. He winked at her and shrugged it over his powerful shoulders. Lord Worthington was so alive, Penelope thought with wonder and happiness. Feeling as proud of him as she ever had of the twins, Penelope had to fight an answering grin.

Giovanni hurried up to them and bowed. "My lord, I have just now found out that you are Worthington. Please forgive me for asking you to—"

"Nonsense, sir. I have had a most excellent time. My compliments to your performers. Perhaps we will see you sometime at Wildoaks."

Giovanni bowed even more deeply. "We are at your convenience, my lord." He backed away with a flourish.

"I suppose we have missed the footrace?" asked Lord Worthington.

Chad pulled out his pocket watch. "By a good quarter hour," he said with satisfaction.

Penelope eyed him quizzically.

"I hate running the footrace, Penny," said Chad.

Kitty, Bodsmead, and Lord Worthington laughed.

"Can we see who wins? Can we?" asked Timothy.

"I do not see why not," said Penelope.

"And after that, I suppose we shall have to feed you two whirling dervishes," Lord Worthington said, smiling and putting a hand on each twin's blond head. He turned to Kitty and Lady Howath. "Do you continue to join us, ladies, Bodsmead?"

"We must look for Sir William," said Kitty quickly. "Is that not right, Bodsmead? But we will catch up to you later at the shooting. Goodbye for now." She hooked arms with her sister and carried them both away, Bodsmead following. Then, some yards from the group, Kitty winked over her shoulder.

The twins' excitement must be infectious, Penelope thought frequently as her group cheered on the racers then strolled back to the fair tents, where they selected tender meat and vegetable pasties, cool cider, and soft wine. Lord Worthington pulled blankets from his horse, which had been tethered nearby.

Jarvis's work, Penelope thought, and wondered idly why she had not seen Jarvis that day. Talking and laughing—even Lady Honoria elicited a few chuckles with some dry comment or other—they settled the blanket on warm grass and picnicked.

Penelope could not remember a better day. For the first time in so long, she felt relaxed and comfortable. As Penelope held out her glass to Lord Worthington for him to pour some wine, she felt drunk at the sight of him. He had taken off his hat. The sun burnished his hair like laughter. Timothy had inched away from Miss

Gregory and now sat next to him. Timothy mimicked one of Lord Worthington's gestures.

The antipathy for her brother-in-law caught her with surprising fury. May you rot in Hades, Eversleigh, she thought, for denying your children a father, and me a husband.

Lord Worthington held out his hand to her. "Do you think that some of Mrs. Smith's shortbread would serve as dessert?"

Smiles spread across the twins' faces.

Penelope let him help her up. "Let us go look."

Mrs. Smith's shortbread had won her a prize. Lucas doubted her round face could have smiled harder, however, than when he had asked her if his party might try a little of it. She had pressed sugar-covered wedges into their hands, and Honoria allowed it was as fine as any she had had, even in London.

After they ate their shortbread, Honoria and Uncle Albert excused themselves. "For you are bound to the archery, Lucas," his uncle said, "and I want to try more sweets."

They wandered over to the archery, where Lucas was pleased to watch Miss Lindon compete with better skill than he himself possessed. He was also pleased to see his tenant Digby win.

"My good man," said Lucas, "like that other prize, I am proud to keep this one at Wildoaks."

Digby's broad chest swelled. "No Perkinses will ever beat me at archery, my lord."

Lucas steered his party back to the fair. He wanted to visit those merchants Miss Lindon had mentioned. They visited the toy merchant first. Carved and painted marionettes dancing along, the twins were willing to let

Miss Lindon look at fabrics without demanding her constant attention.

"How about this ruby, Penny?" asked Chad, holding up a delicate muslin. He then winked at Lucas as his sister bent her head to look at it.

"'Tis a beautiful color," said Miss Lindon wistfully.

The excited merchant would have added his opinion. Lucas shook his head. The merchant nodded, his gaze sharp.

"A lesser woman could not wear such a color, Miss Lindon," Lucas said. "It takes a woman who not only possesses self-confidence, but the ability to inspire it in others."

"You are speaking nonsense, Captain."

"I never speak nonsense. Fribble, perhaps, but never nonsense."

Miss Lindon turned her face up to his, a flower seeking the sun. "Seven yards, please."

"Surely that color is too strong for you, Miss Lindon." Lucas sighed. Cecily.

"On the contrary, I am certain 'twill suit me perfectly," said Miss Lindon serenely.

Lucas wanted to kiss Penelope on the spot. Instead he turned and greeted his family, wondered how Honoria had managed to find her sister-in-law. Except for Cecily, who stood in petulant silence, they exchanged pleasantries about the fair.

"Sir William won the horse race," Uncle Albert said.

"That will gratify him excessively," said Miss Lindon.

"Indeed," Uncle Albert said.

Cecily sniffed.

"And where are you off to now?" Lucas asked.

"We planned to get some light refreshment, then to the shooting field. It is the spectator sport of the afternoon."

"So I am told, Uncle. We will meet you there."

"I am excessive tired. Must we stay through the dinner?" asked Cecily, swaying closer to him and batting her eyelashes.

"Through the very last bite of the sweet course," said Lucas. "This festival is not just for our amusement, *my lady,* but for the tenants."

Cecily leaned closer, her mouth set alarmingly. "As a country gentlemen, Worthington," she said, "you are a bore."

Honoria raised her brows.

"May that be the worst anyone says of me for some years to come. I am picturing a small cottage, no more than ten rooms, somewhere in Northumberland. Does it not sound attractive?"

Cecily recoiled. "You would not dare. Lord Albert?"

Uncle Albert pursed his lips. "I am sorry, my dear, but Worthington is head of the family."

Cecily fanned herself. "This conversation is become wearisome." She strode off toward the next row of booths and turned the corner.

"We shall go after her," Honoria said. "Come, Uncle. Miss Lindon, that ruby muslin would look wondrous on you."

"You are too kind," Miss Lindon said.

"Honoria," said Lucas, bowing.

His uncle tipped his hat, Lady Honoria bowed, and they followed the direction Cecily had gone.

"Why was the pretty lady so mad?" asked Tina.

Lucas patted Tina's head. "My cousin does not like festivals."

Tina was nonplussed by the idea.

"Where is Timothy?" Miss Lindon asked, looking about through the crowd.

Miss Gregory also looked about her. "He was just here."

"There he is," Chad Lindon said, pointing between two of the tents.

"I shall get him, Miss Gregory," Penelope said.

Lucas exchanged a smile with Chad Lindon, then asked the merchant to pull down another sample of cloth, a pale blue. He expected Penelope to be back with Timothy directly, and wanted her to see it.

But she did not come right back. Lucas peered around the side of the tent, saw her straighten from bending down to Timothy. She put both hands on the boy's shoulders, leading him back, her expression grave.

Timothy looked up at her over his shoulder, saying, "But why did Lady Worthington give a bag to the vicar?"

Miss Lindon's gaze quickly met Lucas's. She nodded even as she said, "I do not know, Timothy."

Lucas crouched down so he and Timothy were eye to eye. "Do you remember what size the bag was?"

"Small. Like Aunt Penny's reticule."

"Did you see it?" Lucas asked Penelope.

"I saw them together. I saw a small bag in the vicar's hand. I did not see Lady Worthington pass it."

"I did not mean to get into trouble," Timothy said. "I saw a boy with a carved train. Do you remember the tops you sent us, Captain? We like those tops. I went closer to see the train. Then I saw the vicar, and Lady Worthington."

"Did the vicar see you?" Lucas asked, and Miss Lindon's eyes widened.

Timothy shrugged. "I do not think so. He looked angry."

"You are not in trouble, Master Timothy." Lucas stood up, met Miss Lindon's gaze and found it both persuaded and appalled.

"You do not think—" said Chad Lindon.

"When we saw them on the road," Miss Lindon said, and bit her delectable lip.

"Yes," Lucas said, thinking of the vicar needing to meet someone at The Green Duck and Jarvis also spotting

Cecily there. And Sir William had said the vicar had been spotted near Edmund's picnic site the day Edmund had died.

"We don't know what was in that bag," Chad said.

"Aunt Penny? What's wrong?" asked Tina.

"Nothing, lamb," Miss Lindon said, touching each twin. "It's all right."

"No, we don't know what's in the bag," Lucas said. "But we must find out. It is almost time for us to go to the shooting match. The vicar presides over the event, right?"

Miss Lindon nodded, her expression worried.

"Would you permit me, sir," Lucas said to Timothy, "to put you atop my shoulders? And perhaps your uncle could oblige with your sister. Ladies, shall we have a brisk walk?"

The twins had nothing but enthusiasm for this scheme, and Penelope and Miss Gregory kept up easily. As they approached the field where the shooting match would take place, Lucas sensed the possibility of resolving his cousin's murder. He could not get there quickly enough.

Chapter 16

Penelope could hear the spectators come for the shooting match before they crossed the rise and were among them. The spectators spread themselves before the target field, creating a patchwork of colors against the green grass. One part of her registered her surprise at the number of spectators even as the rest of her mind reeled at the implications of the vicar being involved with Lady Worthington.

Shock, horror, and disgust warred within her, and it was all she could do to maintain her slight smile and allay the twins' concern. And although Lord Worthington also tipped his hat politely, Penelope read his tension in the set of his jaw and the way he looked about him, a hawk sighting its prey.

Penelope spotted Kitty, Bodsmead, Lady Howath, Mrs. Tipplethwaite, and her mother among the spectators, for they reclined at the hill's base, near the shooting area. Sir William paced nearby.

"There's your grandmother, scamps," Lord Worthington said. Then, to Penelope, "We leave the twins and Miss Gregory with Lady Lindon."

"Worthington—" Chad said.

"Mr. Lindon, I beg you to trust me."

"Very well," Chad said.

"It will be all right, Chad," said Penelope, and suddenly she thought that maybe some part of it would be.

They settled the twins and their governess with Penelope's mother and exchanged pleasantries with the others. Penelope saw the speculative glances of Lady Howath and Mrs. Tipplethwaite, but they did not daunt her. The matter of the vicar pressed her.

"Lady Howath," Lord Worthington said, bowing low, "I remember your saying I may compete to win in this event."

"Why, yes," said Lady Howath, fluttering her hand about her throat.

Good Lord, Penelope thought, when he exerts his charm, even Lady Howath is not immune.

Lord Worthington turned to Penelope. "Will you honor me with some token that I might take into battle?"

The light, almost teasing note in his voice coupled with the tension both of them felt drew Penelope's gaze to his as though she were attached to marionette strings he pulled. Nor am I immune, she thought, and said, "If you wish it."

"There is nothing I wish for more."

His fervent tone sent shivers racing along Penelope's back. Her fingers shaky, Penelope unpinned a green ribbon from her bonnet. Lord Worthington accepted it with a solemn bow and bade her tie it on his sleeve. The feel of his hard arm beneath her hands almost undid her.

"Ah. Here comes Jarvis with my pistols. Excuse me."

"What did you give Lord Worthington just now, Penelope?" her mother asked. "I was attending the twins."

"A ribbon from my bonnet, Mother."

"A token?" Kitty inquired.

"He said something like that," replied Penelope.

"Well I never," said Miss Crimpin, tossing her blond curls. "How too, too feudal. Who would have thought?"

"Yes," said Kitty gently, "it does take imagination."

The Crimpin ladies both frowned, although Penelope suspected Miss Crimpin's frown indicated more confusion than annoyance. Mrs. Tipplethwaite hid her mouth behind her fan like the debutante she may have been thirty years ago.

"He makes a fine figure of a man," said Lady Howath.

"You must be very proud of him," Penelope said, "I understand he won the horse race."

"Indeed, congratulations, Lady Howath," said her mother.

Lady Howath blushed. "I did not mean—"

"I only hope my son shoots as well as Sir William rides," continued Lady Lindon with an innocent air Penelope recognized. Was her mother again asserting herself? "Alas, I fear it will not be so. This will be Worthington's sport."

"What makes you so certain, Lady Lindon?" Mrs. Tipplethwaite asked, and so quickly it occurred to Penelope that she had a bet riding on it.

"Chad is very good, bless his heart, but he has not had to defend himself from any Frenchies or pirates lately. I always say it is exigency that creates heroes."

Miss Crimpin sighed.

Kitty leaned slightly toward Penelope and whispered, "Well, she has *some* imagination."

It was all so very normal, Penelope thought, the vigilance of each other, the sniping, and the humor. But somewhere among the mild briars and the flowers, there lay a horrible thorn. Penelope shivered, looked to Lord Worthington, who conversed earnestly with Jarvis. Then Jarvis, seeing her, tipped his felt cap and set off along the hill crest.

Lord Worthington rejoined them. "It looks as if they're getting ready, Mr. Lindon. Miss Lindon, would you be so kind as to walk up there with us?"

"Do you go, Penelope," Lady Lindon said. "The

twins and I and Miss Gregory are quite content here. Wish your uncle and Lord Worthington good luck."

The twins chorused their well-wishes with impudent smiles.

"Scamps," Lord Worthington said, and tousled their hair. He settled his pistol case under one arm, offered the other to Penelope. That support was all Penelope required.

They walked down the hill together. Lord Albert waved to them from a little way across the field. Lady Honoria deigned to nod. Lady Worthington merely pouted.

What had been in that bag?

A group of ten men, Farmer Digby included, surrounded a long table near the vicar, talking as grown men do when they do not want to appear excited. The men doffed caps at Penelope and Lord Worthington as they approached the vicar and said hello.

"Your pistols are by the hedge, Mr. Lindon," said Mr. Simons. "You may join the others loading, then place your pistols here on this table. The rules are you may not touch your pistols until you use one to shoot, or until everyone has shot twice. Everyone reloads together."

Chad nodded.

Lord Worthington set his pistol case down on the long table and carefully took out his pistols, pointing them to the side. "I had not known to keep my pistols with you, Mr. Simons. I feel as if I were bringing gifts."

" 'Tis an old custom," Chad said, carefully, "to leave the pistols with the vicar. I am sorry I forgot to tell you."

Lord Worthington smiled, but Penelope knew how, paradoxically, his smile could contain as much steely anger as happiness. "It is of no matter," he said.

"You may load near the hedge, my lord," said the vicar.

"They are already loaded, vicar," said Lord Worthington.

The vicar frowned. "Surely an unwise habit, my lord."

"Perhaps here in Derbyshire," Lord Worthington responded. "But hard-won habits do not die in a month, or even two. I beg your pardon, Mr. Simons."

Mr. Simons nodded stiffly. "Miss Lindon, perhaps you would now return to the spectators?"

"Was asking her to come with me also a departure from procedure?" asked Lord Worthington. "I must apologize again, sir. 'Tis just that I had asked her to be my luck. Do you see, she has graciously lent me a token of it."

Mr. Simons looked at the green ribbon around Lord Worthington's arm. Other contestants, finished with loading their pistols, had come closer to the shooting table, where they might put them down. Many heard Lord Worthington's comment, and grinned. Penelope smiled back, although her lips felt like wood.

"I think you may also carry a token, Mr. Simons. From my cousin, Lady Worthington."

Suddenly everyone was very alert, and a murmur passed among the assembled men.

The vicar raised his brows. "Do you see such a token?"

"I suspect it is inside your coat pocket, sir."

"How could you know what is inside my coat pocket?"

Lord Worthington smiled and stepped ahead of Penelope. "For some time now, I have been having my cousin watched."

"How monstrous!"

"Murder is a monstrous affair, vicar," Lord Worthington said, his face terrifying in its intensity.

A ripple of tense surprise passed through the men, and Penelope wondered if they realized they were forming a circle around her, Chad, Lord Worthington, and the vicar.

"You suspect Lady Worthington?" the vicar asked in ringing disbelief.

"Not directly. What is in the bag she gave you, sir?"

The vicar said nothing, just glanced between Lord Worthington, Chad, and the surrounding men.

"You there," Lord Worthington said, not looking away from the vicar. "Smithson. Go fetch Sir William."

Although fascinated by the struggle going on between two of the upper class, Smithson succumbed to the authority in Lord Worthington's voice. He ran off toward the spectators.

"Why do we involve Sir William in this?" the vicar asked.

"Because both of us have come under suspicion, in my case through innuendo, in yours through evidence. We need someone impartial to sort it all out."

"You have no evidence against me."

"There is the bag you carry."

"If I carry it. And did I carry it, it might be nothing more than a token."

"From a woman newly widowed to a married man."

Penelope glanced at the men around them, saw they were frowning. Digby, especially, looked grim and wary.

The vicar laughed unpleasantly. "From a man with your past, I must believe your protestations hypocritical."

"Which past is that, sir?" Lord Worthington asked. "The man I was eleven years ago? The man who rose from midshipman to captain in His Majesty's Navy in six short years? Or the man who has tried to correct his predecessor's injustices?"

He looked around the circle of men. "Can any man here say I have threatened one of his? No. Would Miss Lindon be standing here with me today if I were yet inclined to scandal? No."

"You cannot hide your desire for Lady Worthington behind Miss Lindon's skirts."

Impossibly, something managed to tighten further in Lord Worthington's face and back. Penelope took a deep breath, waiting for the explosion.

Chad snorted. "Worthington has as much desire for Lady Worthington as I have for playing dress-up with girls." He smiled. "Except when I'm with my niece, of course."

Several of the men softened, even smiled. Lord Worthington smiled, too, although his gaze did not waver from the vicar. Penelope wanted to take his hand, or lean against his broad back, anything that would let his strength communicate itself to her. She knew she should not, though, and she held her ground, drinking in the potent sight of him, hoping it would be enough.

"I shall not bother mentioning that you are no gentleman," Lord Worthington said, "to be bringing ladies' names into a public discussion. I shall ask you only this: When Sir William comes, will you show us the bag Lady Worthington gave you?"

The vicar's lips curled back unpleasantly. "I am a viscount's son. I do not subject myself to searches."

"Very well, then," Lord Worthington said. "We know where we stand."

"Do we indeed?" the vicar said, and, quick as a blink, he pulled a pistol from his waistcoat pocket. "I will not be harassed by the likes of you."

Penelope gasped. Lord Worthington put his left arm back and pushed her more squarely behind him. Penelope grabbed Chad's hand and squeezed it.

Then something extraordinary happened. Some of the men, led with a sharp nod from Digby, pushed their way between Lord Worthington and the vicar, to form a stout line.

"You won't be shooting Lord Worthington today, vicar," Digby said. "We won't stand for it."

"Get out of my way," the vicar said.

"You will not be shooting any of my tenants today, either, sir," Lord Worthington said, stepping forward into the line of men and putting hands on their shoulders. "My steward, Jarvis, is up on the rise behind us. He carries a very nice Baker rifle. Are you familiar with the Baker rifle? It's exceptionally accurate. He won all our wagers. He's been aiming it at your head since we began this conversation."

"You're bluffing."

"Some old habits do indeed die hard, such as keeping close watch out for pirates. Funny thing about pirates—they are all alike, whether they prey upon the ocean, or the land. Do you wish to test his aim, sir?"

In the face of so much confidence, the vicar faltered. His hand drooped. Lord Worthington stepped forward and took the pistol from him so quickly the vicar looked startled.

Lord Worthington said something to the vicar Penelope could not hear. But the vicar's head snapped up. Lord Worthington took him firmly by the arm and waved toward the hedge along the hilltop. A sudden glint of light on metal did not surprise Penelope. If she had learned anything about Lord Worthington, it was that he was thorough.

Sir William and Bodsmead pushed their way through the circle of men. "Here, now, what is this?" Sir William said.

Lord Worthington let Mr. Simons go and explained.

Sir William frowned. "You say Master Timothy Eversleigh and Miss Lindon saw him receive the bag from Lady Worthington?"

"Yes."

"Could he have made some mistake?"

Penelope stepped forward. "Master Timothy mentioned it in all innocence, Sir William. He had no reason to lie or invent tales. And I saw Mr. Simons put such a bag in a pocket of his coat."

Sir William compressed his lips. "If you have such a

bag, sir, I beg you let me see it, or you shall be searched."

Sullenly, the vicar reached into his coat pocket and pulled out a small velvet bag. A handkerchief came out with the bag.

"Sir William," said Penelope quickly, "you may also want to keep Mr. Simons's handkerchief. You remember the sketch I made of the late Lord Worthington. Among the things there was a handkerchief. It matches this one."

She met Lord Worthington's gaze. His satisfied smile dispelled the chill that threatened to overtake her.

Sir William's brows rose high up his forehead, but he took both bag and handkerchief. He opened the bag, spilled its contents upon his hand. Jewels and gold glittered in the sun.

The men in the circle tried not to look impressed, but several of them nudged each other. Penelope let out her breath.

"Good God," said Chad.

"Mr. Simons, you shall have to come with me. There are questions to be answered. You there, men, take the vicar to my carriage. My lord, you will come with me, if you please."

Lord Worthington bowed. "In a moment, sir."

Two men led the vicar up the hill. Lord Worthington turned to the remaining men. "I cannot express my gratitude for what you did. I am proud to know each and every one of you."

Digby doffed his cap, shuffled, then tilted his head to say, "We think as how you'll make a good lord, my lord. That's all of us, too." Every man around the circle nodded.

Someone screamed. The men parted, as did the spectators on the hill. Penelope strained to see.

Lady Worthington had fainted into a heap of yellow on the green grass.

Lord Worthington turned to Penelope. "Miss Lindon—"

"Go, my lord," she said.

He took her hand, bowed low over it. "I will always be grateful for your trust." Then he walked away up the hill.

Penelope trembled. Chad put his arm about her. "Come on, Penny. Fantastic end to the festival, isn't it?"

Chapter 17

"Yes, Masters," said Lady Lindon, "show them in here. I wonder if they have news," Lady Lindon said.

Two days had come and gone since Sir William had arrested Mr. Simons, two long days of idle speculation. Penelope had never felt so alone. Chad had had to prepare for his journey to Oxford. There was no word from Lord Worthington. Penelope amused herself by thinking that she had fallen off a cliff but not reached the ground yet.

The events had awakened something long sleeping in Lady Lindon. Penelope found her walking in the garden at midday giving orders to the gardener about the trimming of the shrubbery. Then Lady Lindon had decided to count the linens.

"Just to know, my dear," she told Penelope, "not because I do not have implicit faith in you."

As Lady Lindon had bustled up the stairs with two maids in attendance, Penelope had looked around Lindon Hall's foyer and realized how big and silent it was.

Masters returned. "Lady Howath, Lady Bodsmead, Mrs. Tipplethwaite," he intoned.

Lady Howath said, "My dear Lady Lindon, we have news."

"Then please tell us without delay," Lady Lindon said.

"The gentlemen questioned Mr. Simons far into the night and again through yesterday, but Mr. Simons kept insisting that the fact that he had that bag and such a handkerchief did not prove him a murderer."

"Why ever not?" asked Lady Lindon.

"As for the handkerchief," Penelope said, "his being by the river when the late Lord Worthington was killed does not prove he did it. It only makes him suspect."

"Exactly so, Miss Lindon," said Lady Howath approvingly.

"Well then, how did he account for that handkerchief being there?" asked Lady Lindon.

"He said," said Mrs. Tipplethwaite, "that he had been out walking that day and must have dropped it. He suggested that Lord Worthington or the person meeting him picked it up."

"How very unlikely."

"True," said Lady Howath. "But it could have been accurate. Sir William and Lord Worthington then questioned people who might have seen Mr. Simons near the river that day or who could account for his movements. No one could remember seeing Mr. Simons anywhere until quite late in the day."

"What about Mrs. Simons?" Penelope asked.

"She was the first one Sir William called," said Kitty. "She said she had been shopping that day. But Maria insisted that she had never known Mrs. Simons to shop for an entire day."

"I told Sir William he should question her again."

"Maria is not giving herself credit," said Kitty with a smile. "She was very diplomatic about her suggestion."

Lady Howath straightened her already rigid posture. "I hope I know how not to interfere in my husband's business."

"Just so, sister, just so."

"But what happened?" Lady Lindon asked.

"Yesterday evening, the gentlemen paid a visit to Mrs. Simons. I am told Lord Worthington handled her brilliantly, explained everything they had found, and was very sympathetic. Mrs. Simons became upset and told them an incredible story. She has suspected the vicar of this crime since it happened."

"My dear Lady Howath," Lady Lindon exclaimed. "Do explain."

"The story becomes rather indelicate at this point, but some two days before the murder, Mrs. Simons said she found a letter from the late Lord Worthington to the vicar. The letter demanded that Mr. Simons meet Lord Worthington at the place where Miss Lindon later found him to discuss some information Lord Worthington had just discovered."

"I do not understand," said Lady Lindon.

"He was going to blackmail the vicar," Penelope said.

The visitors' eyes all widened in concert.

"Blackmail the vicar! Whatever for?" asked her mother.

Penelope explained everything she and Lord Worthington had seen and guessed.

"This is all very shocking," said Lady Lindon. "The vicar and Cecily Worthington. The difference in their stations. And you keeping secrets from me, Penelope."

"They were not my secrets, Mother. I'm sorry."

"As to their stations," Mrs. Tipplethwaite said, as Lady Lindon sniffed, "there is not the difference you think. Lady Worthington is only the daughter of a minor squire. Mr. Simons is second son to a viscount. His brother is Lord Marblethorpe."

"I had forgotten," murmured Lady Lindon.

"What did they do next, ma'am?" Penelope asked.

"They had Mr. Simons's study searched," Lady Howath replied. "But they could not find a blackmail letter from the late Lord Worthington to the vicar."

"Were I in his place, I would have destroyed such a damning letter," Penelope said.

"I, too," said Kitty, frowning, "but Sir William and Lord Worthington think it yet exists. Lady Worthington claims that Mr. Simons blackmailed her over its existence, threatened to make it public if she did not continue to meet him. Then, when Lord Worthington was having her so closely watched, she said he asked her for jewelry in case he needed to quit the country."

"But, keeping such a letter would give him as much motive as it would her," Penelope said, stunned by it.

"She was very frightened. She knew he had murdered her husband so he could continue seeing her without interference. I do not think she was thinking clearly."

"I am trying to puzzle out where matters rest now," Lady Lindon said. "It sounds as if the evidence against Mr. Simons is Lady Worthington's allegations, the jewels, and the handkerchief. But for the handkerchief's presence there, we could account for some other way, and Lady Worthington's word is questionable. Does the matter rest, then, on proving Lady Worthington gave the vicar the jewels?"

"According to Sir William," said Lady Howath, "the business may come down to that."

Penelope felt her hands shake suddenly. She balled them into fists and stood up, ready to flee the room. "Timothy had no reason to make up stories. But tell me, Lady Howath, who will say I would say anything to protect Lord Worthington?"

"Why, why—" began Lady Howath.

"Oh, Penelope," Kitty said sympathetically.

Frowning, Mrs. Tipplethwaite said, "Sit down, Miss Lindon. No one will say such a thing. We all know you too well to believe such a thing, and no one here could fail to understand how wholeheartedly Lord Worthington's tenants support him. Not after that little scene with the pistols."

"Worthington has established himself," Lady Howath

said, "and no one dare gainsay him. He has let it be known he will tolerate no question of your honesty in this matter."

Penelope blinked.

"It is true," Kitty said. "Bodsmead told me Sir William wanted to question you about it, but Worthington told him he had it from you himself, and his word was sufficient."

The captain and marquess in charge, Penelope thought with warmth and exasperation. But she should not stand there like a moonling. "I am grateful for his confidence."

Lady Howath stood. "Perhaps you may receive more than his confidence sometime soon, Miss Lindon."

Penelope thought of two small children practicing their letters upstairs in the nursery. Timothy's tongue would be set firmly between his lips. Tina's mouth would be puckered like a drawstring bag. "No, my lady, I do not think so. Would you please excuse me?" And Penelope rushed from the room.

The next day Penelope was sitting in the nursery when the underbutler found her. "Yes, John?"

"Lord Worthington has come to call, ma'am."

Penelope looked at her children, their blond heads bent together, although each was painting a picture on a separate easel. Their bodies looked so frail to Penelope. Delicate little necks, thin shoulders. But Timothy could knock her clean over when he ran up to her and wrapped his arms around her legs.

Lord Worthington no longer had anything preventing their marrying. But Penelope did, and regret and guilt piled their weight on her.

She sighed. "Thank you, John. I shall be down in a moment."

"Very good, ma'am." He bowed and left.

Timothy perked his head up. "Captain's here? Can we go say hello? We haven't seen him since the festival. Come on, Tina. Say yes, Aunt Penny. Please? Please?"

Penelope touched his head, felt the fine hair ripple under her hand. "Not today, loves. Maybe tomorrow."

Timothy frowned. "You never let us have any fun."

Penelope sighed. There was no point in arguing when Timothy spoke like that. "May I tell the captain hello from you?"

Timothy handed Penelope his painting. "This is for him."

"Mine, too," said Tina, thrusting out her wet painting.

Penelope smiled at the swaths of colors. "I love them. He will, too, I am sure." She kissed them. "I love you, too."

Tina slanted her a look, then kissed Penelope's cheek. Timothy, not to be outdone, did the same.

Penelope left them, her heart full.

Lord Worthington rose when she entered the drawing room, and the sight of him, standing so calm and strong and immensely tired, almost undid her. She wanted to cast herself into his arms and have him take some comfort from her.

Instead she proffered the wet paintings. "These are presents from the twins, my lord."

He took them by the corners. "They are too kind." He gestured to a table between two cushioned chairs. "May I?"

"Certainly."

He set the paintings down, careful not to overlap them. Then he stepped toward her and back again. "May we sit?"

Penelope came over and sat. "You look tired."

Although he had been about to sit down, he straightened, tugged at his waistcoat. Then, with a little smile, he sat and deliberately put his hands on either arm of his chair. "We have found the blackmail note, in his coat lapel. He confessed, after that. So no one will bother you or Timothy."

"I am told you would not have permitted it, regardless."

He stiffened. "I never want anything bad to happen to you."

Penelope shook her head. "You cannot protect me from everything. It is not possible."

"You will allow me to be stubborn on this point, at least, on my feelings on the matter. The truth is, I have some other news that will distress you. In time it will also distress the twins." He tipped his head, scrunched his mouth, then continued, "But between then and now, it may offer us an opportunity."

Penelope's heart beat fast. "Captain, you are alarming me."

He came and sat next to her, took her hands. She had not realized until then, feeling his warm hands about hers, how cold hers had become. "I have been in Bodsmead's company much these past days. Do you remember talk of his brother, Captain Ghent?"

Penelope nodded.

"Bodsmead is a very conscientious soul. He did not wish to pass on rumors, but he had a letter from his brother just before arriving here in Derbyshire. Captain Ghent has had cause to be sailing in and out of Lisbon and move in society there. It is generally acknowledged that your brother-in-law will not live the year. I am very sorry."

"Poor Eversleigh!" Penelope shook her head, trying to take in the news. She felt immensely sad, not only for him, but for his beautiful children. Her beautiful children. "But what has happened to him?"

"It is some kind of cancer."

"But why did he not come home?"

"I asked Bodsmead that question. He did not know."

"But you believe the story?"

"It explains why Sir Roger Morley ducked some of my questions about his cousin." Worthington pressed her hands, then released them to pace about the room. "It also explains why Lady Eversleigh dispatched Sir Roger to give a report on you and me."

"I do not understand."

"I think Eversleigh is as conflicted about whom to name guardian of the twins after his death as he was when your sister died. I think he would like to keep matters as they are. But there is the matter of that promise you made. He cannot enforce it from the grave. So I think he would like an excuse to take it back now, while he can still tell himself he is the one doing what he thinks best by his children."

Penelope blinked. "I do not understand you. You have never met Eversleigh. How can you know what he might think?"

Worthington set his hands on a blue chair back and leaned into it. "For the same reason I could outwit enemy captains and commanders of forts. I make guesses. They are usually right."

To her surprise, a tear slipped down Penelope's face. "I am sure they are."

"God, Penelope, I cannot bear to see you cry." He came to her, folded her to him. Penelope closed her eyes and found all those places where she matched him exactly.

She could have stayed there all day, except for the niggling doubt his words had sown. "What do you want me to do?"

He set his hands on her shoulders, holding her away from him, his expression intent. "I want you to write to him and tell him I have made you an offer of marriage. You would like to accept it. You know the twins will have a good home there, with us." He paused. "You do know that, do you not?"

Penelope smiled through her tears. "Yes, I do know that."

He dropped to his knees before her, took her hands again. "Are you laughing at me because I am doing this backward?"

"Nothing about you has been what I expected," Penelope said. "Dear Lucas."

"I like the sound of my name on your lips."

She laid her hand on his bright hair, surprised to find it waved crisply. She loved him, but there was one thing she needed to ask. "Should I tell Eversleigh I know about him?"

"No. It would seem, would it not, that you were trying to blackmail him."

"It could, could it not?"

"You are no blackmailer, Penelope Lindon. You could not write such a letter, and I would not ask it of you. I am not Edmund. We are not Cecily and Simons, trapped by our own venality. I told you of Eversleigh to give you the confidence to ask for release."

It was the right answer, the only answer Penelope could have expected. She had had the triumphant thought, when Worthington first mentioned Eversleigh's illness, that she might have her taste of revenge. But it had faded so quickly as to leave nothing but a sick taste in her mouth.

"What if he says no?"

He touched her face, ran his hand lightly along her jaw. She caught her breath and shivered in response. "You must do what you must to keep your children. I could not love you the way I do, did you not feel this way."

"Lucas," she breathed and, wrapping her arms about his neck, drew him down to her mouth. She needed his kiss and as she reveled in it, tasting the salt of her own tears on his face, she felt the pull of the whirlpool forming between them. She drew back and saw the pictures the twins had sent him. Paper, she thought, covering the rocks.

"Scylla and Charybdis, my beloved Penelope," he said, looking at the pictures as well.

"Hold me tightly. Hold me close." But for Penelope, it was no longer enough.

"Penny?" Chad asked. "What's happened?"

Penelope would have pulled away from Lucas's embrace, but he continued holding her against him. "I have been asking your sister to make an honest man of me."

"Well," Chad said, leaning against the door, "she's the only woman who could have kept *me* honest, and I do believe a vision of her angry will keep me honest to my dying day."

"You jest, brother dear," said Penelope. "I have never been angry a day in my life."

"We'll attribute that bit of nonsense to your being in Worthington's arms."

"Wretch."

"Storyteller." Chad smiled. "When do I wish you happy?"

"We must write to Eversleigh," Penelope said.

Lord Worthington's smile warmed her to her toes.

"Eversleigh? What can he have to do with it?" Chad asked. Then he met Lucas's gaze. He seemed to see something there, for he pursed his lips, then relaxed. "Of course."

"Keep this to yourself in the meantime," Penelope said.

"Your exceptionally well-trained brother saw nothing, heard nothing, and never entered the room until this very moment. Would you please give me a small gesture of affection, too? A mere pat on the head and a 'good boy' will do."

"You are absurd," Penelope said, and crossed the

room to her brother. "I could not pat you on the head. You are grown too tall."

Chad hugged her close. "You would be happy?" he asked.

"I would be very happy." Penelope pushed him back. "Entertain the captain, would you? I have a letter to write."

Lucas crossed the room, took her hand, and kissed it. "I shall call again tomorrow."

"Stay, and have dinner with us."

He nodded, assenting.

Penelope paused outside the door, heard her brother offer Lord Worthington something to drink, his deep rumble of a reply, then Chad say gruffly, "Friend bedamned. Never had a proper brother before. Only saw Eversleigh when he and Helen got married and when he brought her home to have the twins. Didn't count, really. 'Sides, you're taking my sister a bare three miles down the road. I'll be the one coming out ahead."

Penelope went into her study, sat down at her desk, and pulled out a piece of paper. With hands barely shaking, she dipped her pen and began, "My dear brother . . . "

Chapter 18

When Lucas returned to Wildoaks that night, Honoria and his uncle had retired. Lucas wanted to do something—fire a salute, run into the small town yelling his news, pick up the twins and twirl them around—anything to publish how happy he felt. But he could not, and so in the midst of great happiness, he paced around his study, frustrated.

May I be granted a swift resolution to the whole business, he thought. The alternative did not bear contemplating. He would have to leave Wildoaks. Even knowing her reasons, even understanding and approving them, he could not stay, see Penelope time after time, and not have her his.

"Cap'n?" Jarvis asked from the doorway. "Masters told me you were in. Might I have a word, sir?"

"How long have you been standing there, man?"

"Long enough to wonder how goes the fort, sir."

"We wait upon treaties, Jarvis."

Jarvis grimaced. "A dashed nuisance, treaties."

Lucas shrugged. "Is there something you need me to address at this advanced hour of a quarter past ten?"

"Well, sir, I wanted to ask permission to marry."

"Good God, man, you don't need my permission for that. Who is the lucky lady?"

"One of your tenants, sir, which is why I bethought

myself of getting your permission on the arrangement."
Jarvis cocked his head. "The widow Bagley, sir."

"Permission granted." He went to the sideboard,
poured two drinks and felt an uncomfortable reverse
sort of *déjà vu*. "You will tell me you fell in love over
the thatch, next."

Jarvis accepted the brandy with a sly smile. "That
thatch gave me occasion to be there pretty much every
day for a couple weeks. She's a friendly woman, is
Marianne."

"I wish you joy," Lucas said, and they clinked their
glasses. "Do you know the cottage about a third of a
mile down the way toward the Howaths? Ivy Cottage,
it's called."

"Aye sir. We inspected it."

"Right. It was customary for Wildoaks stewards who
are married to have Ivy Cottage as part of their com-
pensation. You could trade that thatch for a proper roof."

"I am coming to like the land, Cap'n."

"Congratulations, Jarvis. You will be a happy man."

Lord Worthington, Penelope thought, was late. For
the past three days he had had an unerring instinct for
her neighbors. He appeared at Lindon Hall within a
quarter hour of her greeting callers. He would sit near
Penelope and join the conversation as if daily having an
unmarried marquess with a reputation for scandal in
one's drawing room was nothing to be remarked upon.

Penelope loved him. She loved him fiercely and without compromise. She spent every other minute
wondering what being married to him would be like.
The minutes in between she wondered what not being
married to him would be like.

Marriage certainly suited Kitty. Sitting across from
Penelope, her husband at her side, she glowed. The

Bodsmeads did not touch, but they exchanged many sidelong smiles. Penelope suspected Kitty had told Bodsmead that she was increasing.

They made Penelope happy to see them, and she suspected their effect was working on the others, too, for the party was more relaxed than in previous days.

The news of the day was Mrs. Simons' removal from the town. "The poor thing collapsed before getting into the carriage," Mrs. Tipplethwaite said, "and had to be carried."

"I think she had only so much defiance in her," Kitty said. "She had used it all up speaking to Sir William this week. It is good she had arranged to go stay with her sister."

Masters entered and bowed. "Lord Worthington, my lady."

Penelope never thought she could become immune to her neighbors' raised brows. Only one person's negative opinion mattered to her now—Lord Eversleigh's. Thinking of him doused her with cold, mental water. What would he think of her letter?

But it would be several days, if not weeks, before she could expect a reply from Eversleigh.

"Penelope, do attend," Lady Lindon said. "Here is Masters trying to tell you an express has come for you. Were you expecting a letter?"

"Your pardon, ma'am," Penelope said automatically, motioning Masters to her. He held out a salver. Penelope recognized Eversleigh's handwriting on the letter's address, his crest in the wax. So soon! How could it be possible? It could not be possible. Eversleigh was writing about a different matter altogether, perhaps.

But perhaps not.

She took the letter in trembling fingers and stood.

Lady Howath, Mrs. Tipplethwaite, Kitty, and Lord

Bodsmead were all looking to her. Lord Bodsmead and Worthington stood.

Penelope could not have imagined a more public forum to receive such news. She met Lord Worthington's eyes. The letter resting in her hands likely affected him. One way or another, the neighborhood would know of it.

"My lord Worthington, I believe this is a matter I could use your assistance on." She turned to encompass the group with her request. "Would you excuse us for a moment, please?"

His polite smile masked some of his wariness. "Please excuse me, ladies, Bodsmead."

Penelope led the way from the room. No one spoke until she had closed the door behind Lord Worthington, then she heard an excited buzz. Lord Worthington folded his arms.

"Let us go into the study," Penelope said, and walked to it across the sunny foyer, where she closed the door.

"Is it from Eversleigh?" he asked.

"It is indeed. But too soon. My letter cannot have reached him yet. What does he reply to?"

"Likely to the note I wrote him before the festival."

"Why would you do such a thing? What right did you think you had?" Penelope asked furiously.

"For all the reasons I mentioned before, chief among them the fact that I love you and want to spend the rest of my life with you. Given my reputation, however, I suspected what your response to my proposal would be. And was I not correct?"

Penelope wrapped her arms around herself.

"Eversleigh's opinion was the only one that mattered to you. So I took a calculated chance. I wrote him that I did not know your feelings, which was true when I wrote, but I wrote him of mine and my concerns. For all I know, he has had a fine laugh at my expense."

Penelope looked at the letter, then back to his face.

"I can tell you feel a fool for saying you respected my understanding. You need not. I do understand. I understand that if this letter contains bad news, you will never speak to me again, and I will leave the Four Corners. I meant it when I said you were my anchor to this place. I could work the estate, make it grow, but without you it would mean nothing to me. And I have never done well when what is before me means nothing to me."

"You would blame me for your failings?" Penelope asked indignantly.

"No," he said. "I would not blame you. I want you to understand that I am as nervous about what is in this letter as you are. I wrote it knowing what I could lose and that I tried to protect you as best as I could. And I knew that might not be enough." A muscle twitched near his mouth.

Penelope let herself see that sign for the deep emotion it represented. Her indignation drained from her, and she went to him, set her hand upon his upper arm. He stiffened, and she ran her hand up and bowed her head. The ruffles of his shirt betrayed how deeply and quickly he breathed.

She met his gaze again and said softly, "When Lord Bodsmead praised your boldness and your daring, I thought I would explode with pride in you. How can I expect you to be less than you are, any more than you have expected me to be what I am?"

He shook his head. "I have never dared with anything so important before."

"Was there not a time, my lord, when you did as you pleased with no thought to anyone?"

He nodded, compressing his lips. "Have I not admitted it openly to you?"

Penelope touched his face. He closed his eyes and took a deep breath. She waited for him to look at her

again before saying, "That was your past. You may hold
our future." She touched his hand, felt the letter's
smooth paper. "I cannot bear not to open it. Nor could I
bear to open it without you."

He folded her in his arms. Penelope felt complete, but
the comfort attendant on such a feeling rapidly turned
into desire. She loved him. She wanted to be his wife.
She wanted everything.

"Let's sit down," he said, "or you shall undo me."

Penelope laughed, although shakily, as he drew her
toward a sofa near the window. He broke the seal, re-
vealing another sealed letter inside.

"He's written in Chinese boxes," Lord Worthington
said with a hint of disdain. "Sorry. Let's read the end
first. Here. 'I wish you well however you proceed.'
Damn, that's ambivalent."

"We'll start at the beginning," said Penelope.

Lord Worthington nodded and turned the paper over.
They read. Eversleigh expressed himself as startled by
Lord Worthington's writing to him, and even more startled by his very request to approach Penelope with a
proposal of marriage. "For," he wrote, "I had heard that
you could turn any woman up sweet, no matter the circumstances."

"I think I dislike your brother-in-law," said Lord
Worthington with a growl.

"Perhaps he means it as a compliment. Helen said
no one paid much attention to him until she set her
sights on him."

"Hmph," Lord Worthington said.

"From all reports, my sister-in-law has done excellently by both children. I cannot imagine separating her
from them. However . . ." It was the last word on that
side.

Penelope gasped.

"Steady, my love." Lord Worthington turned the letter over.

I have long wondered what effect having had little contact with a man, someone who could be like a father to him, will have upon Timothy. I have not filled that role for him, and now I cannot. I am dying. The physicians give me less than a half year. Since I know that Sir Roger has plans to ask a young woman of fine family to marry him, I had thought to change my twins' guardianship. It would not be a happy occasion either for my sister-in-law or the twins, but they were going to need to adjust to changes anyway. I thought it a likely time.

Your letter gives me hope that I will not have to separate them from Miss Lindon. She has become their mother, as my dear Helen would have been had she been able. And having lost Helen, I am reluctant to deprive my children of the only mother they have ever known.

"Worthington!" Penelope said, squeezing his arm.

You wrote that you worried whether I could consent to an arrangement where you would have a husband's rights over the guardian of my children. The short answer is no, for two reasons. I have heard much of you from friends within the navy who account you honorable.

"It is nice to know he would now take my word on something," Lord Worthington grumbled.

Second, when I first met the Lindon family, I thought Penelope the more comely of the two sis-

ters, and as they were barely a year apart, I did not give much weight to seniority. But I soon learned that Penelope has much stubbornness in her.

"Gracious," Penelope said, half-laughing with embarrassment and annoyance. "I hope he loved Helen for more than her sweet temper. And what shall you think of me?"

"Have I not said you had the mind of an admiral disguised as a lieutenant? But look, your stubbornness is an asset to him."

Penelope read,

> *You will not have happiness in your household if she is unhappy with you, and since her happiness has been in making a fine home for my children, it will perforce become a requirement of your household. Whatever your former reputation, you could not withstand her for long. I wish you well however you proceed.*
>
> > *Your servant,*
> > *John Michael Wallace Carruthers,*
> > *Earl Eversleigh*

Lord Worthington laughed. "He thinks me crazed, but is too polite to say so."

"I would be angry," Penelope said, "did he not give me everything I want."

Lord Worthington drew Penelope up beside him. "It would not be a great burden to you, to marry me, that is?"

Penelope smiled, loving his single note of doubt. She touched his hair, ran her fingers through it while he closed his eyes and breathed deeply. Penelope felt as though she were soaring. Tears came to her eyes even as she smiled. She could not imagine having lived without such happiness for twenty-five years. "I will marry you, Captain Lord Worthington, and when our new vicar says 'will you take this man?' I will say 'yes' with every breath in my body."

"My dearest, my lovely one . . . " he murmured. He stroked her hair. Penelope closed her eyes, overcome with feeling. Then his lips were on hers, and she felt a sweetness and a heat she had never known before. How could she have ever imagined he would be like Gerald!

Lord Worthington drew away, holding her by the shoulders, smiling in a curious, bemused fashion. "Go easy on me, my dear. I am but a man."

Penelope laughed. "You are more than a man. You are my best friend and my lover. So when the vicar says 'will you take this man?' I will not only say 'yes,' I will say 'yes, I will take this exceptional man.'"

He drew her to him so she could nestle her head against his shoulder. "Had we not been talking so soberly before," he said, and she could feel his suppressed laughter, "I would accuse you of being drunk."

Penelope lifted her head so she could look into his eyes. "All I know is that I love you, Lucas, and I trust you with my life. More, I trust you with my twins' lives, too."

His arms tightened about her. "I would marry you day after tomorrow by special license, but I think my tenant expert would tell me to wait until the banns have been read."

Penelope sighed. "I think 'twould be best. Besides, we must run my father to ground."

Lucas laughed. "My eminently practical lieutenant. You will never bore me, Penelope Lindon, not even when we are old and have been married for decades. At least we can tell your mother, your brother, and the twins today."

"And Jarvis."

"And Jarvis."

Penelope laughed. "And do you know, I thought I heard Masters announcing the Crimpin ladies. If we are very lucky, we may also announce to the entire Four Corners."

"You have an odd idea of luck, darling."

Penelope shook her head, smiling. "You will enjoy this, Lucas. For once we will render them speechless."

Lucas smiled. "I love you, Penelope Lindon."

More Regency Romance
From Zebra

いぬかみっ!
I·NU·KA·MI

Volume 1

story by **Mamizu Arisawa**
art by **Mari Matsuzawa**
character design by **Kanna Wakatsuki**

STAFF CREDITS

translation	Rhys Moses
adaptation	Lorelei Laird
cover design	Pablo Defendini
lettering & retouch	Igor Cabbab
layout	Bambi Eloriaga-Amago
copy editor	Erica Friedman
editor	Adam Arnold

A Tor/Seven Seas Publication

INUKAMI! VOL. 1
Copyright © Mamizu Arisawa / Mari Matsuzawa 2006
First published in 2006 by Media Works Inc., Tokyo, Japan.
English translation rights arranged with ASCII MEDIA WORKS.

Visit us online at www.gomanga.com and www.tor-forge.com.

ISBN-13: 978-0-7653-2146-6
ISBN-10: 0-7653-2146-7

Printed in the USA

TOR ®   Seven Seas

10 9 8 7 6 5 4 3 2

CONTENTS

Step.1 Boy Meets Dog

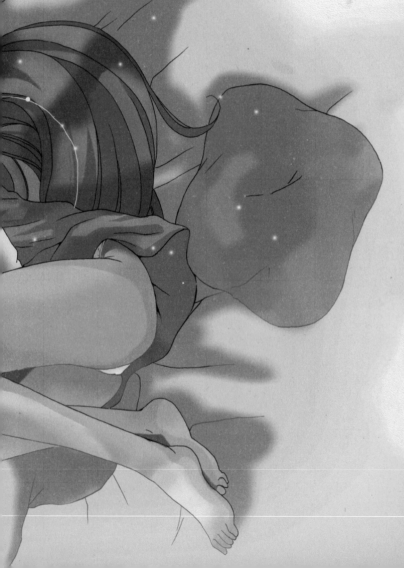

WHOOSH

MY MASTER, HUH?

MY BODY...

SMILE

AND MY SOUL...

I WANT TO BE NEAR YOU AT ALL TIMES!

LOOM

I AM KEITA-SAMA'S INUKAMI, AREN'T I?

UH...

BA-THUMP

YES.

YOU CALLED ME HERE.

IT'S A BIT COMPLICATED.

WHAT IS IT?

SHUT UP AND LISTEN.

I KNOW, GRANDMA! YOU WANT TO GIVE ME MY *INHERITANCE* WHILE YOU'RE STILL ALIVE, AM I RIGHT?

WHO, WITH THE HELP OF THE *INUKAMI* CLAN, WENT TO THE MOUNTAIN WHERE THE DEMONS DWELLED, AND--

IN THE BEGINNING, IT WAS OUR ANCESTOR, A PRIEST NAMED *KAWAHIRA EKAI...*

GOT RID OF THEM, RIGHT?

EXHALE

OWWW!

FOR GENERATIONS, THE KAWAHIRA FAMILY HAS BEEN CHARGED WITH THE DUTY TO SERVE AS TRAINERS OF THE INUKAMI, THE DOG SPIRITS OF THIS MOUNTAIN.

TO BE PRECISE...

THEY WORK WITH US FOR THE GOOD OF THE WORLD.

HAVE WORKED FOR US, THE KAWAHIRA FAMILY.

AND FROM THEN ON, THE INUKAMI WHO LIVE IN THE MOUNTAIN...

I'VE HEARD THAT A MILLION TIMES SINCE I WAS A KID.

IT IS THE INUKAMI'S TRUE NATURE TO VANQUISH EVIL AND PURIFY THE LAND.

FOR IT IS ONLY BY FIGHTING THE EVILS IN THIS WORLD THAT WE CAN ACHIEVE OUR *TRUE* WORTH.

AND WE INUKAMI TRAINERS WORK TO RIGHT WRONGS.

DEJECTED

IT'S GOT NOTHING TO DO WITH ME.

I COULDN'T EVEN FIND AN INUKAMI.

WHAT-EVER.

14

WHEN I WAS THIRTEEN, I WENT TO THE MOUNTAIN AT NIGHT...

I GOT A ZERO.

I RAN ALL OVER THE MOUNTAIN THAT NIGHT.

NOT EVEN A **SINGLE** INUKAMI CAME TO ME.

TO BE EVALUATED BY THE INUKAMI.

IT WAS THE WORST SCANDAL TO **EVER** HIT THE KAWAHIRA CLAN.

COUGH

AHEM. SINCE YOU MENTION IT...

DO YOU STILL WANT TO BECOME A TRAINER?

WHAT GOOD IS IT BRINGING IT UP NOW?

16

SPARKLE

WHO'D PASS UP SOMETHING LIKE THIS?!

BREATHLESS

OF COURSE I DO!

I DON'T THINK YOU *UNDERSTAND* WHAT IT MEANS TO BE AN INUKAMI TRAINER.

OH YES, I'VE *ALWAYS* DREAMED OF HAVING AN INUKAMI OF MY VERY OWN!

AH, IT'S BEEN SO TOUGH DOING MY OWN COOKING AND CLEANING ALL THESE YEARS.

WAIT!

ISN'T IT OBVIOUS?

WELL, I'M OFF!

I'M OFF TO MEET MY INUKAMI-CHAN!

WHERE DO YOU THINK YOU'RE GOING?

HEY!

SLIDE

KEITA!

17

HMM... THIS MUST BE KEITA'S DESTINY.

SIGH...

IS IT ALL RIGHT, MATCHING KEITA-*SAMA* WITH *HER*?

HE'S GONE, JUST LIKE THAT.

WHAT WILL BE, WILL BE.

HA HA HA! JUST A FEW MORE MINUTES, INUKAMI-CHAN!

YOKO.

OKAY, LISTEN, YOKO.

I AM KAWAHIRA KEITA.

I AM YOUR MASTER. FROM NOW ON, CALL ME "KEITA-SAMA."

I'LL DO ANYTHING.

PLEASE TAKE CARE OF ME FROM NOW ON...

KEITA-SAMA.

SMILE

YES.

AND YOU DO WHAT I SAY...

NO MATTER WHAT.

IF I BLOW THIS WHISTLE, YOU COME TO ME, NO MATTER WHERE YOU ARE.

YES.

24

DON'T WORRY.

WITH THAT NECKLACE ON...

YOU'RE FREE TO COME AND GO AS YOU LIKE.

I CAN'T GO PAST THE BARRIER SURROUNDING THIS MOUNTAIN.

HMM...

LET'S SHAKE FIRST.

WELL...

SHAKE, GIRL!

?

YOU DON'T KNOW... HOW TO SHAKE?

SMILE

AND YOU HAVE THE FACE OF A MONKEY.

YOU ACT LIKE YOU JUST BARELY LEARNED TO STAND UPRIGHT.

SO I'LL *ACT* LIKE YOU'RE MY MASTER.

YOU SHOULD BE SATISFIED WITH *THAT*.

BUT I *WOULD* LIKE TO SEE THE WORLD.

SNAP

TOKYO TOWER... AND I WANNA EAT SOME *CHOCOLATE CAKE*!

HEY! ARE YOU LISTEN-ING?

HEY, HELLO?

TAKE ME THERE.

FIRST, I WANT TO GO TO *TOKYO TOWER*.

PROBABLY INTO TOWN.

BAM

THAT DAMNED DOG.

WHERE THE HELL'D SHE GO?

--BUT...

BY THE TIME I PULLED MYSELF OUT OF THE RUINS, SHE WAS ALREADY GONE.

I DON'T KNOW FOR SURE.

INTO TOWN?

I'LL SHOW HER JUST WHAT...

THEN I'LL *FIND* HER.

SHE ALWAYS DID SAY THAT SHE WANTED TO SEE THE CITY.

BUT...

HUMANS ARE MADE OF.

WAHHH!

PURPOSE!

I WAS A LITTLE *UNPREPARED,* YOU KNOW.

NOW YOU TELL ME?!

WHY DIDN'T YOU GIVE IT TO ME BEFORE?

THIS BOX CONTAINS YOKO'S WEAKNESS.

?

WHAT'S THAT?

THEN YOU SHOULD TAKE *THIS* WITH YOU.

WHY IMMEDI-ATELY

HMM?

IMMEDI-ATELY

KEITA, YOU *MUST* FIND HER.

THAT WAS FROM THE GARBAGE PILE DOWNSTAIRS.

EWW...

THUNK

SPLAT

HERE'S MY ANSWER.

I CAN PICK UP ANYTHING, EVEN IF IT'S A LITTLE WAYS AWAY...

AND BRING IT WHEREVER I WANT.

IT'S ONE OF MY MAGICAL ABILITIES.

GIGGLE GIGGLE

OH.

THAT TRICK I JUST DID WAS CALLED "SHUKUCHI."

HEH HEH HEH HEH...

HEH...

DON'T GET TOO EXCITED.

44

BLUSH

DON'T BE STUPID!

IF YOU WILL, I'LL SAVE YOU.

WILL YOU BE MY SLAVE?

ALL RIGHT!

ALL...

TAKE CARE THEN!

ズ...

ズ

STAGGER

STAGGER

STAGGER

YOKO-SAMA.

YOKO-SAMA?

AND THAT'S HOW...

I AGREE.

WE STARTED TO COME...

SHAKE

TO A MUTUAL UNDERSTANDING OF EACH OTHER.

Step.2
With a Hot Springs, a Cat, and a Buddha Statue: Part 1

72

SHABBY...

ボ ゛ロ □ □ □

THERE ARE HOLES EVERY-WHERE.

温泉有猫屋

CAT HOUSE HOT SPRINGS RESORT

IS THIS A HOUSE?

WHAT THE...?

IT'S LIKE SOMEONE'S BEEN DIGGING ALL OVER THE PLACE.

THIS HAS GOT TO BE THE *WORST* POSSIBLE SPOT!

AND IT'S BUILT IN SUCH A *LONELY* PLACE.

ヒュオ

SHEER CLIFF

オ オ
FROOOO... オ

DOES ANYONE EVEN *LIVE* HERE?

THOSE OF US WHO *TRULY* UNDERSTAND THESE THINGS GIVE INUKAMI TRAINERS THE GREATEST RESPECT!

THAT MAKES ME FEEL A LITTLE BETTER.

THANKS.

OH, BUT DON'T WORRY, I WOULDN'T JUDGE YOUR SKILLS...

JUST BASED ON HOW YOU LOOK.

MUNCH...

TO PERFORM THE MOST *AMAZING* TASKS.

LIKE HOW YOU UTILIZE THE POWERS OF YOUR INVISIBLE INUKAMI...

YOU SAY PEOPLE HAVE SEEN *A STRANGE CREATURE* AROUND THE HOTEL...

WELL THEN, ABOUT THE JOB...

AND WHO IS *THIS* YOUNG LADY?

BUT I IMAGINE RIGHT NOW, YOU HAVE YOUR INUKAMI IN THIS *VERY ROOM*, UNDER YOUR CONTROL.

OF COURSE, I CANNOT SEE IT.

MY ASSIST-ANT.

HE MEANS HER.

CHOMP CHOMP

EH... EH HEH.

SIP...

AND ESPECIALLY IN THE *OUTDOOR BATH?*

YES, ALL KINDS!

AND HAS IT DONE ANY SERIOUS DAMAGE?

SOME PEOPLE SAY... THEY SAW A SMALL, SHAGGY *MONSTER.*

YES, THAT'S RIGHT.

IT *COMPLETELY DEVOURED* A MULTI-COURSE MEAL SET FOR TWENTY PEOPLE!

WHILE OTHERS SAY IT WAS A SQUISHY BALL OF MEAT.

WHAT DID IT LOOK LIKE?

AND ON TOP OF THAT-- THIS IS DELICATE...

A LARGE AMOUNT OF *UNDERWEAR* FROM OUR FEMALE GUESTS.

BUT THE DEMON SEEMS TO HAVE *STOLEN...*

AT THIS RATE, OUR GUESTS WILL STOP COMING.

IT STEALS PANTIES?

HMM...

OH, KAWAHIRA-SAN, THERE *MUST* BE A WAY FOR YOU TO TAKE CARE OF THIS!

GRAB

Step.3 With a Hot Springs, a Cat,
and a Buddha Statue: Part 2

94

KEITA-SAN...

PAT

HE'S BEEN ON A VERY LONG JOURNEY.

NO, NO. I'M A TRAVELING CAT.

ARE... ARE YOU A NEKOMATA*?

I'VE COME TO ASK YOU FOR A FAVOR.

TRAVELING CATS TRAVEL.

MEOW MEOW

TALK ABOUT A WEIRD CAT...

*IN JAPANESE FOLKLORE, A *NEKOMATA* IS A DEMON CAT WITH A FORKED TAIL.

FIND A *BUDDHA* STATUE?

YOU JUST WANT US TO HELP YOU...

SO LET ME GET THIS STRAIGHT.

ONCE, LONG AGO... THERE WAS A TEMPLE THAT GUARDED ONE-HUNDRED AND EIGHT *PRICELESS* STATUES OF THE BUDDHA.

YOUR MISSION? RIIIGHT.

YES.

THIS IS THE *FULFILLMENT* OF MY MISSION AS A TRAVELING CAT.

THEY WERE *VERY* IMPORTANT TREASURES.

THIS LOSS WAS A *HEAVY* BURDEN TO THE GREAT PRIEST.

WE DON'T KNOW HOW, BUT IT LED TO THE DESTRUCTION OF THE TEMPLE.

UNFORTU-NATELY, THEY WERE *LOST.*

HE MOURNED THE STATUES UNTIL THE DAY HE PASSED.

AND VOWED TO RECLAIM THE SCATTERED BUDDHA STATUES...

SO MY ANCESTOR BECAME THE FIRST TRAVELING CAT...

WHO SWORE TO CARRY ON HIS WORK.

BUT THROUGH-OUT THAT TIME, THE GREAT PRIEST TOOK GOOD CARE OF MY ANCESTOR...

BUT OF COURSE!

HE'S A NICE KITTY, ISN'T HE?

HUNH. FOR A DEMON CAT, YOU SURE HAVE A STRONG SENSE OF DUTY.

HOW LONG IT TAKES.

NO MATTER...

PURR PURR...

CLINCH

IT FELL INTO THE HANDS OF THE PREVIOUS OWNER OF YOUR HOTEL...

YES. I JUST DISCOVERED THIS MYSELF.

AND...

WHO BURIED IT WITH HIS FORTUNE, SOMEWHERE IN THIS AREA.

YOU BELIEVE ONE OF THE STATUES IS BURIED NEARBY?

BUT I HAVE TO DO IT IN SECRET.

CRAFTY...

SO I'VE BEEN SEARCHING ALL AROUND THE MOUNTAIN AND THE HOTEL.

SO, IN OTHER WORDS...

SCRITCH...

OHHH! I GET IT.

WHAT YOU REALLY WANT FROM US IS YOKO'S SHUKUCHI!?

I REALIZED THAT IT WAS MY *BEST CHANCE* TO PULL A BURIED STATUE FROM THE GROUND QUICKLY.

YES, WHEN I SAW HER *SHUKUCHI*...

YOU ARE VERY PERCEPTIVE.

UH, TOME-KICHI...

AND I WOULD BE HAPPY TO *PAY YOU BACK.*

IF YOU COULD HELP, I WOULD BE *ETERNALLY GRATEFUL.*

BLINK

BLINK

DO YOU LIKE WOMEN'S UNDER-WEAR?

MEOW?

FIRST, *COME WITH ME.*

MEOW...

I'LL HELP YOU, BUT...

カキーン

FREEZE

THEY WERE A PRESENT FOR GRAND-MOTHER.

BUT REALLY...

BLUSH

ORIGINALLY...

WHAT?

WE WERE THE OWNERS OF THAT HOTEL AND THIS *ENTIRE* MOUNTAIN.

WHY DID YOU TAKE *UNDER-WEAR?*

THE HOTEL OWNER? HE DIDN'T LOOK THAT BAD TO ME.

HE *SWINDLED* ME OUT OF EVERYTHING I *HAD.*

BUT I WAS TRICKED BY A *BAD MAN.*

NO. THE *NEW* OWNER TOOK OVER LATER.

IT *HURT* TOO MUCH TO JUST STAND BY AND *WATCH.*

BUT...

THE THIEF WHO DID THIS *DISAPPEARED* A LONG TIME AGO.

MUNCH

チャラリ〜
チャラ〜♪

MNCH

MNCH

PLIP

I HAVE TO GO, YUKIKO.

HAVE A GOOD DAY, MY HUSBAND.

Step.4 A Date with Yoko

EXHAUSTED

WHIMPER

TOO CLOSE...

THAT... WAS A CLOSE ONE.

OH... HAKE.

KEITA-SAMA?

DAAAAHHH!!

DON'T YOU HAVE SCHOOL TODAY?

JUMP

I HAD A REALLY ROUGH MORNING, SO I JUST STAYED HOME.

REALLY ROUGH, HUH?

I SEE THAT YOKO ISN'T AROUND...

I CAME TO BRING A *GIFT* FROM MY MASTER.

SHE WENT OUT ALONE?

SHE WAS ALL MAD FOR SOME REASON.

OH, *SHE* LEFT.

IT WAS SUPPOSED TO BE FOR YOKO, THOUGH.

OOOH!

SO WHAT DID YOU COME HERE FOR, ANYWAY?

YEAH.

MAN...

YES! RICE WITH CHEST-NUTS!!

HAKE-CHAN?

YOU ALWAYS HAVE THE *BEST* TIMING, HAKE-CHAN.

WHAT'S *UP* WITH YOKO, ANYWAY?

THERE'S SOMETHING I'VE BEEN MEANING TO ASK YOU.

OH.

WHAT I WOULDN'T GIVE TO HAVE A GREAT INUKAMI LIKE YOU.

Sigh...

GRANDMA REALLY HAS IT *GOOD.* SHE SURE HIT THE JACKPOT WITH YOU.

SHE DOESN'T EVEN *TRY* TO LISTEN TO WHAT I SAY.

THEN WHAT'S HER *PROBLEM?*

DEJECTED

I MEAN...

FIRST OFF, WHY DID SHE COME TO *ME?*

AND ON TOP OF *THAT,* SHE DOESN'T KNOW *ANY-THING* ABOUT THE REAL WORLD...

AND CAN'T REALLY *DO* ANYTHING.

SHE PLAYS *TRICKS* ON ME...

EATS HER WEIGHT IN FOOD...

BECAUSE SHE CHOSE YOU AS HER MASTER, OF COURSE.

BUT SHE IS TREATED *SPECIALLY* BY THE CLAN.

I CAN'T GO INTO ALL THE DETAILS...

SHE LIVED IN ISOLATION FOR MANY YEARS...

SO SHE DOESN'T REALLY UNDERSTAND HOW THINGS ARE DONE.

PLEASE, I HUMBLY ASK YOU TO MAKE HER INTO A FIRST-RATE INUKAMI.

THE WAYS OF HUMAN SOCIETY.

SOME-HOW, YOU MUST TEACH HER...

BUT FROM MY PERSPECT-IVE...

I AM TRULY SORRY FOR ANY TROUBLES YOU'VE HAD...

SO I GET THE DAMAGED MERCHAN-DISE.

TO PUT IT BLUNTLY...

I HAVE HIGH EXPECTATIONS OF YOU, KEITA-SAMA.

I THINK I'LL GO HAVE A LOOK FOR HER.

BUT HASN'T YOKO BEEN GONE KIND OF A LONG TIME?

PROBABLY NOTHING.

HUH? WHAT IS IT?

YOU THINK I'M NOT TRYING TO TRAIN THAT DUMB MUTT?

IT'D BE MUCH EASIER IF SHE HAD STARTED OUT WELL-BRED, THOUGH.

VANISH

ス

ス

STAND...

SIGH...

YOU WORRY TOO MUCH.

LEAVE HER ALONE AND SHE'LL BE BACK EVENTUALLY.

ISOLATION...

SHE LIVED IN ISOLATION...

THAT MEANS SHE WAS **ALONE** FOR YEARS.

FOR MANY YEARS.

ALONE.

ALL...

Step.5 Enter Nadeshiko

CHATTER

CHATTER

WELL, HOW ABOUT SOME *ICE CREAM* AFTER A HARD DAY'S WORK?

HAKE-SAMA, I'LL BE ON MY WAY NOW.

MAYBE YOU'RE RIGHT.

YEAH, I WANT SOME, TOO!

CHATTER

CHATTER

NOW SAY GOOD-BYE TO ONII-SAMA.

WE'RE LEAVING.

TURN

YOU ALREADY HAD SOME FOR BREAK-FAST!

EVERY-ONE.

YES...

CLACK
CLACK
CLACK

SIGH...

THEY CERTAINLY HAVE A LOT OF *ISSUES*.

THEY NEVER TOLD *ME* ABOUT IT!

AND ANOTHER THING! WHY *EXACTLY* DO YOU HAVE *ANOTHER* INUKAMI COMING TO YOU, KEITA?!

SHE'S IN THE SERVICE OF ANOTHER MASTER RIGHT NOW.

BUT FOR *SOME* REASON...

AND SHE SEEMS TO *LIKE ME*, JUST LIKE *YOU*.

I JUST HEARD MYSELF.

ARE YOU KAWAHIRA KEITA-SAMA?

UM, EXCUSE ME...

BUT... WHAT ABOUT *OUR CONTRACT?!*

WHAT CONTRACT?

Y... *YOU*...

コホ
POUR

コボ
POUR

OH, KEITA-SAMA, DON'T TROUBLE YOURSELF.

I'LL POUR THE TEA.

I'M SO *EMBARRASSED.*

POUR

POUR

ピキ゛ン
TRAITOR...

SHE'S *SOOOOO CUTE~!*

OOOH~!

LAY IN YOUR *LAP* WHILE YOU... CLEAN MY EARS.

I CAN...

ポ
BLUSH

HUH?

AND *YOU...*

THWACK!
チョップ

WHAT THE *HELL* ARE YOU SAYING?!!

OH, YES, I'D LOVE TO!

OH!

PLEASE USE THIS!

SHIVER

BURN DOWN THIS CITY.

IF THERE ISN'T, I REALLY *WILL*...

LET ME PUT IT LIKE THIS...

WE WANT YOU TO BECOME AN INUKAMI WHO ACTS THE WAY AN INUKAMI *SHOULD*.

AND *GO HOME!*

JUST TAKE THAT *USELESS* OLD MAID...

I DON'T WANT TO.

WE HOPE YOU CAN LEARN TO *CONDUCT YOURSELF* IN A MORE *LADYLIKE* MANNER.

NOW, THIS IS *ONLY* FOR A SHORT WHILE...

BUT NADESHIKO WILL STAY HERE TO SET AN *EXAMPLE* FOR YOU.

YOKO.

HRMPH

CLENCH

I GUESS THERE'S NO OTHER OPTION.

THERE'S NO *WAY* HE WON'T TRY SOMETHING!

WITH A *CUTE GIRL* IN FRONT OF KEITA...

TELEVISION'S HIT DRAMA! "DIARY OF AN EVIL MOTHER-IN-LAW"

ARE YOU TRYING TO KILL ME?!

OH HO HO HO!

OH MY, MACHIKO-SAN, WHAT IS THIS FOOD?

おーほっほほ MWA HA HA HA!

IT'S TIME TO PUT ALL I'VE LEARNED TO GOOD USE!

GET READY TO *SUFFER,* NADESHIKO!!

I'M SO SORRY, OKAA-SAMA...

THAT SMELL...

IS THAT...

DAD...?

MISO SOUP?

AH!

GOOD, YOU'RE FINALLY AWAKE.

YES.

THEY'RE COUSINS.

BUT THAT MEANS KEITA AND HE––

HIS NAME IS KAWAHIRA KAORU.

INCLUDING ME, THERE ARE TEN INUKAMI THAT BELONG TO MY MASTER.

HE'S THE GRANDSON OF THE HEAD OF THE KAWAHIRA FAMILY.

HERE, LOOK AT THIS.

WOW...

SHE ISN'T JUST SOME TYPICAL INUKAMI.

THERE'S A RING FOR EVERY ONE OF THEM?!

KAORU-SAMA WEARS ANOTHER JUST LIKE IT.

THIS IS THE SYMBOL OF OUR CONTRACT.

DON'T JUST MAKE UP A BUNCH OF **CRAP**!!

SURE.

JUST LIKE YOU SAW ALREADY, KEITA'S A **PERVERT** AND IS FULL OF **NON-SENSE**!

WOULD YOU MIND TELLING ME A LITTLE ABOUT KEITA-SAMA?

NOW IT'S YOUR TURN.

HELP... I NEED AN AMBULANCE...

WELL, HE *IS* A PERVERT.

SIGH...

SMACK

WHACK

BY THE WAY...

WHIRRRRRR

UM...

DO YOU REMEMBER SOMEONE NAMED *SOTARO*?

EH?

GONE.

WHERE ARE KEITA-SAMA'S PARENTS?

To Be Continued

Afterword

I'M **MARI MATSUZAWA**, AND I DO THE ART FOR THIS MANGA.

THANK YOU!

HELLO TO **EVERYONE**, BOTH NEW AND RETURNING READERS!

BUT IN NO TIME NOW, IT'S ALREADY OUT AS A TANKOUBON!

THUMP
BLUSH...
THUMP

IT SEEMS LIKE WE ONLY JUST **STARTED** THIS SERIES...

EXCITED

I'M SO HAPPY!

Inukami!
Behind the Scenes!

YES, I KNOW IT'S A STALE JOKE.

PATCHIEMON...

WITH THAT OLD VOICE...

OKAY, ENOUGH OF THAT FOR NOW.

BOSS

GET OUTTA HERE!

Kick

AFTER I WAS CHOSEN TO MAKE THE MANGA, I OFTEN CALLED UP THE TWO ORIGINAL CREATORS TO ASK ABOUT LAYOUTS AND HOW THE ART WAS DONE.

MEETING

I HAVE A QUICK QUESTION...

HELLO. MATSU-ZAWA HERE.

Pi

TEL... TEL...

I CALLED THE ORIGINAL ARTIST, ARISAWA-SAN.

AH!

THE... THE DIRECTOR'S GONNA BE PISSED!

OH NO! I DOZED OFF.

EEEK!

beep

CLICK

beep

BUT I CAUGHT HIM NAPPING...

UH... HELLO?

HE NOTICED THE CALL ON HIS PHONE'S LOG.

HORROR

THIS IS ARISAWA. UM... DID YOU CALL ME?

SEVERAL HOURS LATER...

DOES HE NOT REMEMBER IT?!

FOR SOME REASON, I CAN'T SEEM TO GET HIM BACK ON THE PHONE...

LATER...

HORROR

beep

DID HE HANG UP ON ME?!

beep

I REALLY DON'T REMEMBER...

ARISAWA-SAN IS A LITTLE *SPACED OUT.*

IS THAT LIKE A MOE CHARACTER?

VERDICT

BUT FOR SOME REASON, WAKATSUKI-SAN ALWAYS GOES OFF ON A TANGENT, FORGETS WHAT I ASKED AND TALKS ON FOR HOURS.

I ALSO OFTEN CALL WAKATSUKI-SAN, THE CHARACTER DESIGNER.

HAPPY

HAPPY

meow

meow

▶ THAT'S THEM TALKING.

IT FEELS LIKE THEY ONLY GET IN THE WAY.

I'M REALLY SORRY!

HMM...

ME, JUST NOTICING THIS NOW.

INTERRUPTING MY NAP AND MY WORK!

: : : : :

TRY TO KEEP LONG CALLS TO A MINIMUM.

VERDICT

HEE HEE HEE...

FLUFF

BAA

FLUFF

BAA

Snuggle

TOO SLOW.

Special Thanks ♣

MAMIZU
ARISAWA-SAMA
KANNA
WAKATSUKI-SAMA
KISHO
FUJIYO-SAMA
ALL THE
DIVISION CHIEFS.
MY FAMILY.
AND
EVERYONE!

INUKAMI'S MANGA WOULDN'T EXIST WITHOUT THE HELP OF SO MANY PEOPLE. I'D LIKE TO GIVE MY SINCEREST THANKS TO EVERY ONE OF THEM.

AND TO ALL MY READERS: I'D BE SO HAPPY TO LEARN THAT YOU GOT EVEN A LITTLE ENJOYMENT OUT OF THIS MANGA.

I KNOW I'VE STILL GOT A LOT TO LEARN, BUT I'LL KEEP TRYING.

SEE YOU IN THE NEXT ISSUE!

REALLY.

 SORRY FOR WRITING SO MUCH.

177

······· **From the Creator and Character Designers** ·······

CONGRATULATIONS ON THE FIRST VOLUME OF THE MANGA! ORIGINAL CREATOR ARISAWA HERE. THANK YOU FOR YOUR CONTINUING SUPPORT, EVERYONE.

WHEN I FIRST HEARD A WOMAN WOULD BE IN CHARGE OF MAKING THE *INUKAMI!!* MANGA, I WAS A LITTLE WORRIED. "WOULD A WOMAN BE OKAY WITH WRITING A MANGA FULL OF RISQUÉ JOKES LIKE THIS?" WAS MY FIRST THOUGHT.

MY SECOND THOUGHT WAS, "I HAVE TO APOLOGIZE TO HER." BUT WHEN IT WAS FINISHED AND I OPENED IT UP, WHAT SHE'D PREPARED FOR ME COMPLETELY EXCEEDED MY EXPECTATIONS. I CAN SAY THAT WITHOUT EXAGGERATION OR FLATTERY. THIS MANGA IS MORE INTERESTING THAN THE ORIGINAL LIGHT NOVELS.

OOPS, I SAID IT...

I KNOW IT'S NOT SOMETHING A WRITER IS SUPPOSED TO SAY, BUT THAT'S HOW GREAT MATSUZAWA-SENSEI'S *INUKAMI!!* MANGA IS. YOKO IS A PERVERT! KEITA'S A REAL DUMMY! FROM THE ACTION TO THE CUTE STUFF, WITH A LITTLE GUTTER HUMOR THROWN IN, THERE ISN'T A PART THAT DOESN'T FIT. I HOPE YOU'LL ENJOY IT.

AND, IF YOU CAN, PLEASE TAKE A LOOK AT THE ORIGINAL *INUKAMI!!* LIGHT NOVELS. THE *INUKAMI!!* ANIME IS ALSO STARTING IN APRIL IN JAPAN, SO IF YOU LIKE THE MANGA, PLEASE GIVE THE ANIME A TRY. I HOPE THAT YOU WILL PICK UP THE NEXT VOLUME OF THE MANGA, TOO!

MAMIZU ARISAWA

AM I THE ONLY ONE WHO THOUGHT THAT? HI THERE, THIS IS **KANNA WAKATSUKI**. CONGRATULATIONS ON THE FIRST VOLUME OF THE *INUKAMI!* MANGA! I WISH I COULD'VE BEEN IN BETTER SHAPE, MENTALLY AND PHYSICALLY, WHEN SHE CALLED ME. SORRY! I'M REALLY WORN OUT. I HAVE TO THANK MATSUZAWA-SAN FOR ALWAYS BEING THERE TO CHEER ME UP, EVEN WHEN SHE WAS UNDER DEADLINE PRESSURE. I HOPE SHE CAN GIVE ME PIGGYBACK RIDES AGAIN. (HEE HEE!) AND, AND...! WHEN WE OPEN THE MANUSCRIPT, LET'S GO TO A HOT SPRING. I'LL TRY TO BE FREE TO GO ALONG.

P.S. I'M SO *HAPPY* THAT HAKE HAS A LOT OF SCENES. HAKE!

(IN THE MANGA.)

 06.3

HONORIFICS

To ensure that all character relationships appear as they were originally intended, all character names have been kept in their original Japanese name order with family name first and given name second. For copyright reasons, creator names appear in standard English name order.

In addition to preserving the original Japanese name order, Seven Seas is committed to ensuring that honorifics—polite speech that indicates a person's status or relationship towards another individual—are retained within this book. Politeness is an integral facet of Japanese culture and we believe that maintaining honorifics in our translations helps bring out the same character nuances as seen in the original work.

The following are some of the more common honorifics you may come across while reading this and other books:

-san – The most common of all honorifics, it is an all-purpose suffix that can be used in any situation where politeness is expected. Generally seen as the equivalent to Mr., Miss, Ms., Mrs., etc.

-sama – This suffix is one level higher than "-san" and is used to confer great respect upon an individual.

-kun – This suffix is commonly used at the end of boys' names to express either familiarity or endearment. It can also be used when addressing someone younger than oneself or of a lower status.

-chan – Another common honorific. This suffix is mainly used to express endearment towards girls, but can also be used when referring to little boys or even pets. Couples are also known to use the term amongst each other to convey a sense of cuteness and intimacy.

Sempai – This title is used towards one's senior or "superior" in a particular group or organization. "Sempai" is most often used in a school setting, where underclassmen refer to upperclassmen as "sempai," though it is also commonly said by employees when addressing fellow employees who hold seniority in the workplace.

Sensei – Literally meaning "one who has come before," this title is used for teachers, doctors, or masters of any profession or art.

Oniisan – This title literally means "big brother." First and foremost, it is used by younger siblings towards older male siblings. It can be used by itself or attached to a person's name as a suffix (niisan). It is often used by a younger person toward an older person unrelated by blood, but as a sign of respect. Other forms include the informal "oniichan" and the more respectful "oniisama."

Oneesan – This title is the opposite of "oniisan" and means "big sister." Other forms include the informal "oneechan" and the more respectful "oneesama."

HAYATE
CROSS
BLADE

SPECIAL PREVIEW

SHIZURU
HAYASHIYA

I'M SO GLAD YOU DIDN'T CHICKEN OUT.

THE TIME'S FINALLY COME.

MUDOU AYANA!

IF THERE'S ONE THING I DON'T THINK I'LL EVER BEAT HER AT, IT'S INSULTS!

RRG!

I'D ALMOST COMPLETELY FORGOTTEN ABOUT YOU.

80% OR SO FORGOTTEN, I'D SAY.

I'M GLAD, TOO.

STAB

SOMETHING'S NOT RIGHT...

HMM...

Hang on a sec...

WAIT.

"50,000 YEN"?

50,000 YEN!!

WE'LL NEVER LOSE TO THE LIKES OF YOU...

WE *DO* HAVE REAL NAMES, YOU KNOW!!

Yeowch...

OH YEAH!! THAT'S FOR THE *PAIR*. YOU'RE EACH ONLY 25,000 YEN!!

¥50000

IS IT NECESSARY TO BE *THAT* FRANK?!

¥25000

¥25000

2.5 poo.

CONTINUED IN *HAYATE X BLADE* VOL.1

THE END

YOU'RE READING THE WRONG WAY

This is the last page of *Inukami!* Volume 1

This book reads from right to left, Japanese style. To read from the beginning, flip the book over to the other side, start with the top right panel, and take it from there.

If this is your first time reading manga, just follow the diagram. It may seem backwards at first, but you'll get used to it! Have fun!